Storm of Fire
SAM SUFFRAT

DEDICATION

To the one who was always by my side.

CONTENTS

CHAPTER ONE

I was a nervous wreck.

I couldn't stop staring at Chessie's lips that held a shine from the streetlight outside her window. I watched as she leaned forward and placed a cool hand on my arm- I silently prayed her sweet perfume masked my sweat stink. I cupped the side of her face with my hand and moved in for a kiss.

Suddenly, the old vinyl seat under my butt made a fart sound. My eyes went wide in shock. We both paused. "It seriously wasn't me, it's the seat," I said quickly. I wanted to laugh and make an old joke out of it, but I wasn't sure how this new Chessie would react.

Chessie nodded, wrinkling her nose. I looked away awkwardly but she cocked her head to meet my eyes.

Before I knew it, she pressed a hand on the back of my neck and parted her lips- I mirrored hers. Our lips touched and a tongue began roaming inside my mouth.

I tried to get into the rhythm of kissing, but it was awkward as hell. My lips kept knocking against her teeth while she tried nibbling on my lips as we kissed. Worse, everything was feeling wet and slippery. As our bodies pressed together, her nauseating perfume almost made me gag.

Chessie's cold hand found its way up my shirt and it slowly traveled down south. I jumped. Chessie's laugh pulled me away.

"You're so shy," she teased. My face grew hot. Was she laughing because she knew I was inexperienced? This was not how I pictured my first kiss. Especially here in front of Gavin's house.

I watched her open the visor mirror and unclasped her bag. She revealed a cherry lip gloss. The transparent bottle glistened like slime under the streetlight. I vomited a little in my mouth as she smeared an extra layer on her lips.

She rounded to me. "Okay, so once we get inside, Mack, lead me around the cheerleaders, Laura and Ashanti. As soon as we find the jocks we have to dance and put all the other couples to shame." I opened my truck door to air out my armpit sweat.

"Don't call me that, Chessie," I retorted. "How about we turn the truck around and watch A Charlie Brown Christmas like we used to? Since winter break started I was hoping we could stay in and watch some Christmas reruns."

She closed her compact powder with a snap and shoved her lip gloss inside her bag. "Mack," she started slowly, "we're not kids anymore. Second," she flashed two fingers up in front of my eyes for emphasis hissing, "Don't ever mention to anyone we used to do that. We're trying to be king and queen of Dormant High, not the jesters."

"Correction, you want to be queen, Chessie. I want to be your boyfriend of Dormant High." I tried to say it plainly but I suspected she could hear the ache in my voice. "Would you stop calling me Mack?"

Chessie pouted cutely. "Seth, please. Do it for me?"

I rolled my eyes but a smile tugged the corners of my mouth. Chessie stroked the side of my face with her hand and I leaned in closer. I was itching for more of her.

My smile fell as I stared back at those wide brown eyes. I wanted to start kissing again.

"We can hang out for a couple hours, right?" she said.

I cleared my throat. "Sure, we can stay for a bit."

Chessie leaned back into her seat. "Alright, let's go." She paused. "Am I the one who's going to open the door?"

I grimaced. "You have the hands for it."

Chessie gave me a look.

"Fine, my queen." I made a short bow with a flourish of my hand and I slipped out of my seat into the warm breeze. I went around the truck and swung open her door from the sidewalk curb. Chessie stepped out, eyeing the house.

Stretching across a quarter acre of land was a stone lit pathway that curved toward a great black gate and metal fence. Gavin's house was obscured by palm trees decorated in Christmas lights and lanterns.

Once we neared we could see the party inside. Huge tall glass windows covered the side of the house. Chessie and I cut through the circular packed driveway and walked up the short steps leading up to the front doors.

I caught a glance at my girlfriend.

Girlfriend. My heart made a somersault. That word was a new and unknown territory.

With a confident smile, Chessie linked her arm with mine and opened the front door.

Gavin Martin, A.K.A. Meathead, was throwing an end-of-the-year party. Anyone who held an ounce of dignity, like the geeks, nerds, overachievers- weren't on the guest list. Gavin invited Chessie and that was enough reason to come.

Inside was chaotic. Loud music poured through every part of the house and into my eardrums as high school and college kids guzzled down beer. A couple danced on the pool table and bodies danced on the living room floor.

We shimmied our way past a couple drunks who were using the sofa as a surfboard. Several guys I knew by face welcomed me by name and offered a beer. In the midst of the crowd, Toby Armand stalked toward us. The guy hated my guts since I grabbed his forward position on Dormant's soccer team. I clenched my jaw as he neared. He gave a half nod and strode past. That was a first.

We finally got to the food table stationed across the dance floor. Chessie shrugged off her tan jacket and tossed it to me.

I raised my eyebrows at her pink halter top that stretched tightly over her chest. She smoothed her hands over her little white skirt that exposed her slender tanned legs. I openly looked her up and down with an approving nod. She rolled her eyes at me. "Shut up."

"What?"

"I can tell what you're thinking. It's all over your face."

"I was only thinking those legs could kick a soccer ball across the field."

She scoffed and rolled her eyes again. Her legs were very nice to look at. They were strong and slender, the result of playing volleyball for years. Chessie was a tall girl but her pink heels made her short skirt look mini.

I didn't trust my eyes not to linger any longer and made myself busy with the fruit punch. I offered her a drink but she declined. She was eyeing the dance floor. People were starting to notice she had arrived and she was enjoying it.

Some guys noticeably paid less attention to the dates they came with. I knew what they were thinking. Chessie's old phone number was still displayed all over the guys' locker rooms. I set my jaw.

Chessie casually stood with a hand on her hip, nodding to the beat of the music. I shifted closer and coolly wrapped an arm around her waist. Some of the guys took the hint and looked away, but the girls were eyeballing her hard.

"Hey, Chessie. Mack." Someone greeted us from behind. Gavin's buddy, Ross DeMaio wobbled towards us. His arm hung around his date's neck to keep himself from toppling over. "You made the party," he slurred with surprise. He gulped down the beer in his right hand. It wasn't even nine o'clock and he was already trashed.

"Chessie dragged me here, it's not like I had a choice," I said over rap music. Ross laughed loudly and his date winced, tilting her head away from his mouth.

"C'mon Mack, don't be like that. You always go ghost, man. Did you even show up to Gavin's Halloween party?" Ross turned to his date with a sly grin on his face. "You remind me of that chick who dressed as the hot nurse. She went bobbing for apples." He squinted at her. "She was hotter."

The girl's mouth dropped and she quickly shoved him. "Jackass!"

Ross went knocking into the punch bowl, spilling it and his beer onto the hardwood floor as he fell. He laughed himself stupid after the girl pushed through the crowd and disappeared.

The two girls who were sitting on the sofa, rushed to Ross's aid. He was ready to reject them, but one look at their chests and the smirk slicked right back on his face. They helped pull him up to his feet. Ross wiggled his eyebrows at his new company.

"Wanna have some fun?"

After he left, I turned to Chessie. "Why are we here?"

She sighed. "Don't start. You should take Ross's advice and have some fun." She replaced my cup and thrust a cold beer into my hand. "Loosen up."

I looked at her. "I'm driving, remember?"

She let out another exasperated sigh and grabbed it back. "Whatever."

She twisted and popped the top off with a napkin and gulped it down. A gigantic burp erupted from her lips. I laughed. "That's cute."

Her scowl shut me down. "I'm coming right back."

A frown settled on my face. "Whatever happened to putting other couples to shame?"

She flipped back her bangs with a hand and straightened her posture. "Maybe later." She jutted out her chest and shrugged. "Go out there and mingle." Before I could answer she was already leaving. "I'll be right back," she yelled behind her as her slender frame was sucked into a sea of sweaty bodies.

After I watched her leave, I took a seat next to a couple making out on the tiny couch. I ran my fingers through my thick black hair, trying not to feel annoyed.

Our soccer team won first place in the nation and took home the trophy last week. Chessie had agreed we could celebrate it together this weekend until she got the invite to Gavin's party. Now we were official and I wanted to celebrate my victory even more with her.

"Hey, sexy."

I gazed up and watched Marion Aguilera and her girl pal Odessa something, plop on either side of me on the couch. Odessa's drink sloshed in her cup and fell on the girl making out on the couch.

"What the hell?" she squealed.

"What?" Odessa said, taken aback. She stared down at the girl's wet blouse. "I'm drinking vodka, it's not like it shows on your dress."

The girl glowered as her make out buddy pulled her away from the couch. Once the couple was gone, I stared straight ahead, nonchalant, as bodies grinded on the dance floor.

A pair of legs blocked my view and jumped into my lap in one motion with an arm swung around my neck. I stared up at Marion's eager face. This habit of hers was getting old.

Right after I kicked the winning goal during nationals, the cheerleaders dropped their pompoms and ran in the middle of the field. Marion suddenly leapt into my arms. As if that wasn't enough, she stuck her tongue down my throat, macking me right in front of hundreds of shocked eyes. For the record, that didn't count as a kiss.

Odessa sat beside me and giggled while she started petting my hair.

Don't get me wrong- Odessa and Marion looked better when they weren't drunken hot messes. Odessa was a thin black girl with dark brown eyes and a boob job larger than she was two summers ago. Marion was a white girl with long black hair that ran down her back and had the most perfect full lips.

Someone distinctly whistled before shouting out loud, "Mack Daddy!"

I wanted to sock David Gaetti in the mouth.

"Marion, get off." I gently tried to pull away, but she wouldn't take the hint. She pulled closer and started playing with an earlobe with her finger. That sent an involuntary shiver up my arm and several places I wouldn't mention out loud.

"Seth, babe, you're hot," Marion slurred. "I think it's the Spanish in you that gives you that hot factor."

"Your brown eyes are to die for," Odessa cooed in my ear. "Are you half Brazilian? You have sexy caramel skin."

Their pickup lines hit me cold and I immediately stopped thinking with my junk. I shrugged Marion off me and untangled from them. I stood.

"Seth," Marion cooed, "you don't have to pretend you don't like me. We can make your time worthwhile."

"No thanks." I glanced around for Chessie.

"Hey, man!" Carl Sardinia emerged from the dance floor. He knocked me hard on the shoulder.

"Hey to you too, man." I shoved his arm away. His neck visibly tensed. Carl was a head taller than me and outweighed me by fifty pounds of muscle. His shaggy red hair covered his square face and gave him the look of a predator. He only attacked when he smelled fear.

"What are you doing here, Castillo? I don't remember your ass on the guest list."

"I'm not in the mood. Go fetch a ball to occupy your time."

Carl cracked his knuckles threateningly. "Get out of my face, Mack."

He wasn't worth a fight. "You met Marion?" I told him. "Marion wants to talk someone," I said, turning to her confused face. "Didn't you and Odessa want to speak to someone hot?"

Marion straightened herself in her seat. Odessa leapt from the couch and staggered to Carl's side. "Do you want to sit with us? Seth is no fun." Carl glanced from Odessa to me.

"Come over here," Marion patted the empty seat beside her. "I promise we'll make it worth your time."

Carl's frown widened into a sickening grin. He groped Odessa's behind and she giggled. Just like that, Carl quickly forgot I existed.

I seized Chessie's jacket off the couch and walked away, checking my watch. A half hour passed since Chessie and I arrived. As soon as I found her we were out of here.

I went through the living room then traveled to the backyard where a bunch of guys were smoking weed and playing beer pong. I moved to the kitchen area. She wasn't there either.

I doubled back through the house, headed up the stairs to catch a bird's eye view of the crowd, and leaned over the banister. It wasn't long 'till I caught sight of Chessie making her way from the bedroom with Ashanti and Laura. My jaw automatically clamped together when I spotted Gavin behind her, laughing over something she had said. Chessie smiled back at him, stumbling through the mass. Gavin took the opportunity to wrap his arm around her waist, tugging her close.

I blazed down the stairs and cut in front of them, pulling Chessie towards me.

"Hey, Mack- Hey!" Chessie shoved me. "Why'd you pull me so hard?"

"Oh snap," Laura said. Ashanti smirked. "I love it when guys fight over me, too."

I ignored them and handed Chessie her jacket. "Time to go." Chessie snatched it from my hands then looked at Ashanti. Her eyes sharpened back to me. Her voice was low. "What are you doing? We just got here," Chessie hissed.

I nodded my head. "I know. We have to go."

I turned, leading Chessie behind me. "Seth, what's the matter with you?"

We sifted our way to the front door. Ashanti followed with company in tow.

"Mack," Gavin called after us, "That's how you treat your girl?"

I managed to keep moving.

"You're leaving, Chessie?" Ashanti called behind us. "See if you make the squad if you do."

We were causing a scene. I turned in time to see Ashanti's green eyes flicker a challenge. Chessie yanked her arm free from my grasp. "Geez, what's your problem? I'm not leaving." She rounded on her heel and returned to Ashanti's side. Ashanti smugly batted her fake eyelashes.

"No one wants to leave with this poor pussy," Gavin laughed. "Smart move."

My jaw loosened. "Shut up."

"Seth, leave it alone," Chessie urged.

Leave it alone? I rounded at her. "I came with you and I'm not planning to leave you with him."

Laura started giggling. It pumped up Gavin. "I don't know why someone as hot as Chessie would do with someone like you," he said. "You know what? I bet she's better in bed with me than Erving!"

Chessie blinked as if he punched her. I saw red.

I lunged at Gavin and he spun away in time. I ran past and collided into a pair of bodies. People parted, giving us space.

"Fight! Fight! Fight!" Voices chanted around us.

Music pounded in my ears, fueling my anger.

"Yo ass is getting kicked today, homeboy," Gavin said. He eyed his Meathead friends Manny Johnson and Carl Sardina who joined on either side of him. Gavin raised his chin with a confident sneer. I clenched my fists, ready to square up in his face. Chessie placed a hand against my chest, shoving me back.

"Seth, would you stop? He's just messing with you." She flashed Gavin a look. "No one's fighting. Call your guys off," she started but I cut her off.

"This trash was the one who spread those rumors about you and you're hanging out with him?" Chessie jerked back as if I stung her.

"Let's talk outside," I tried gently, but she pulled away again.

Her tone grew stern. "Leave me alone."

I looked at her.

"That burns bro," someone laughed.

I gave Chessie one last look. She was on the Meatheads' side.

Fine.

I scowled at Gavin then rounded to leave. "Get out of the way," I yelled to the tight crowd and they unrelentingly let me through. Cheers and boos led me out of the house.

I departed the property and went stomping around the block for several minutes. When I finally returned to my old Ford blue truck, I was sweating from the humidity. I unlatched the glove compartment and nicked a cigarette from a half pack of Marlboros. I pulled out a lighter.

I never appreciated people smoking and coughing and hacking around me. Growing up, I feared ruining my lungs the way Aunt Evangeline ended up with lung cancer. When mom started seeing her boyfriend Logan Roth about a year ago, I developed an acquired taste for smoking.

I closed my eyes to relax my muscles in my neck and leaned against my truck. I took in a deep drag. I needed to get a handle on my anger until I could go back inside and haul Chessie out of there.

I glared at the house. I imagined what I would have done to Gavin if my fists touched him.

I took another drag and exhaled. I turned my attention towards the sky. Lightning streaked across the stars. A storm was brewing and I was about forty minutes away from home- I had to drop Chessie off, too. I thought about how I had to go back in that circus and find her. I glared at the stars.

As much as Chessie knew I loved her, I didn't think she understood how she hurt me. Last spring, the person spreading the rumor she was a slut, was Gavin. And here was Chessie, flirting with the enemy.

But Erving started it all.

A second flash of lightning streaked the sky as the wind picked up. I would have called Chessie on her cell right now, but I doubted she had her phone on vibrate.

A sudden bright burst of lightning pierced the sky. In the next moment, it crashed into the ground in a rumble. I didn't see where it struck but I pushed off my truck in surprise.

My eyebrows rose as lightning zigzagged across the sky again. What was weird though, was the lightning flash hadn't faded. Instead, it expanded into a beam of light, plummeting straight for the earth.

BOOM.

Lightning struck and pounded into the asphalt, rattling cars, homes, and trees. Several car alarms went off again; dogs barked wildly. There was a complete blackout in the neighborhood.

When lightning struck, I collided into my truck and held onto my rearview mirror for support with one hand, cigarette long forgotten, as my other hand shielded my eyes from the flash of light. The left side of my ribs throbbed where I hit them. My ears were ringing. I blinked.

There in the middle of the dark road an old man stood. Blue lights ran through his black trench coat as his black hair stood on end; each strand of hair pulsated in golden light. A visible halo of electric energy crackled around him.

I didn't have time to make sense of what I saw. He was bright and terrifying. I felt the exact moment his eyes fixated on me in the dark. A chill ran down my spine.

Suddenly he sprinted at a speed I was sure a professional track runner couldn't maintain. He was coming for me. Fast.

I stumbled a few steps as he slithered around my truck. His steely gaze trained on me like I was someone who kicked puppies for a living- I hardly made another step when he leaped over and landed behind me.

I spun around- I found myself staring into a golden face with white eyes burning with electricity. The old man placed his hands firmly on my shoulders and for a fraction of a second, intense heat coursed through them. Electricity jolted through my bones; the man's jagged yellow teeth widened into a cartoon character. I fought him off and clawed at his eyes, but my cries were caught in the wind My body sagged and my vision darkened.

I blacked out before I hit the pavement.

CHAPTER TWO

My eyes were stinging and crusty by the time I opened them. I took in the annoying machine beeping beside my bed. The disinfectant scent lingering the air and the middle-aged man lying in a metal bed across the room, snoring. Where was I?

A face hovered over me. Eyes brimmed with tears.

"Seth!" Someone hugged me so swiftly my vision was clouded by a mass of black curly hair.

"Mom, you're hurting me," I rasped.

"Lo siento, mi amor." She apologetically stroked my right arm.

"Pobrecito, how are you feeling?"

I didn't know how to answer her without spitting. My chest and left arm I realized were neatly bandaged in a sling. My skin burned and rubbed raw like matchstick on a striker underneath the dressings. Breathing triggered sharp needles through my ribs.

"Where am I? How long was I out?" I croaked. I was so sore it hurt to blink.

"Saint Mary's Hospital," Mom answered. She helped me sit. She began fluffing the cardboard pillows against my back. "You collapsed after a lightning strike last night."

Like a firecracker, several images bounced and ignited in my head and I quickly bolted that door to my mind shut. I shifted in bed as though the old man with glowing eyes was lurking in the corner of the room.

No. He couldn't be here. None of it happened.

Her fingers trembled as she lifted the bed sheets and covered my exposed toes. Her brown eyes regarded me soulfully. "It is three a.m., the morning after your party. *Preocupe mi mucho, mi amor.*" You worry me very much, my love.

I preferred her to yell. "I didn't think-"

Her eyes turned misty. "You went to an underage drinking party with no supervision. I trusted you, Seth."

I hated seeing her hurt because of me. Especially after Dad. "I didn't drink," I assured, stroking her hand. "Chessie and I were going to leave-"

Mom shook her head. "You know better."

I sucked in air and quickly regretted it. My breath was carving my name with a knife into my ribs. I strained to say the words out loud. "I'm sorry."

Her frown lines deepened. "It will be a long time before I can trust you again. You can't use the car or stay out late with your friends."

I nodded. The motion felt like I was jiggling loose change in my head. I laid back and waited for the room to stop spinning. Mom smoothed my hair with her fingers. "I am glad you're okay. You are all I have."

The snoring across the room cut through the moment. Mom and I caught each other's eye and we started to laugh. My laughs soon turned into fits of painful coughs.

A little while later there was a knock at the door. A doctor in white scrubs walked in and greeted us.

"How are we doing today?" She said this without waiting a reply. She halted at my metal bed and peered down.

"This week alone there were several lightning strikes reported in Dade County. You were struck close to the heart and you're very fortunate to be alive. You have a few shallow burns to show for it." Dr. Renaldo, I learned from her nametag, explained.

Mom gently rubbed my shoulder as the doctor informed me. "While you were unconscious, we performed a CT scan, and I have shown the results to your mother. So far, your bones are in good shape. After we schedule an MRI and EKG test, we'll know if you're ready to be discharged later on today."

"Thank God," Mom said.

"What's an MRI and EKG?"I asked.

"An MRI can spot if there are any damage to your tissues," Mom said. "The EKG will check if your heart is healthy."

Dr. Renaldo only clicked on her penlight and peered closer to my face. "Look directly at me." She pointed the laser in my eyes. "Do you remember what happened to you?"

She alternated to my left eye. Guess I would be blind in that eye too.

It was an innocent question to ask, but I thought of what would happen if I told the doctor what I believed happened. I was aware whatever I said bought me a one-way ticket to the psych ward.

"There was a lightning storm," I said carefully. "Next thing I know I'm here in a hospital bed." Dr. Renaldo straightened and retracted her penlight.

She looked down at my arm. "Let me see how it's doing." Dr. Renaldo helped me remove the arm sling. She frowned. "There seems to be little swelling," she said, checking my arm. I glanced down and my mouth almost dropped. The parts of my arm that wasn't bandaged was covered in purple welts and scars. It looked burned and disfigured. Mom gasped.

"The color and bruising will change over time but I will prescribe something for the pain and swelling."

"Is he going to be okay?" Mom asked wearily.

"The injury to his arm is to be expected but we'll keep a close eye on it. We also need to do an MRI just to be sure," she told Mom. "Do you want him to take one now? I can schedule an EKG right away if the room is available."

Mom glanced down at me for a reply. "Okay," I said.

Two hours and a throbbing headache later, I was back in bed. The man across the room, Daniel O'Keeffe, was awake. He wasn't very friendly and he didn't speak a word. He loudly turned up the volume on the television, probably because he didn't want to make small talk. Instead, he joined along the laugh tracks of I Love Lucy.

After the nurse gave O'Keefe a sedative, I got up and grabbed the remote from his side of the nightstand and shut off the T.V. Finally, I had peace.

Weary by my aches and pains and irritated from the jackhammer snores across the room, Mom later called in a nurse for pain meds. She soon left the hospital to pick up my truck from Gavin's. Once the drugs kicked in, a nightmare began.

I laid in the dark as I intently listened from my chambers. The speakers were all maids, cooks, guards, and attendants, were gossiping about my sudden refrain from kingly meetings and dwindling appearances. My daughter Vaora, my son Sixa, two trusted Awcers, Chancellor Melwimik, and a few of my royal consorts knew the truth. I disappeared for two days in Alchord on business. The recent attack on the Bror Passage had to be addressed.

I sent my hearing two floors down the main corridor. I nearly missed Vaora's frustrated sigh as she opened the door to her sleeping quarters.

Sweet fields of honey. I was also losing my hearing.

Her brother's footsteps traipsed inside her chamber and halted. Vaora waste no time for pleasantries. "How is Father?"

I could imagine her stature: her black, thick hair in disarray with her golden skin glowing with restless energy.

"The king is still unwell, but he is trying his very best to keep up appearances," my son responded. Sixa was sure to be wearing a dignified scowl on his round, golden face. With his black hair pulled taut in a fashionable ribbon, he was severe as his speech.

"He was seen walking diligently to the alcove for his daily reading meditation. No one seemed any wiser he is ill."

My body howled out in discomfort; I could not raise my head more than an inch. The three-floor journey to and from the alcove nearly drove me down into the burrows with the worms. It would have been wise to heed Melwimik's counsel to stay put, but I was obligated to deflect raising suspicions. A dying king was as good as a dead king in the eyes of the people. Panic and usurp arose in such times. These were the worst of times.

Vaora's faltering voice brought me to the present.

"What is ailing him?"

"Lower your voice, Vaora," my son chided her. "We cannot speculate what has happened to him."

"How can you stand here after what Parpagg did?" Vaora said in

spite. "That cockroach betrayed the kingdom and stole the Po'luxnann."

"I'd be damned if you call ripping the Po'luxnann Gejruvhet from the king's body is similar to losing a sock," Sixa said impatiently. "We sent our best men, Vaora," he said. "They will find Parpagg soon enough."

"And he will pay in blood," Vaora vowed.

"I'll see to it he does," Sixa swore bitterly.

"A beheading or slicing off Parpagg's fingers one by one wouldn't be enough," she suggested.

"I admit I am not at my best but we mustn't lose our very own heads," Sixa told her. "We have to be strong for Temcaltiaf. For Father."

A pause followed. "For Father," Vaora agreed solemnly.

I tried very hard to snuff the cry in my throat. If I made a sound or shifted in my bed they would know I was listening. For I could not trust my own children...

Similar to the after effects of riding a Tilt-A-Whirl at the Youth Fair, my head and stomach were churning. I dizzily shrugged off the sheets, dragging zombie-style to the bathroom, and puked my guts out. My liver threatened to join the slosh in the toilet. Semi-wet and dazed after a hot shower, I slowly shuffled back into bed.

The beeping sound blared through my eardrums and the scent of disinfectants in the room tossed my stomach. The faint smell of pee wafted from the other end of the room. With every passing moment the scent grew stronger. A migraine beat against my temple. I wanted to bury my head into the pillow and shout.

Between Daniel's snoring and the television he turned on in the middle of the night, I didn't get any shut-eye 'till the sun's first rays peeked through the window. I didn't trust the shadows on the walls.

It was that Saturday afternoon my best friends, Karin Jung and Eli Goodchild, came to the hospital for a visit. They cautiously poked their heads past the door frame. Relieved they found the right room, they entered with somber faces.

"Guys, I'm not dying."

"Of course not," Eli said with Karin following behind. He lightly punched my right shoulder.

"You weren't barbecued last night. You look burnt and boney as usual."

"You know all the right things to say," I said to Eli. "Keep telling me those sweet nothings."

"I worried about nothing," Karin said, standing beside him. Through her razor cut bangs, she glared daggers. Her eyes were puffy as though she hadn't slept much. It was the first time I saw her without her raccoon eyeliner. Eli looked a mess as well. His strawberry blonde Mohawk wasn't spiked up with products and he was missing his typical six earrings from his empty ear holes.

"I didn't mean to make y'all worried." I struggled to sit. Karin helped me up slowly.

"Thank you," I told her gratefully.

"Is that where you got hit?" Eli pointed at my arm.

"Yeah," I winced. Aside from the needling pain lancing up and down my arm the bandages were itchy and hot.

"How did it feel?" Eli said.

"Being electrocuted?" I asked. "It tickled."

"Nice."

"Are you feeling okay?" Karin looked concerned.

"Meh," I shrugged. "I'm good."

With my arm bandaged and in the sling, it was a good thing they couldn't see the swelling, the welts, and the funny colors that came with it. Even I was afraid to look at my arm; once was enough.

There was a knock on the door and before I could ask who it was, Chessie walked in the room. Her lips pursed into a thin line when she saw my visitors.

"I need time alone with Seth," Chessie announced. Karin with her five-foot-nothing to Chessie's five-ten, looked at Chessie as though she drowned a rat in her cereal.

"*Giseki*, I don't care what you need," she hissed *bitch* in Korean. "Got a problem, jump off a bridge."

"You first, bitch," Chessie advanced.

"Both of you stop," I warned.

Karin looked around the room incredulously. "I'm the dog here? Oh hell no, honey." She popped her neck in ghetto fashion. "Did the school whore forget whose bed she woke up in this morning?"

"Okay puppies, you can chew on each other's ear later," Eli said, pulling Karin back.

"Right now we need to chill the hell out." He motioned to Daniel snoring at the other side of the room. Karin and Chessie glared at one another. Karin resolutely stormed out of the room. Eli shrugged and followed her out. That went better than I expected.

Chessie wheeled around. "Why did you let her speak to me that way?"

I grimaced. "What am I, Karin's keeper?"

Chessie glowered. "Someone needs to put her on a leash."

I set my jaw. "Listen, you came in here demanding her and Eli leave the room. You already know how Karin is."

Her voice rose. "So you're saying I started it?" Chessie sounded shocked.

I adjusted the pillow against my back. "I'm saying pick your battles, 'kay?"

Chessie stood with her arms crossed. It was a couple of moments before she sat down on my bed.

"I wanted to see you," she finally said. "I didn't know if you were really hurt," her voice wavered. "After you left the party I went to look for you and the p-paramedics were working on you. You were on the g-ground. I thought you were," she cried so loud Karin exclaimed, "What a drama queen!"

I tried my best to console my girlfriend. "Chessie, I'm alright. See? No broken bones."

"And we fought!" Chessie blubbered. "I wasn't doing anything with Gavin, I swear. He was just showing me around his house and introduced me to Ashanti- you know the head cheerleader? And then you popped out of nowhere, telling me to leave."

I snorted. "I popped out of nowhere? What am I, a daisy? I'm your boyfriend."

"You know what I mean."

It was bad enough we went to Gavin's party but she was also hanging out with him. Her choice to stay back at the party made me look like I was some controlling boyfriend instead of someone who cared about her. I bit back my words. "Gavin is an asshole and I was trying to get you away from him."

Her watery brown eyes hardened. "He wasn't going to pull anything. I can take care of myself." She placed a cold hand on top of mine. "I didn't do anything with Gavin, Seth. I didn't cheat on you."

That isn't the point, I wanted to say, but she went on.

"I ran outside and saw you on the ground." She shook her head at the awful memory. "I thought you were dead. I didn't think I'd have a chance to tell you."

She put her face into her palms and started to cry again. I wrapped an arm around her and she shuddered. Daniel snorted in his sleep.

"Chessie, everything's fine now," I said, stroking her hair. "If you keep crying these people in the hospital would think I really died."

I felt her nod. She gazed up at me. Her mascara ran down her face. "You okay now?"

She pulled away and sniffed, wiping her eyes with the back of her hand.

"Yeah, I'm good. God, I probably look like such a hot mess, don't I?" She kissed me on the cheek. "Thanks, Seth." If that quirky smile didn't stop my heart I don't know what would.

Chessie started rummaging in her bag and pulled out her makeup. She patted her face with a sponge. "I have to take a picture of us. We need to let people know you're okay."

"Chessie," I started.

"Oh c'mon, Seth. I know you've got the worst luck taking pictures, but I'm sure this one isn't going to end up in a disaster." I rolled my eyes as she put away her makeup and replaced it with her phone in hand.

"Remember our eighth-grade class picture?" she said. "Before we took the photo we had lunch. You had food poisoning from the cafeteria food and didn't know it. Your lips were so swollen and red."

I remembered one upper lip was dramatically larger than the other. My tongue was so swollen it made the front of my mouth appear long and wide. "I looked like a fish out of water trying to breathe," I said. "How was I supposed to know I was allergic to pineapple?"

"Oh!" She bobbed up and down on the bed. Suddenly I started seeing the old Chessie. "Remember the time we were at the fair on the Ferris wheel? When that bird flew into our passenger car right at your face?" She started to laugh.

I winced at the memory. "Yeah. It got so frightened it started to poop. Everywhere. All over us."

Chessie laughed even harder. "It scared the living daylights out of me too!" She wouldn't stop giggling. "How many people can say they have a picture of that?" Her joy made me smile, even if it was at my expense.

When she finally calmed down, she looked at me. I noticed a couple of tear drops clung to her lashes. I wiped them away with my thumb.

Time slowed down until all I could see was her beaming smile. Chessie laid her head on my shoulder.

"Say cheese!"

She held up her phone and snapped continuous pictures. When she was done, Chessie gently pushed me against the bed and I lay back, mesmerized. She ran her fingers through my hair and massaged my scalp.

Very slowly, she inched her head towards me and puckered her lips, meeting mine. I was glad I brushed my teeth after I showered this morning.

Her body pressed against me as something floral and sour filled the air. She slid her tongue into my mouth and I accepted it, taking it in. My arm gripped around her waist and the floral scent poured through my nose.

Heat, rising from my chest, intensified as Chessie's body rubbed into mine. Her sweet scent soured. I yelped, breaking the moment.

Chessie stopped and shifted herself to get a better look at my face. "What? Did I do something wrong?"

I bit back another cry as my eyes began to water.

"You're on top of me- chest hurts."

"Oh! Sorry!" She backed away. "Are you alright?"

"I will be." Right after I stopped seeing stars. "Are you wearing flower-scented perfume?" The scent was starting to give me a migraine.

Chessie winked. "Lilac. You like it?"

I could have sworn I smelled something different. She lightly rubbed my chest with her hand. "I hope you'll get better once school rolls around in a couple weeks. We have to start practicing making out in the halls."

I opened my mouth as the door banged open. Karin marched up to my bed. "Times up."

Both girls turned to me in unison. Chessie stood. I looked at Eli who was right behind Karin.

Eli spoke up, receiving the message. "We need to talk to him, Chessie. Alone."

"Whatever." Chessie glared at Karin and bent over my bed. She met my lips again. Karin and Eli gawked.

My heart monitor sent sporadic beeps to the machine. The smell of sour milk grew more distinct in the air and I held my breath, revolted.

What the heck?

Chessie blew me a kiss and closed the door behind her. I took a cautious sniff of the air. The smell was gone, but my headache remained.

"Does your mom know you're dating?" Karin said.

I narrowed my eyes at her. "Not until you say something about it."

"And on top of that," she continued, "you ditched your Game Night with Eli for her?"

"Don't forget they went to Gavin's party together," Eli pointed out to Karin who scowled. "It's like he doesn't have any pride."

"Chessie's girlfriend material, don't get me wrong," Eli started to say over Karin's snorts, "But why now? After all these years she pretended your feelings didn't exist?"

"Just because someone doesn't stick their tongue down your throat right away doesn't mean they'll never be interested," I said, recalling a few minutes ago.

"You made Dormant High news," Eli said. "We found out about your little fun last night because you're on everyone's news feed." He pulled out his phone from his pocket, pressed a button and tapped his screen a few times before passing it to me. "Some dude at the party caught the lightning strike on his phone."

I had a sinking feeling. Eli handed me his cellphone. It was a video that was no longer than five minutes. I hit play. I quickly knew where this was first shot. Whoever was recording this video was outside Gavin's parking lot when lightning first struck.

They didn't catch the first strike, but the camera began rolling right after. "Oh my God, oh my God! You see that? Lightning hit the ground!"

The guests inside the house started to holler in annoyance because the lights were turned off. The cameraman walked briskly in the dark, camera flashlight on. Car alarms were blaring. The shot was shaky but the cameraman changed coarse down a familiar road and caught the second lightning strike. "No! No way! Oh God it's like the apocalypse," he said dramatically. I squeezed Eli's phone tightly. Maybe they'll see him on video. Maybe it was real.

"Did you see that? Man!" The cameraman pointed the camera at his face. "Guys, this is so crazy. Lightning crashed down. I'm going to check it out." He continued down a road. Car alarms and voices filled the background.

"What was that?" Someone shouted. There were more voices. The cameraman stopped in his tracks and turned to the speaker who caught up to him. "I don't know bro, but lightning hit the ground twice."

"Is that even possible? I thought lightning never strike in the same spot?"

"I don't know."

There was a howling scream. I knew it was me.

They were going to see the attacker. I thought as my heart beat wildly. I was about to see me lying on the ground.

Neighbors started pouring out onto the street. The cameraman, now more afraid than excited, slowly picked up the pace.

Not more than a few yards to the right was a bright blue light in the corner of the screen. The cameraman missed it the first time.

There was a sudden loud sound; it sounded like a roar under the clap of thunder. The camera swiveled around in surprise. The blue light was gone.

"Man guys, I don't know," the cameraman sounded fearful. The street was dark and empty. As I watched the video with growing anticipation the hairs on the back of my neck rose. That was the end of the video.

I wanted to hit the replay button. I wanted to shout at the cameraman. He was so close to catching this guy on camera. Why didn't he keep rolling?

"There's another clip," Eli mentioned. He grabbed the phone from my hand and found another video. He handed it back and I quickly hit play. This video was longer.

It was the event after the lightning strike. There were sirens heard in the background. Bright cop lights and fire trucks glared on the screen. This cameraman had a front row seat of the action behind the yellow tape police. "Yeah, there's that kid from that soccer team. He's down for the count. He's probably dead." He was speaking to a friend as he recorded the scene. I didn't hear what the other guy said.

There I was on the ground being worked on by paramedics. My shirt was torn off. A bag valve mask went over my face to help me breathe. I couldn't watch anymore. I handed Eli his phone.

"That was the first video we saw," Karin said. "I thought you died."

She locked eyes with mine. I held her hand.

"Chessie and her cheerleader groupies blast texted the entire student body about the party." Eli took a moment to sort through his phone.

"Ashanti texted this one," Eli pointed to his screen.

I was already dreading what I'd see. "How bad is it?" He gave a slick smile. "Just read."

I read the message posted in a group chat:

@ Gavin Prescott's that soccer guy Seth Castillo
got roasted by lightning! He's in the ambulance
right now-cops r on the block n power
lines r down- dis is freaky!

It wasn't bad as I thought it would be, given how the cheerleaders tore people's reputation apart as a sport.

"It's even on social media," Karin said across from me. "Show him Chessie's message."

Eli took his phone back. "I screenshot it. He handed it back to me. I read with apprehension:

My boyfriend Seth got struck by lightning
@GavintheBuffKingPrescott party!
Ouch! no worries! his mom says he's ok.
My kisses will heal him faster ?
#Dormanthigh #boyfriend #soccerplayer
#party#lightningstrike#ambulance
#scary#cool

I sighed, relieved. There was nothing about an old man or any strange magic that night. There wasn't any proof what happened last night was real.

"Her tweet isn't as bad as Ashanti's text."

"The lightning strike fried his brain," Karin told Eli.

"What's the big deal," I said. Karin motioned to Eli. "Show him Chessie's recent status updates."

"Hold on a sec." Eli swiped his phone a few times before handing it over. I read:

10:32am: Gonna c my bae @Saint Mary's
hospital. I hope he's alright!
#boyfriendgirlfriend#accident
#girlfriendtoastar #SaintMarys

12:26pm: I hope this dress doesn't look too

inappropriate for a hospital visit to c

my bae! #islay

Image:

Chessie wore a short blue mini skirt and a sleeveless white blouse where she left unbuttoned at her cleavage. The top she wore was transparent. I hadn't noticed she wasn't wearing an undershirt before. I scrolled further down. My thumb paused at another picture and the bottom of my stomach dropped.

I had to check the time stamp to make sure this was what I was really seeing: 2:17pm.

The image captured a close-up side profile of Chessie and I locking lips right here in the hospital room. My eyes were closed as we kissed- I could practically see the sleep crust from the corners of my eyes. Underneath the picture was a caption:

My kisses do heal him faster! Don't u agree?!

#myboyfriend#spontaneouskiss#hospitalvisit

#SaintMarys

It was the best kiss I ever had and the whole world had a front-row seat. My cheeks were on fire.

"She wanted you as her boyfriend after you won nationals and now she's blasting your status all over the Internet," said Karin. "I can't believe you kissed her."

She somehow looked upset and hurt. Eli grabbed back his phone and pocketed it. "What Karin is trying to say is, she doesn't believe Chessie's worth the heartache."

"I think you misinterpreted what I was trying to say Eli and it's not very hard," Karin said. "Chessie is the slut who will rip Seth's heart out."

I already had a headache and my whole body was throbbing in pain. I wasn't in the best mood. "Karin, whatever crap you have against Chessie has nothing to do with my relationship with her."

"Why are you always defending her?" Karin accused. "You don't get it, do you?" she burst. "You're an accessory- a game to her. God, I don't understand why you're so blind!"

She stomped her way back to the door. I was about to say something I probably would regret, but Karin surprised me. She wheeled back on her heels at the last second and sat on the hospital couch instead. She crossed her legs and arms, furious.

"Let's drop the subject, deal?" Eli said lightly but his eyes were hard.

"Whatever," Karin said. I didn't respond. It was the same conversation I had with her every week. It never went anywhere.

There was an abrupt knock on the door and Mom came in with a large brown bag with coffee and my soccer bag. She kissed me on the cheek and greeted my friends.

"You left your phone in the truck." She handed it to me.

"I bought you a new change of clothes and some warm food. I don't think you will enjoy the hospital food more than a coffee with a turkey and cheese sandwich."

I perked up. "With mustard and jalapeños?" Mom passed over the greasy brown bag and smiled. "Of course."

"Awesome. Thanks, Mom." I placed it on the nightstand. I'd eat right after I removed the gown. "I'm leaving today, right?"

Mom nodded. "Yes. I will be downstairs signing you out. Come down in half an hour in the lobby." She placed my soccer bag beside Karin on the couch and departed. I glanced at Karin. "Can you leave the room?" Her expression hardened in alarm. "Why?"

"I need to change into a shirt and jeans. Got a problem with that?"

She scoffed. "Please. I've seen you in your underwear."

I looked at her confused. Eli's face fell.

"Oh, for crying out," she smacked her head with an open palm then stood abruptly. "Alright, I'll let you change in privacy."

"When did you ever see Seth in his underwear?" Eli asked her.

"Halloween," Karin said as if it were obvious. "You guys were dressed as fat baby angels in diapers."

"Diapers then, not underwear," Eli said. Karin smiled. "It wasn't as funny as the home video when you were a baby." She winked at me.

"My mother showed you that?" I sounded irritated.

"I told her," Eli corrected. "I simply gave Karin the play by play."

"Why'd you do that for?"

Eli grinned at the memory. "It was a cute video of your Mom changing and bathing you, rubbing ointment on your dangly parts-"Karin was laughing so hard O'Keeffe rolled over in his bed. The door opened and Chessie walked in and heard the last part of the sentence.

If an earthquake opened up in the center of the room, I would have taken a leap.

CHAPTER THREE

While Mom discharged me downstairs, Eli and Karin left the hospital early to hang out. I collected my personal effects that were left in the hospital closet. In the plastic bag was one thing salvageable-Dad's old watch. I wonder if Mom told him where I was.

I doubt it. She probably wouldn't have called him unless I was in a coma.

I inspected the watch. Its worn leather was a darker shade of brown and it splintered against my hand. A large crack centered on the dial. The hands were frozen on 9:57.

I glared at it, forcing it to fix itself. I had the sudden impulse to throw it away and forget about it. I scowled again and carefully placed it into my bag and strolled out to of the room.

I headed towards the elevator with Chessie. She reached out a hand and gently squeezed my palm as we went down the hallway.

"What are you up to today?" I asked.

Chessie grinned. "Why? You want me to nurse you back to health?"

I raised an eyebrow. "I think my Mom got that part, thanks. I'm seriously asking."

She shrugged. "Just gonna go hang out with some friends and chill. I'll probably meet with Ashanti later."

We paused before the elevator. She removed her hand from mine and dug into her pocket. She started checking her phone messages.

The elevator arrived and we stepped inside. Chessie suddenly squealed out loud. I almost went into cardiac arrest.

"Aww, Ashanti and Lauren liked the picture of us kissing! That is so sweet of them!"

"What?" Once my heart calmed down enough, I asked, "Are you talking about the picture you took of us earlier in the hospital room?" Her head bobbed up and down. "Yes!"

I pushed the button for the lobby floor and said nothing.

"Oh! Ashanti just commented!" She read the message. "'Hot.'"

"You shouldn't have posted it," I muttered. Chessie continued scrolling through her phone. I went on. "Moments like that, don't you think it should be, you know, between us?"

She didn't glance up and shrugged instead. "It's just a photo."

"Chessie, you already know I hate taking pictures. Then you show one of the most private things in my life for cheerleaders to comment?"

She rolled her eyes up at me and linked her arm with mine. "Seth, it's just a photo of us kissing," she said again, sounding exasperated. "It's not a big deal. I sent it already so let it go."

We stared at one another until the elevator doors opened. An uneasy silence passed between us and I unlinked my arm. She looked at me crossly. "Really?"

I motioned towards the front desk. Mom didn't know about us and I had to figure out a way to break the news to her.

"I am almost finished. Do you have everything?" Mom asked as we neared.

"Sure," I said. I maintained a two feet distance from Chessie.

"Chessie, do you need a ride home?" Mom said.

"No thanks, Ms. Sanchez. I borrowed my mother's car."

Mom nodded then turned to me. "Logan's in the parking lot waiting for us."

My shoulders tensed. "Why is he here? You came in his truck instead?"

Mom sighed. "Seth, please. He just came from work and offered to pick us up."

I highly doubted he did it out of the kindness of his heart.

"Seth? See you around?" Chessie said, already leaving. I gave her a nod. "Sure."

"Bye, Ms. Sanchez," Chessie waved. After Chessie left, Mom tried again. "Why don't you go out and meet Logan out in front? You don't have to wait around here while I finish."

"Whatever you say." I turned and marched out of the hospital. It didn't take long 'till I spotted the red Chevy idling in the ambulance zone. What an ass.

Logan watched from his side view mirror as I walked beside his truck, hesitated, and opened the back door. I slid inside and shut the door with a snap. Aside from working in construction, Logan worked shipment in seafood and his truck always smelled of rank fish that matched his attitude.

"The way Beth was going on how hurt you were I'd swear you'd be walking in a wheelchair," he joked. "You look well enough to walk home."

"I don't want to be in this truck."

Logan was a fit bald man in his forties. He was at least two inches taller than I, standing at six-foot-three. He looked intimidating but I wasn't about to show it.

He turned in his seat. His moustache bristled. "Then get out."

"I would if I could." We both knew we tolerated each other because of Mom.

Mom's gaze swept across the parking lot and spotted Logan's truck. I gradually leaned back in my seat and clamped my mouth shut. Logan wore a cool expression by the time she climbed in. The only indication he was still stewing from our conversation was the vein throbbing at his neck.

"We are ready to go." Mom beamed at Logan and gave him a peck on the cheek. "Thank you for picking him up," she said.

"Yeah, sure," Logan shrugged and shifted to drive. "We also have to make another stop at the drugstore," Mom said. She gave him an apologetic look.

"Why?"

"He was prescribed medicine for his injuries. He also needs his ointment cream." Mom dug into her bag and handed me the doctor's note of prescriptions.

"And he needs to get them now?"

Mom wore a wounded expression. "Yes. I know he could always go get them."

"Hey Mom," I called out from the back seat, "I was planning on stretching my legs for a bit. I can get them later. Kill two birds with one stone."

Mom's shifted in her seat. Her face softened as she met my eyes. "You just left the hospital."

"I'll only be gone for two hours, no biggie."

"You're not allowed to stay out late and use the truck."

"Yeah, I know." I leaned an arm on the doorsill and placed my head in the crook of my elbow. I stared out the window. The sky was murky gray. I thought of something.

"Don't you have work today?"

Mom shifted again in her seat. "Ms. Hutchinson's daughter came to visit her for a few days so they won't need me for work."

Mom worked as a CNA for old folks. For two years she's been an in-house caregiver for Ms. Hutchinson, an eighty-three-year-old woman. Her family never visits her, according to Mom. This was the first time I heard she had a daughter.

Logan turned into our uneven driveway, passed the crooked mailbox, and parked in front of a small orange and white house where weeds and wild grass grew in the front yard. The numbers to the house were so chipped and worn the nail holding the number six flipped into a nine. I stepped out of the car before the engine cut off. I headed inside the house and retreated to my bedroom.

Two of Karin, with her fingertips touching from opposite ends of the room, would be able to measure the size of my bedroom from all four walls. Posters of my favorite band Grunge Steak hung over a gaping hole in the wall that was here before we moved in. A few posters of my favorite Korean dramas Karin got me for my birthday last year: Happy Happy Face, Lovers Across the Stars, and The Gentlemen's Way, pinned the walls.

I kicked off my shoes and shoved them under my bed where over a dozen soccer trophies lay (I didn't have any space to put them anywhere else).

I sat on my creaky bed. On one side of the room was a small computer desk with an ancient laptop handed down from Dad. Two small picture frames stood beside it.

The first frame was the immediate family: Dad, Abuela Antonia, Abuelo Miguel who passed away when I was ten, and my Tía Evangeline with Mom and I at a party. I was six in that picture, the year I came from Cuba to the States. Back then, Mom and Dad dragged me to family gatherings at Abuelo and Abuela's home every weekend.

Fiestas were a time when my aunts, uncles, and their friends played castanet, dominos, and mancala while Spanish music filled the block. Their white neighbors didn't mind the noise because they always crashed the party and stayed for the food.

Looking back, I wanted to be born into a traditional American family because they weren't forced to meet ten or so of their extended families on a daily basis. Funny how the very thing I didn't want then is the very thing I miss now. Mom and I couldn't visit Abuelo and Abuela's house the way we used to. It'd be too complicated.

The second picture frame was with Dad, Mom, and I when I was twelve. We were at our old house before we moved to Little Havana, Hialeah, and then landed in North Miami. Dad and I were leaning on the hood of his shiny new Hyundai, both our arms waving high as if we were prince and king of the world. Mom was hanging out the window, waving to the camera. The picture captured a moment in time when life was good. If I had known Dad would have left that summer, I wouldn't have been smiling so hard.

I don't know why I still kept that picture; maybe it was because I wanted to remember the good old days. Maybe I kept it because it was one of the last pictures I had of Dad with us. Or maybe it was the only proof I had of a time Dad wasn't a lying, cheating asshole.

I threw my arm sling on the ground and lay stiffly in bed, wincing. The car ride from the hospital drained me. My arm was swollen and throbbing and all I wanted to do was sleep off the pain. I fell into an uncomfortable nap.

Sixa's deep rumbling alerted my ears. He stopped Vaora in the corridors and pulled her behind him until they reached her chambers. They had been arguing.

"You are to stay in your chambers and accept no other visitors but myself, your ladies-in-waiting, and Chancellor Melwimik," Sixa ordered. "The rumors surrounding you have reached the ears of the Council," he seethed.

"All baseless," Vaora snapped. "You know this."

"It may be baseless, but you are on dangerous grounds," Sixa warned. "Your ladies-in-waiting, the royal guards, and the servants out in the hall reported they heard you shouting in the library, a few days before the king collapsed."

Vaora sounded affronted. "They all heard incorrectly." She began to pace. "I admit I was in the library at the time but I never said such vile things! I never said I hated Father's reign, I swear it. I never declared I was happy he was dying by my hands-"

"Control your tongue!"

"You bark as though I truly uttered those heartless words!"

Sixa seized a moment to restrain himself. He lowered his voice. "Speak to your lawyer of this case; do not present it to me."

"But you are my brother," she moaned. "Whom better could I express

to?"

Sixa sounded dignified. He maintained his composure.

"I am speaking as heir of the crown. There are ears all around us. Speak to your lawyer. He is better suited to free you from this.

"More than a moment went by before Vaora spoke quietly.

"I understand."

"Good. You are fortunate the Council merely confined you to your chambers and not a cell," he said. "Keep your head low. I will handle all that I can for your sake. I will look after the king in your stead."

I reviewed what I had heard from Sixa and questioned his words of diplomacy and sincerity. Was he my true enemy? Or was it my daughter?

I stopped listening to them and focused on Chancellor Melwimik. He rooted patiently over my bed. He wore a crimson shirt that matched his eye color and cottoned gray pants. His jaw pursed tightly as he stood still, staring straight ahead at nothing.

"What is the next report, Melwimik," I demanded. Melwimik straightened, breaking into a live stature. He discerned I was listening and knew better than to ask what I heard. Sweat dotted his silk shirt as he revealed his following report.

"Yes, my king. Under heavy interrogation we learned there was someone else who was involved in poisoning your food. Debnard, the head chef."

Fury consumed me. He was an old friend after two hundred and four years. This same man made tonics and medicine when my children were sick and wanted to poison me. The man had been in this castle longer than I've been king and he planned to commit murder. For his treachery the punishment was death. I would mourn him when Parpagg and all involved were found.

Right after the dream, I had a nightmare about the old man from that night.

My head throbbed and my arm and chest burned like crazy. I should have gone to the drugstore when I had the chance yesterday.

I rolled to my side and glanced at the clock on the desk. 4:15 AM. I slept the whole day away. A sudden thought echoed in my head.

Sixa.

I shuddered. I tossed and I turned, trying hard to fall back to sleep. My nightmares were blurring the lines of what was real or imagined.

I peeled the covers off and headed to the kitchen for a glass of water. I downed my first glass- the water barely hit my stomach. I was parched again.

Vaora.

My chest and arm felt like they were on fire and I was so thirsty.

I ended up downing several glasses in a row, attempting to quench a bottomless well. I went to the freezer and filled up a plastic bag with ice. I tied it and started icing my arm first- the swelling still hadn't gone down. In fact, it looked a little bigger than before I went to sleep. It wasn't normal, any of this.

King Razhatlab.

My knees started to shake. I had to get a grip on myself. I could blame all this on the lightning strike; there was no other way to explain what was going on with me. I held on to the kitchen sink with my head hanging low. It was getting harder to think clearly.

I took off my bandages and started stripping my shirt off on the way to the bathroom. I quickly hopped into the shower and blast it on cold.

I was in the bathroom for a long time. Tired of standing under running water, I climbed out of the tub and headed to my room.

I rammed my feet into my running shoes and was out the front door in under three minutes.

I started down the road. I didn't shoot off as fast as I would have liked since my arm and chest were still sore so I began at a slow jog. Once I found my pace, my feet drummed against cement as the cool wind warmed against my skin. Soon the world became a blur. Adrenaline pumped in my veins as the heat that stuck to my bones disappeared.

Now feeling more alive, I started shouting as I flew down the block, expelling frustration and fear. My feet gradually stopped in front of Emilio's Café that stood on the corner of a busy block right beside a gas station.

It was a weird location for a small Cuban restaurant to sit next to a McDonalds and a Pizza Hut, but Emilio was a genius. He catered to a demographic that still appreciated their *café con leche* and their Cuban bread fix. A line of people would come up to the window before Emilio opened while other customers waited in plastic chairs and tables outside on the gravel lot. It was too early in the morning for customers but it was odd seeing the cafe emptier than how I remembered it.

Mom wasn't much of a coffeemaker so Dad used to come here in the early morning before he would drop me off at school and head to work. I hated standing in the line for some stupid café con leche Dad obsessed about. He wouldn't drive anywhere else, not even when they built a Starbucks a half-mile away from home. He wanted the "original Cuban flavor."

I wondered if I stayed a little longer if I'd catch sight of him here. I quickly buried that stupid thought. Last ⁻ heard Dad lived in Sunrise, a city about an hour from here. Maybe his new wife bought him a fancy espresso machine and made him coffee every morning. I hoped she made terrible coffee.

I didn't drag back home until it was half past eight. Aside from the headache that hadn't left me since yesterday, due to runners high, I was feeling okay. After I had my second longest shower of the morning, I caught my reflection in the mirror and stopped. My round face had a darker tan and my high cheeks were flushed which was normal after a run. I looked the same as I always did, with new dark circles resting under my eyes.

The peculiar thing about my reflection was my hair. It was dry as a bone. I slowly rose a hand to my head as my reflection did the same. I rubbed my hair between my fingers. It felt wet, sticking to my face and neck, but here my reflection had already styled his already dry hair. I rubbed my eyes. I was definitely tired.

Hard knuckles pounded the bathroom door. I flung the door open to Logan. He loomed in the hallway, eyeballing me. "When were you going to come out of there?"

I stood tall, staring back at him. "Whenever I felt like it." He glared back.

"Don't you have your own place? Your own bathroom?"

His mouth worked again. "If it weren't for her."

For a brief second he was ready to finish his statement with a threat, but another thought took a hold of him. Logan advanced with his teeth bared. He shoved past me and snapped the bathroom door shut.

I put on a fresh pair of jeans and a long black t-shirt before I went to the kitchen. I filled up my water cooler and an empty water gallon to the brim and gulped it all down in one go. Next, I started rummaging the fridge for breakfast.

Mom's bedroom door opened and my back stiffened. I flipped the frying pan a little too hard as someone neared.

"Buenos días, mi amor," Mom greeted. "Did you have a good night's sleep?"

I relaxed and turned around to plant a kiss on her cheek.

"I'm making half dozen eggs scrambled with some cinnamon toast and sausages. I'll make extra for you."

She nodded as she placed her empty bottle of Nyquil on the kitchen counter.

"¿Cómo sientes?" How are you feeling? She peered up at me, eyes full of apprehension.

I managed a smile. She didn't look like she had much sleep either. Dark circles rested below her eyes and her black curls were haphazardly tied in her Scrunchie. I gave her a side hug as one wrist picked up the cup of cut bell peppers. I dumped them in the frying pan and watched them sizzle. "It's a better morning now," I winked at her.

She self-consciously tucked a curl behind her ear. *"Ah, mi amor."* My love. She giggled and placed a kiss on my cheek. "Don't forget to pick up your prescription today. While you are there, please get me a bottle of Nyquil."

"They check ID's for that," I told her, adding eggs into the pan.

"Oh," she remembered, nodding. "Then I will have Logan buy it instead. Did you go running?"

"Yes I did, but trust me I'm fine," I said quickly. "I don't need to wear the arm sling and bandages anymore. The prescriptions will be a waste of money."

She seemed insulted. "They are not a waste of money."

"I am getting better without them," I said. I didn't want to argue.

"*Mijo*, don't worry about silly things, eh?" She gripped my hand and shook it firmly. "I am your mother and I will provide for you. If the pills will make you better it is worth every peso." I knew there was no point to convince her otherwise. "I understand. Can you help stir the cinnamon toast batter?"

She watched me, knowing I was changing the subject. "I really can't cook without you," I added. That made her smile.

When I was ten years old and Mom worked crazy evening and morning shifts, she tended to forget to stock on food while Dad worked as a manager at a cellphone store all day and crashed at home during the night.

After a few nights of eating cereal for dinner, I decided I'd make food out of anything from the cupboard. I started off with making little things like adding peanut butter to pancakes or mixing Ramen noodles with cold chicken nuggets from McDonalds. Dad came home one evening with a bunch of cookbooks from a bookstore and placed them in the cupboard. He never said anything about it and I never did ask. We both knew at that point cooking was something I was interested in. It wasn't long until I enjoyed it. A couple of those cookbooks were hidden deep inside my closet.

We were chowing down our breakfast when Logan entered the living room and turned on the T.V. He dialed up the volume.

"Beth, you hear this breaking news report?" Logan called out. "Some nut job was digging graves in the local cemetery and left the corpses on the highway."

"It's not like we're eating," I said drily.

"*Ay, dios mios,* what is the police saying?" Mom asked in shock.

"Nothing, as usual. What a sick and twisted world we live in." He strolled into the kitchen and kissed Mom on the lips before he sat and helped himself with the food in the middle of the table. He eyed my plate.

"You sure you're going to eat all that?" He pointed at my five slices of toast, three sausage links, and half dozen scrambled eggs.

"It's on my plate. What do you think I was gonna do, frame it?"

"Seth," Mom warned. The house phone interrupted. "Will you please see who is calling?" I stared at her. She held my gaze for a moment before she looked away. I shoved my chair back and picked up the receiver.

"Hello," I said gruffly.

"Hello? Seth?"

I frowned. "Yes?"

"Hola, Seth! ¿Cómo estás?" Hello, Seth! How are you?

It took me a moment to recognize who was on the other line. The voice was something between a cough and a wheeze, the same way someone would sound if you smoked cigarettes for the past twenty-two years.

"I'm good. I haven't heard from you in a long time. How are you?" I turned towards the dining table. Mom watched me as she picked at her eggs.

"I'm living, just living," Aunt Evangeline chuckled. At least I thought it was a chuckle. She started coughing away from her receiver. It took a few moments before she returned. "You do well in school? Play soccer still?" she asked.

"Yeah, I am."

"Who is it?" Mom finally asked.

"Aunt Evangeline," I told her, motioning her to the phone. I watched as her face fell. Her eyes became drawn and a slight panic set in her frown lines.

Mom dropped her fork and scooted back her seat. Tell her I'm not here, she mouthed. She squeezed Logan's forearm before she left the kitchen table. Logan continued to eat.

"Was that your mother?" Aunt Evangeline said.

"Uh," I started, but Aunt Evangeline already knew.

"When will she stop avoiding my calls?"

Great. I hated lying to her. "Actually, Mom stepped out. I'll just let her know you called."

"And I'm sure she will." I caught the bitterness in her tone. "She has to talk to me. God knows I do not have much time to say my goodbyes to everyone. I need my sister-in-law, *sobrino*. You understand what I am saying?" Aunt Evangeline coughed again. I nodded, my throat suddenly feeling tight. "I understand, auntie."

There was a pregnant pause. "You said you still play soccer?"

The shadow of the kitchen chair flinched. I frowned as I answered her. I was seeing things.

"Yes. We won nationals not too long ago."

"Aye, yes! You tell your Papa?"

My jaw automatically set. "Nope."

"Hmm. I will tell him, then."

"We won 3 to 2." I wanted Aunt Evangeline to pass on the message to Dad I was doing great without him.

"Aye!" She burst out again. She started coughing uncontrollably.

"I know you're happy for me. I wish you could watch me play, like you used to," I said.

"Yo también cariño, yo también," she agreed.

There was an awkward pause. I didn't know what else to say to carry on the conversation. "I have to go now. I was about to eat breakfast," I said lamely. *"Hasta luego,* Aunt Evangeline and take care."

"Love you," she said between a fit of coughs. "Please tell Beth... call me. I miss her," she rasped. "Call your father, too. *Adiós.*"

Click.

I looked at the receiver long after she hung up. I couldn't stand hearing her so sick and weak. Mom avoided Aunt Evangeline like the plague the same way I ignored Dad- who was I to judge? I couldn't blame her for feeling the way she did against Aunt Evangeline.

Mom was once a best friend to Aunt Evangeline, Dad's sister. After Dad's side of the family defended him when they knew he cheated on Mom, things changed. I knew Mom was hurting over Aunt Evangeline's health, but she just couldn't bring herself to see her. It was a typical Cuban mentality; the woman was the reason why the man stepped out on his family so she had to make it right. Mom also wasn't Cuban, but Española, and it already made her an oddball in the family.

Since I was little I'd always hear my jealous aunts say because my Mom and Dad married five months after meeting, their marriage wouldn't last. That comment still upset years later.

Back in the day, Dad visited Spain once with a few of his cousins and his two older brothers. Mom was a tour guide in Barcelona and Dad happened to book the tour last minute.

Because Dad kept making her laugh during the trip and he asked the most questions in his tour group, he caught mom's attention. Pretty soon they were taking a few private tours together around the city. Dad stayed in the country after his family had gone back to Cuba. According to Karin, that story sounded like something out of a romantic movie. And for Mom, it was. I remember when I was little how she would describe herself as a princess and Dad was the prince in the story. There was a happy ending every single time she told it.

A few months after meeting, Mom and Dad married in Spain and I was born a year later. My grandmother held a grudge that my Dad stayed in Spain and didn't go back to Cuba until I was two years old. My grandparents owned a farm in Cuba that needed taking care of, but my Mom didn't want to live in Cuba with Dad.

My parents finally came to an agreement they'd work hard to get their green cards to live in the States for a better life together as a family. Mom stayed in Spain while she got her green card for the U.S. while Dad went back to Cuba to help support his family. I was too much responsibility for my Mom at the time. I stayed with Dad and my grandparents for the next four years of my life.

I don't remember much of my time in Cuba but there was an old house that stuck in my memory. It had a large backyard with bananas and plantains we always ate and there were chickens scattered all over. I named a few chickens but one of them was a pet. I called it Tiki.

It took a few years but my uncles and aunts who were already living in Florida, helped Mom, Dad, and I get our green cards for the States. Dad left Cuba first so he could get everything ready for when the time came I could have a proper home in America. My grandparents ended up passing the farm to two of my Dad's older brothers. I was six years old when I first came to the States with my grandparents.

I hadn't laid eyes on my Mom since I was two years old so it was a weird reunion seeing her after so long. I was used to hearing her voice or seeing her on video calls. When my grandparents and I came off the plane, Mom was waiting at the gate. I remember someone ran up to us with tears in their eyes. I was scared at first, but suddenly she fell on her knees and hugged me tight. I suddenly knew who she was.

After all this time apart, here was Mom, live and in color. Then suddenly there was Dad, dropping on his knees, taking part of the hugging circle. I remember tears.

I think it was in that moment I understood. Both my parents were reunited with me. It felt like they were never going to let me go.

I grabbed my food and left Logan alone in the kitchen.

I stumbled back into my room in the dark and dropped on my bed, spilling some of my drink. I ignored the mess and placed my cup and plate on the floor.

I laid back in bed, suddenly feeling in worse shape. I was fine before I picked up the phone but now I was struggling to breathe. It felt like someone dumped a vat of jalapeno peppers on the upper half of my body was experiencing the burn. I looked down at my throbbing arm.

It was so swollen it looked grotesque; it was noticeably bigger than my right arm. Horrified, I was starting to feel like Quasimodo from *The Hunchback of Notre Dame*. I lifted my arm, twisting my wrist front and back. Scars stretched from my collarbone down to my wrist were irritated and red. When I inspected it closely, the red welts and scars had some sort of pattern that looked like I went to a tattoo shop and asked a ten-year-old to draw me a tattoo.

My power-

I sat abruptly.

My ears didn't pick up anything but the television and sounds coming from the living room. My eyes wandered to my closet, the floor, and back to my desk. I shifted up towards my window and widened the blinds. Sunlight pooled into the room.

I was sure I heard someone. It sounded like the person was standing right above me.

My vision went out of focus. I squeezed my eyes shut, trying to hold back the nausea. Somehow my thoughts swam back to my dreams. I relived a different tale.

For the fifth time today, Melwimik came with a new report. "My king," *Melwimik said diplomatically. "Our Passagekeepers are holding up the* *battle to safeguard our Passages, but they are losing in numbers. The* *R'uttri have been relentless."*

I chose my words carefully. "How are the humans?"

Melwimik's face grew somber. "The Bror Gate has been under more *attacks in the past four nights. Passagekeeper Emikrili has reported a* *dozen R'uttri and ghouls have entered the Bror Passage." It will only get* *worse, I feared.*

"How are Temcaltiaf and the people reacting to the broken Gate?"

"The forests are slowly dying as our suns are going out," he answered. *"The people of Temcaltiaf are worried but they are not panicked. The* *people still believe in the king." He bowed his head. I looked away.*

Bless them all. Bless the poor souls who have me for a king. Melwimik *paled, turning dusk yellow. "In relation to, the Council is having difficulty arranging another meeting with Lord Lagredi and Countess Ubu. The Council is hoping to negotiate any terms of assistance against the R'uttri who are breaching through-"*

"Lagredi and Ubu believe saving Temcaltiaf and the humans are up for discussion?" I exclaimed.

Melwimik faltered. "My king, due to the conspiracy murders of Imudmid's Council leaders as of late, they believe it is in their best interests for us to prevent our suns from waning." His eyes tightened. "Imudmidians are not affected by the lack of sun as we are," he reasoned bitterly. "The loss of the suns would only help expand their territory into ours."

I held up a hand. I heard enough. Though Lord Lagredi and Countess Ubu were Imudmidians I had no reason to believe they were sending R'uttri through the human world. I believed Mag. They were not responsible. "I will join in the next Council meeting."

"My king, you're unwell," Melwimik sounded alarmed.

"I will be in worse health the longer I allow the Council to handle affairs."

The Po'luxnann was robbed from me, and soon in effect the walls between the human world and my world D'uthne, would be gone. Blood and war would be as common as a sigh carried off in the wind. I adjusted myself on the duvet and turned my head on the pillow.

I gazed up at the ceiling. Stars and galaxies of swirling cosmic lights danced above. I found it hard not to be lost in the majesty of the grand design. It reminded me the universe was far greater than what lay ahead.

I blinked from the light in my eyes. The sun shined brightly through the glass window, high in the sky. There was nothing here in my room. No king, no chancellor.

I shakily sat up on the bed. I couldn't stop feeling grief that was not my own- I was seeing and hearing things that weren't there. I was going to drive myself crazy if I stayed in one place.

I texted Eli. I asked if he could pick me up and he soon replied he'd be down my block in an hour. That's one of the things I loved about Eli; he was always there when you needed him, no questions asked. After that was done, I heavily sat down on the floor, catching my breath. I glanced down at the cold plate of breakfast left untouched. I completely lost my appetite.

Eli texted me after an hour and said he was parked outside. I had the list of my doctor's prescriptions in hand and started out the house.

"Where are you going?" Mom called out from the living room. She was watching television. She was curled up against Logan on the couch with an arm wrapped around him like a life raft. My mood deepened.

"Eli's."

"News says there's a cold front moving in tonight. Coldest it's ever been in Florida in seventy-five years," she said. I could tell she was trying to make conversation. Mom rose off the couch. "Wait a moment. I want you to take something before you leave." She disappeared to my bedroom. I ignored another frustrated buzz in my jeans.

"How many times you need to shower a day?" Logan muttered. "Are you that dirty?"

I gave him a confused look. Logan's grip tightened around the remote as he glared at me. "Five showers. That's how many it takes to get you clean? Do you know how many gallons of water went down the drain because of you? Do you think we're made of money?"

My fist clenched. "Last I checked my Mom paid the bills. You don't live here," I said. "You are not my Dad- you don't get to school me."

Footsteps entered the living room. "Tell your boyfriend this isn't his house and he can't run me," I said, eyes set on Logan. Mom handed me my waterproof jacket, frowning. "I leave for one minute and you start an argument."

"I didn't," I retorted. "He has a problem with me taking a shower where I live." I gave her a look that asked, why are you still with this clown? She turned to Logan.

"He's running the hot water," Logan said. He rounded at me. "Are you going to take care of the bill come next month? You the man of the house?"

I lost my cool fast. "Since when was this your house?"

Logan threw the remote on the couch. "The bills and your mother say I am. You best shove that attitude somewhere else."

"Logan, calm down," Mom started.

It took so much of my control not to jump across the table and knock the man out.

I looked at Mom. She was shocked what Logan said but she was staring at me. She was more afraid of what I'd do next. My arm started to feel heavy and my headache wouldn't let up. I had to get out of here.

Kill-

I rounded on my heel and shut the front door behind me. Down the block, a black Toyota parked on the side of the broken driveway.

I threw my bag in the back and collapsed in my seat. Eli frowned at me. "What took you? You busy putting on makeup?"

I ignored him and clasped on my seatbelt. I reclined my seat and concentrated on breathing through my nose.

Eli shifted into reverse. "He's still sticking around?" he nodded to Logan's truck parked in the driveway.

I nodded grimly and shut my eyes. I was growing sicker.

"Just drive."

CHAPTER FOUR

We made a pit stop at Walgreens Pharmacy to pick up my prescriptions. After I dragged back to the car I heard, "Dude, you need to down those pills when we get to my place, stat." I knew I looked as bad as I felt.

Eli lived in a middle-class neighborhood with his dad, his ten-year-old sister Susan, and his mom who were both away on a trip to see his grandparents for the holidays. Eli parked beside his dad's patrol car in the driveway.

In the Goodchilds' front yard, inflated snowmen aligned the walkway that was filled with artificial snow, and a fat Santa in a sleigh stood in the middle of the yard. Colorful Christmas lights adorned the eaves on the roof, a wreath decorated the front door, and rope lights wrapped along the porch rails. All this reminded me when Mom, Dad, and I used to put these kinds of things up for Christmas. Eli was lucky to have that.

Before we made it up the front steps, a forty-two-year-old man with a five o'clock shadow stood in the doorway under the mistletoe, fully dressed in his police uniform.

"Haven't seen you around, Seth." Mr. Goodchild's wrinkles crinkled at the corners of his eyes.

"Hello, Mr. Goodchild."

"Has soccer been keeping you busy during winter break?"

"No, I just finished up the season," I said politely. The world tilted from where I stood. I had a hard time focusing.

"Can we chat away from the threshold?" Eli pointed up at the mistletoe. "With three dudes standing under it I'm getting a tad uncomfortable."

Mr. Goodchild gave Eli a look.

"You working again, Dad?" Eli asked.

"Yeah, it's always crazy this time of year. The station needs more hands on deck." He started to leave.

"I hope you catch the Graveyard Digging Loser," Eli told him. His father sighed. "Me too, son. Say hi to your mom for me, Seth."

Eli shut the door behind us and I followed him to his kitchen. "What was that all about?" I dropped into a barstool. I rested my head on the cool counter. Ahh. That was better.

"Dad and his precinct have been working around the clock. Holidays are the worse seasons for him; he's gotta deal with so many people wasted and he has to break up fights, and the accidents," he explained. He grabbed a glass from the cabinet and went to his fridge to the water dispenser. "The Graveyard Digger is the name people are calling the criminal who's digging up graves and leaving corpses off the sides of roads."

Eli handed me the glass. "Thanks. I heard about it," I mentioned, remembering what Logan said earlier about the news. I started twisting the caps off the prescribed pill bottles. I didn't want to apply my ointment yet.

"Police believe it's a prank, like 'To hell with Christmas', sort of thing. And if it is, it's an effed up one," he grimaced. "Some kids found the corpse of a two-year-old kid in a park. The body was missing an arm, a leg looked like it was chewed off like some dog got to it. The eyes were gone."

"What the heck," I said.

"Dad said the dead girl's parents were already going crazy when they came down to the station. They had just buried their daughter last week, and now they're going to have to bury her all over again." Eli's jaw tightened. "What a screwed up Christmas."

"That's horrible, man."

What those parents of the girl were experiencing must have been hell. The situation brought me back to King Razhatlab's sorrow.

No.

I quickly stopped myself.

We went up to Eli's room as soon as I was done. Eli's room, three times bigger than mine, had posters of video game vixens tacked onto every inch of his walls and ceiling.

Eli's parents weren't thrilled he had a half dozen piercings and dyed his hair into a flaming cockatoo, but they figured it was better for Eli to express himself this way than with drugs- not that he did any. Eli booted up his Xbox Live and handed me a controller.

I was feeling better after taking my medicine, well enough to play Call of Duty with other gamers online the entire day. In the middle of the game, Karin called Eli and said she was coming over and showed up around seven with a new recipe she'd made. Eli and I scarfed down her pasta on the double.

"How long have you guys been at it?" She nodded to the game.

"'Bout eight hours," Eli said. "Seth's been going at it all day. My buddy here hadn't taken a break until you came."

"You're going to blow your entire winter break on video games like you blew your summer?"

"Pretty much."

"Yup," I agreed.

She let out an exasperated groan. "What a waste. So how is it?" Karin motioned to the bowl of food.

"It's okay," I said between a slurp.

"Don't screw around. Tell me the truth," she said.

Eli sighed. "We're guys, Karin. We're going to tell you it tastes like food." He pointed at the floor to the two empty bowls of chips, the five empty boxes of microwaved deep-dish pizzas, and the bowl of chicken nuggets that was almost gone. "We fart, we scratch, and we eat."

Karin snorted. "I need the food critic to tell me how my food tastes, not you, the rabid caveman."

"Seth was the caveman that ate everything in my fridge today," Eli informed her.

Karin looked at me. "What can I say? I'm a growing boy," I told her.

"Whatever," she waved my comment away. "What do you think of my food?"

I slowly slurped my food, allowing the flavors to dance around my tongue. Karin waited impatiently for a response. I put the bowl down, coming down to a verdict.

"Well, you put too much basil- it's overpowering on my tongue. You dumped garlic cloves into the pasta at the last second, right?"

Sure enough, Karin averted my eyes, proving me right. "It tastes as though the garlic was undercooked. The pasta is overcooked, though. Then there's the uneasy balance of too much tomato sauce than the quantity of pasta. They're supposed to work in harmony, not duel it out in a cage we call my mouth."

"I doubt the quantity of pasta sauce makes a difference," Karin grumbled.

"But it does," I said. "It's almost as if I'm drinking tomato soup. Would you prefer dry old tofu or undercooked eggs?"

Eli snickered. "I love how Seth goes all manly with kitchen talk." I gave him a look. "You're hilarious, Eli."

Here's the thing. In middle school I tried to hide my cooking from Eli until Mom let slip I cooked the meals I took with me to school for lunch. Eli thought it was a joke but after he came over the house and tasted one of my dishes, he became a believer. Karin became friends with us in eighth grade, and it turned out she wanted to practice cooking because her mother, a traditional Korean woman, believed girls had to learn to cook no matter what. Not that Karin cared to uphold cultural ideals. She only wanted to please her mother, not that she'd say it out loud.

"Why are you cooking pasta?" said Eli. "Shouldn't you be working on *kimchi* or *jjapchae*? I mean, they're Korean food."

"It's my mother's way of training me to cook. She wants to keep 'Korean foods sacred' until I can learn how to cook properly,'" she air quoted. I picked up the bowl and sniffed, sensing something else.

I turned to Karin. "You added liquor?"

Karin's jaw slacked open. "No, I didn't! I- geez. I used grape vodka for an extra kick."

"Karin," Eli said, "If I start heaving up a lung,"

"I only added a tiny bit, I swear," she said again. "How did you know I added vodka?"

"I can taste it," I said.

"I was watching a cooking show and the woman put in grape wine and we didn't have wine so I added a little vodka," Karin said apologetically.

Eli put down his bowl and I did the same. "I swear you want to kill me," Eli said. Karin looked a little hurt.

Eli had liquor intolerance and found out the hard way this past summer at a party. He stayed away from that stuff like the plague.

"Karin, vodka is liquor," I said.

"You know," Eli began, lightening the tension, "speaking of food and bathrooms,"

"We never mentioned bathrooms," I pointed out.

"I mentioned throwing up which leads us to bathrooms. Anyway, have you ever sneezed while taking a dump? It's an interesting combination of shooting-"

Karin threw a pillow at him. "Remember when I said you talked too much?" she said and changed the subject. "So guys, what are you doing for Christmas besides playing video games?"

We both shrugged. "We already said nothing," Eli said.

"Perfect." She clasped her hands together. "Remember when I told you ages ago my mother had this New Year's Eve gala at the Del Riel Hotel?"

"Either the food was poisoned or there was a catch," Eli said. "I should have known."

"Why do we have to go?" I asked.

"It will be a nightmare if you guys aren't there to keep me from strangling my mom and she's dragging me there to show me off. She hopes I'll be a big shot businesswoman and the gala will be the perfect environment for me to form some company relationships. I know you guys already said no,"

"And yet you keep bringing up the subject," Eli muttered. My phone vibrated in my pocket. I brought it out and read the caller ID.

"Look at him," Karin winced. "His face lit up like a thousand Christmas trees." I ignored her and pushed the talk button on my phone.

"Hey, Chessie, what's up?" I attempted to keep my voice casual but my heart was hammering a mile a minute. Karin rolled her eyes and lay flat on her back on the bed. Eli started whistling and resumed the game. I covered the mouthpiece and pressed my ear to the receiver.

"Hey boyfriend, I was wondering why I haven't heard from you." I heard soft music playing in her background.

"Yeah? I'm good. I called you twice and left you a voice message today," I said.

"Oh? Well, I guess your calls didn't go through. I was pretty busy texting Ashanti all day," she chirped.

I frowned. "If Ashanti was on the phone with you all day, you would have seen my calls," I said, but she went on. "What are you doing right now?"

"Playing video games at Eli's."

"Let me guess; Karin's there too?"

I decided to allow the silence speak for itself. After a beat, Chessie continued. "I was wondering," she said coyly, "did you eat dinner yet?"

"Nah, I didn't have dinner," I said.

Eli tore his eyes away from the game and winked deviously. Karin prodded me hard on the shoulder with her foot. "Liar."

I covered the mouthpiece. "Shut up, guys. Karin, when was the last time you washed your feet?"

Karin smirked as I adjusted the cell to my ear.

"Well, do you want to have dinner with me at Black Tie?"

"Sure, sounds like a plan."

"Great! See you in half an hour?" Chessie asked.

I checked my phone for the time, already standing.

"Alright."

"Bye."

She hung up.

"What'd she want?" Karin said coolly.

"A date," I said.

"So, you were talking about some gala," Eli said as he resumed playing Call of Duty.

Karin pursed her lips. "My Mom's gala. I already bought four very expensive tickets last summer, remember? And each dinner plate costs money, and if bodies aren't at the reserved table my mom will throw a fit."

"Why'd you buy four tickets- damn, man! Who the hell keeps clipping me from behind?" Eli glared at the screen. "Yo, Dballin', why aren't you covering us?" He spoke into his head mike.

"Karin was still friends with Chessie when she bought them," I said. Karin narrowed her eyes at me. "Did I say anything wrong?" I told her. "I'm willing to go if Chessie is invited."

"You must be really high."

"And if Chessie isn't invited, Eli's not going," I said. "Right, Eli?"

"Yes! Eat my fire, asshole," Eli shouted then rounded to me. "What?"

"You'll go to the gala if Chessie comes," I said. "Sure, whatever," Eli said, his attention back to his game. Karin was heated. "What are you trying to prove?"

I sighed. "The crap between you and Chessie needs to stop."

"You expect me and her will make up at the gala?"

"I'm hoping for a Christmas miracle," I said drily. "You're not stupid to risk a fight with Chessie in front of all those suits coming to the gala. When's the party?"

"You are full of it, you know that? *Napoo nom*," she muttered bad guy in Korean and took a few seconds to deliberate.

I knew Karin hated being alone at big events, even school parties. If she didn't have Eli or me around, she'd be left at the mercy of her mom, but deep down I also knew she missed Chessie. If she didn't, she wouldn't be angry enough to care.

Karin pulled out two tickets from her pocket and slapped them on my open palm. "Next week Saturday. Doesn't mean I'll be talking to her," she said coolly.

I pocketed both tickets. "As long as she's invited, I'm good." Karin gave me an aggravated look. "The attire is formal, no slacks," she warned.

"We're going to have to dress up in suits like penguins?" Eli said. He turned back to the screen. "I'm not talking to any of y'all," he addressed the gamers online.

"What'd you expect?" Karin said. "It's a black-tie affair, loser." She dangled her feet in front of his face. Eli shrugged it off. "So does black tie also mean we'll be seeing you in a dress?" he asked. There were sounds coming through his headphones.

"Man, I wasn't talking to any of you, jokers," he said into his mike.

I could hear the players laughing on the other end. Karin slid off the bed and sat beside him.

"So, you'll be in a dress?" he asked again.

Karin's face softened. "It's not as though I can go to a fancy gala in shorts."

Eli went quiet for a moment. He nodded.

"Cool." He continued playing the game.

I checked under Eli's bed, searching for sneakers. Karin got up and sat on the bed, moving out of the way. "I have to meet Chessie in a half hour at Black Tie," I said.

"Shouldn't you be heading home now?" Karin said. I had mentioned earlier about Mom's recent ground rules.

"I can stay out a little later. Mom said Logan was going to buy a bottle of Nyquil today. She must be knocked out by now." I emerged from under the bed with one sneaker.

"You know," Eli thought, "you've been holding out so long to date Chessie that Marion stole your first kiss."

I looked at him. "Seriously, why man?" Karin lay on her stomach and propped her head beside Eli's. "It's true, Marion was his first kiss."

"Marion wasn't my first," I said defensively.

Eli grinned. "The whole school saw you on the field, bro."

"Even a three-year-old can tell the difference between what's a kiss from his mommy and one from a guy snogging a slutty cheerleader," Karin said. "Seth didn't look like he enjoyed it though," she recalled. "Even I was embarrassed for him."

"Are you blind?" Eli said. He paused his game and turned off the mike. "Have you seen Marion? The only thing that should have been awkward was revealing a boner in the middle of the field."

"Guys, would you shut up?" I found both sneakers and shoved my feet inside them. I remembered something. "Eli, can I borrow your car?"

"Sure, bub. As long as you disinfect the car after you do the freaky with

Chessie," he joked.

"You've got issues, man."

He grinned. "I know, but you got a bigger problem than me; you haven't been laid in seventeen years. Don't you ever feel like you've been a deprived man searching the desert for water?"

Karin grabbed a pillow and bopped him on the head. "You act like being a virgin is a sin. Ever thought some people want to wait for the right person?"

"Anybody's the right person," Eli said. "It's all about the timing."

"Eli," Karin warned.

I straightened. "Yeah, it's all about the timing." That headache started creeping up again. "You think what happened to Chessie with Erving was 'all about the timing?'"

Eli's shoulders stiffened. Karin propped herself up on her elbows and stared at me then Eli.

"Your keys are on the key hook?" I said to Eli, trying to keep my tone even. I didn't wait for an answer and left the room.

CHAPTER FIVE

It wasn't Eli's fault I was peeved over what he said, but my knuckles whitened as I clutched the steering wheel. Chessie was one of the most important people in my life. I know I wasn't there when it happened, but it was still my fault.

Headlights swung at me as I made a sharp turn. The traffic light turned red and I nearly plowed into a vehicle coming in the opposite direction. I shook my fury off like a winter coat. I had to nip that memory in the bud, at least for tonight.

I pulled in front of Black Tie, a restaurant Chessie's family owned in downtown Miami. I sat in the parking lot for a few minutes before I pulled out a cigarette and the lighter from the glove compartment. I stood outside on the side of an alley, relieving stress as I puffed on a cigarette.

Rain started to fall. I stomped the bud underneath my shoe and chewed some mint gum. I pulled my jacket over my head and ran inside.

Black Tie was a large red and black building. Inside, mellow lights hung overhead in yellow, blue, and red. Bars, tables, and booths were deep chestnut and brown. Chairs were faded cream from years of wear and tear.

Chessie's sister, Charlene, A.K.A Charlie, met me at the front entrance. She swept past her customers waiting for her to seat them and crushed me into a hug. Charlie was five-foot-three with the same wavy brown hair as Chessie but she wore it above her shoulders. She also had on this heavy eyeliner around her hazel eyes. Charlie graduated high school more than a year ago but she chose to take time off school. I had no idea what her plans were. According to Chessie, her sister wasn't in a rush to figure her life out.

"Charlie," I said, trying to slip gently out of her grasp. "How you been?"

"How have *you* been? It's about time you and Chessie started dating!" She jumped up and down on the soles of her feet. Her customers in front grew irritated. I leaned down closer to her ear and whispered.

"Charlie, if your dad sees you doing this he'll say you're being unprofessional." Not to mention he'd boot me out for promoting her unprofessionalism. Charlie rolled her eyes. "Puh-lease. As if I care."

I shook my head. "Is Chessie out there?" I said, moving toward the booths. "You don't have to seat me. I'll catch you later," I said, leaving Charlie pouting.

"You will tell me how you asked her out, right?" she called out.

I waved behind me and smoothed my fingers through my messy hair. Suddenly I was self-conscious over my stained jacket and jeans I wore. Mr. Jensen wouldn't be happy seeing the guy dating his daughter a wild mess.

Another thought hit me. He must have known about our relationship. Charlie was hardly someone who could keep a secret.

I cast a glance around in case Mr. Jensen lurked in the corner with kitchen knives. Chessie sat in the back where three long tables took most of the space. I frowned. These tables were usually reserved for customers celebrating birthdays or meetings with family members and friends. She smiled, motioning me over. My heart lodged in my throat and my palms were getting slippery every step I took.

Chessie was stunning as usual and the light ambiance made her look irresistible. She wore this blue and white dress and a blue flower clip let her wavy hair fall completely to one side of her face. I noticed she wore a lot more makeup than usual. I wished I had borrowed something nice from Eli to wear before I came. She was so beautiful.

Chessie stood and grabbed my hand, pulling me close and met my lips. When she let go, I officially wanted to rid the world of lip gloss. Chessie sat and I pushed in her chair. I grabbed the seat across from her.

"How are you feeling?" She motioned to my arm and chest. "No arm sling?"

"I'm fine without it," I responded.

"That's good. So boyfriend," Chessie murmured, "I already ordered you your favorite. Or would you rather the special?"

"Sure," I winked as she propped her elbows on the table then folded her hands under her chin. She flashed a wicked smile. I raised an eyebrow. "If the special is you." Chessie laughed. "You are such a tease."

"Nah, I'm just trying to be cheesy," I said, leaning forward. I paused, feeling a frown crease my forehead. "Is it really okay to kiss here? With your family around?"

She raised a brow. "What are you afraid of?"

"Your dad, for starters." Chessie peered down at my hands and began making tiny circles on the top of my right hand with her finger. She sent electrifying shivers through my shoulders. "I won't let Daddy get in the way of us."

Her gaze and soft voice had me fighting the urge to pull her into my arms. Instead, I placed her hands in mine. I wanted to ask her out to the

New Year's Eve gala, but I wanted to do it somewhere else. "You want to go for a walk after dinner?"

Chessie pursed her lips together. "It's getting late. Daddy expects me to be home by midnight."

I snorted. "When was coming home without your dad knowing ever a problem? Just climb up your tree to your bedroom. It's no big deal, right? It's not the first time you've done it." I leaned over the table and lowered my voice. "Then later I can sneak into your room and cuddle," I said, playfully serious.

Chessie smiled and removed her hands from mine. I suddenly missed her touch. "We'll see."

Code for, I don't think so.

I tried not to let it get to me. Maybe Chessie wanted things to go slow. I could do slow; I waited four years for the love of my life.

"Hey Denis," Chessie greeted him.

The waiter they hired three months ago approached with our food. He halted at our table and nearly dropped the dishes onto the floor as they clattered onto the table. Some of the pasta slipped off the plate and onto the tablecloth.

"Sorry," he mumbled and gulped like a frightened kitty. He was only nineteen-years-old, but he hung his head low like a kid called out for getting into trouble.

"Um, here's your Cajun chicken Alfredo and Caesar salad."

"Actually, I ordered the Alfredo for Seth and that's my salad," Chessie pointed.

"Sorry," Denis muttered, and passed over my plate as some of the escaped pasta dragged onto the tablecloth. I winced.

Chessie addressed me with a grin. "Do you want any dessert?"

She hadn't noticed the guy was staring at her with an unwavering gaze.

My back stiffened. "No, thanks." I gripped Chessie's hand on the table and lightly squeezed. Denis quickly looked away and pretended not to notice.

"Thanks, Denis." Chessie dismissed him and he scurried away to the kitchens. Chessie's gaze wandered to me. "What was that all about?"

I didn't know how stupid I sounded until the words flew out of my mouth. "The guy has a crush on you."

"So?"

I blinked. "What do you mean, 'so'?"

Chessie rolled her eyes. "You're worrying about something that doesn't even matter," she said matter-of-factly. "It's not like I'm interested in him."

I didn't know why her answer bothered me, but it did. "Look," I started but Chessie was distracted. There was a loud clamor of customers hooting and hollering at the front of the restaurant.

Chessie's eyes flickered nervously.

"Okay, don't freak out, but I invited a couple people to eat with us."

"What?"

She leaned over the table and whispered hurriedly. "Okay not a couple," she admitted, "but a group of people. Just be nice, okay?"

"What are you talking about?" The noise was coming behind me. I turned to follow her gaze. It's when they got closer the muscles in my stomach tightened. Gavin, Ross, Carl, and Manny came into view, making a show of themselves- in tow were the cheerleaders. Ashanti, Odessa, Marion, and Laura wore sweaters over their bikini tops, booty shorts, and wore flip-flops. They were all soaking wet.

I faced her. "Chessie, what are they doing here?"

"I invited them," she straightened as they neared.

"Seth, be nice. Do it for me?"

Gavin smirked as he arrived at our table. He knew I would have rather eaten a bowl of live roaches than dine with him. He threw a slick smile at Chessie who returned it. "You know it took us forever in this rain to find this hole in the wall?"

"Glad you found it okay," she said. "Don't worry about my promise; ten percent discount on whatever you eat here."

Gavin pulled into a seat beside her. "Fine by me." He slicked back his wet hair and inched closer to her in his chair. He made sure he brushed arms with Chessie and cracked open his menu. I imagined myself cracking it through his skull. The rest of Chessie's guests joined the table.

"This food better be worth it," Ashanti commented before she sat down. "Can someone turn up the A/C? It's raining cats and dogs outside, and it's freaking cold." She began to wrung out water from her long hair with a table napkin.

"Really cold," someone agreed.

"Seth! I can't believe you're alive," Laura exclaimed. I looked at her.

"Everyone at the party thought you died," Laura said.

"I once got zapped when I plugged in my straightening iron in an outlet," Ashanti shuddered. She looked at me sympathetically. "I know how you feel."

"Did it hurt?" Ross asked. "Some guys posted pics of how they found you knocked out on the ground. You looked trashed," he grinned. I grunted a response.

A portly man with thinning black hair drew out of the kitchens to check what the commotion was.

I swore I saw dollar signs flash in front of Mr. Jensen's eyes when he saw our crowded table. He fixed his crooked tie, halted before Chessie, and personally reserved a rotten glare catered towards me. Last I saw him he was consoling Chessie's mom after Chessie's incident and screamed at me to get out of his house. I guessed the memory didn't fade between us.

"Welcome to Black Tie," he nodded to the group. "I am Edgar and I'll be your server tonight," he said in a slight Dutch accent. "Chessandra, who are your friends?"

"Daddy," Chessie said sweetly, "you know my friend Seth, and the rest are the football team and the cheerleaders from my school. They wanted to try out a new restaurant so I invited them."

It wasn't Chessie inviting Meathead that killed me. The fact she introduced me as a friend was the bullet that did me in. Gavin beamed as if Christmas had come early.

Mr. Jensen nodded. "If you need anything at all, please do not hesitate to ask." He gave Chessie a meaningful look before he left.

"Is there any good food here?" Ashanti asked.

"You can get the special; it's salmon tonight," Chessie encouraged. Ashanti's upper lip curled. "I hate fish." Chessie looked hurt.

"What do you have that's heavy, greasy, and meaty?" Carl asked.

"I'm looking at it," Gavin directed at me. Meathead's goons laughed and agreed. Chessie immediately gave me a warning look. I chewed my words and picked up a menu. I was ready to hurl it at someone's face.

"So what were you guys doing before you came here?" Chessie asked casually.

"Nothing much. We hung out at the beach until out of nowhere it started to rain and got cold," Laura shivered at the memory.

"My toes are so frozen I think they're falling apart," Ross said.

Laura went on. "Then we went over to Ashanti's house to chill out." Her eyes lit up as she looked at Ross. "I think Ross got a little too chill with Marsha Santiago, if you know what I mean."

Odessa gasped. "That's why she suddenly needed to go home?"

"Y'all were making out in the bathroom!" Marion exclaimed. "I knew it!"

"No we weren't," Ross grinned across the table. "I hooked up with her straight to third base."

"Ew. Gag me," Odessa said.

"That's what she said," Ross nodded supremely.

"Ross, in my bathroom!" Ashanti exclaimed in disgust. I completely lost my appetite right then.

After the girls were through squealing, "You're so gross!" and the guys were congratulating him as though he won a medal, Gavin started again.

"Mack, how far have you ever gone with a girl?"

I slapped the menu on the table. "How far have you gone with Carl?"

Ashanti and her pep squad squealed in shock and amusement. Carl growled from the end of the table. "I'm gonna-" Gavin held him back. Carl sat back down, staring me down.

"He ain't nothing but a pussy," Gavin told him. "Right Chessie?" he directed the question to her. Chessie blinked.

"Don't you agree he's pussy, Chessie?" Ashanti said, egging her on. Chessie's eyes fleeted to Ashanti then met my gaze. She was nervous.

A waiter came in and interrupted what Chessie was going to say. She paused at our table looking visibly upset. I noticed there were some patrons in the restaurant from the surrounding tables that were equally unhappy.

"Would you all keep the noise level at a minimum?" the waiter hissed. "There are customers complaining of the disturbance. We'd appreciate if you would mind respecting others."

"Yeah, yeah," Gavin said. "We got it," he waved dismissively at her. The waiter gave him an aggravated look and squarely walked away. Gavin licked his lips at Chessie. "I don't get how a fine ass girl like you wants to stick around his small dick."

I snapped my fingers several times at him. "Hey! Hey Gavin, eyes over here."

He glared. "What, Small Dick Mack?"

Now I had his undivided attention, "You should check your own damn dick. Matilda swore up and down you were built like a girl- must be why you prefer sitting on the toilet."

"Ooh, he handled you, bro!" Ross boomed.

"Do you piss on your balls when you stand?" I said.

The guys at the table went ape, banging the table with their fists as they clowned Gavin. Gavin went red in the face. Last spring rumor spread Gavin wasn't exactly built for intimate relationships, according to Matilda Warwick, a freshman.

"You wanna know who the real man is?" he provoked. Everyone was waiting to see what he was gonna do. Gavin leaned into Chessie's chair and cupped her chin in his hand. Chessie's eyed widened in frozen shock as Gavin locked lips with hers and stuck his tongue down her throat.

Dad always told me when I had a problem to handle it when it happened right then and there. I should have pulled out Gavin's intestines and shoved them up his ass long ago.

I stood, knocking my chair backwards. Odessa and Marion began cheering and clapping while the guys got rowdier, disturbing the restaurant's atmosphere.

"Three cheers for the slut queen!" said Ashanti.

"Yay for the slut!" Odessa said.

"That's your girl, Mack! Whatcha gonna do?" Ross taunted.

I was gonna snap Gavin's neck into a twig, that's what.

My head felt like it was about to explode as Chessie kept her lips moving as Gavin's body pressed into hers. I was going to kill him.

Do so, a voice whispered.

A sudden sharp pain stabbed me in the chest and I wheezed in surprise. I fell back in my seat and my head bounced forward, slamming into the Alfredo sauce.

Tears brimmed my eyelids. At first, I couldn't hear. When I did, I heard laughter. I slowly gazed up.

"Look guys! He's going to cry," some girl said.

"He's about to wet himself!" Carl laughed. I wiped the Alfredo sauce out of my stinging eyes. My blurred vision steadied on Gavin's hand on Chessie's cheek. They continued snogging each other. An eerie cold presence crawled over my skin.

Kill him, the voice insisted.

As though he heard, Gavin's eyes darted around the room. His eyes finally fell on me.

Let her go. Do it now, I growled. *Or I kill you.*

A vision of Gavin burned alive flickered in my mind. The image vanished as soon as it came.

Gavin's expression filled with horror. He immediately pulled away from Chessie, skidding his seat backwards.

My fingers clenched the tablecloth to buoy me over the pain- down crashed water glasses, plates and silverware on the floor. The spilled water droplets on the table hissed and condensed into steam. I watched as the tablecloth glowed bright ember. In a sudden spark, the table caught fire.

The power and lights in the restaurant cut off. There was a chorus of surprise as everything was shrouded in darkness. Gavin tumbled out of his chair and ran.

Lights feebly flickered on as the fire quickly engulfed the table. Ross followed closely behind Gavin, shouting and clearing for the exit.

I don't know why I didn't pass out right then- my head banged and my heart beat hard. My limbs felt like they were being pricked with needles by an insensitive masseuse- I was drowning in an endless wave of agony.

I blinked through my burning eyes. Suddenly, I realized I was staring at Chessie, cornered against a wall. She was dangerously close to the fire.

"Get out of the way!" I shouted, but my voice sounded so far away, so muffled. I tried to move but the pain wouldn't let me.

I will ease your discomfort.

My eardrums felt like they were about to burst as the alarm rang out like a thousand angry school bells. The overhead sprinklers went off, pelting like bullets. Customers who hadn't already left, hurried for safety as waiters ushered them through the emergency exit doors.

In the midst of chaos, Charlie ran to us, brandishing a fire extinguisher. She squeezed the trigger and let out the foam to pacify the fire but it wasn't enough. She chucked the extinguisher aside and dove to Chessie who was still in the corner, shaking. I watched in a daze as Charlie threw her uniform shirt over Chessie and pulled her away from the fire, rescuing her. I threw up.

"Chessie!" Charlie yelled, rattling her shoulders. I cupped my hands over my ears. It was as though Charlie was speaking through a megaphone.

Chessie was too stunned to answer quickly enough. "I'm fine," Her voice boomed in my skull. Charlie nodded gravely. "Let's go!" she told us.

I pulled myself off the ground, stumbling after Chessie and Charlie. The restaurant cleared out except for us, the two waiters ushering everyone out the doors, and a man. He stood in a black shirt, gray jeans, and a black baseball cap obscured his face. Through all the shouts and moving panic, he remained calm. It wasn't until I looked his way did he lift his head. He rounded on his heel and disappeared.

Rain fell overhead as we stood outside with firefighters, police, and paramedics. Most of the shock had evaporated and Mr. Jensen, along with the police, was asking Chessie and I a few legit questions about how the fire started. We didn't know what to say and Chessie's guests already left the scene. Once the EMT's confirmed to Mr. Jensen Chessie was alright, Mr. Jensen, busy with police matters, reluctantly allowed me take Chessie home.

By then, I could walk in a straight line. Most of my weariness had faded away. Chessie lived about twenty minutes away from Black Tie, but the downpour and wailing wind felt like a two-hour journey to her house tonight. I clenched at the steering wheel, trying to keep it together.

Chessie almost got burned. I had to look at Chessie several times to see she was safe in her seat beside me. My mind flickered back to images of Gavin burning.

His screams echoed in my head like a broken record. I could almost feel the heat blazing off his body as he reduced to ashes. And the smell… My stomach revolted.

I pulled up to Chessie's driveway and shut off the wipers. I turned up the heater. We hadn't spoken to one another after we left the restaurant. I broke the silence.

"I'm glad you're safe and no one got hurt. Chessie continued to stare out beyond the dark windows. I tried again.

"Your father's place is going to be okay. Knowing your dad, I bet in a day or two he'll be ready to open for business again. I'm sure he has insurance-" I cut off.

Chessie started bawling. Then she began to laugh, shaking her damp hair from side to side.

"Are you okay?" I flipped on the overhead light. Once she regained some self-control, she started giggling. "I can't believe it!" She threw her hands up in frustration. "My one shot at getting them to like me."

Once I got over my confusion, I measured my words.

"You almost got burned, your dad's restaurant is completely soaked, and all you care about is if Meathead and his drones *like you?"*

She bristled. "I can't show my face around Ashanti," she glared. "You were supposed to be a good boyfriend cheering me on, but all you cared about was having your stupid fight with Gavin. Don't you care about me?" she screeched.

I stared at her. I was a deer caught in freaking headlights.

"Of course I care, Chessie. I cared enough to go to Gavin's party and I ditched Eli and Karin tonight to spend time with you." My voice rose. "I cared enough to stick around when you invited Meathead and his dream team to our dinner date. *For you.*" My hands rattled the steering wheel but I ignored them. "I cared enough when he put his hands on you and you sat there, *making out with him!*"

I expected her to apologize. I expected her to deny it. Chessie rounded in her seat and faced me, wet mascara running from her eyes.

"Do you know why I invited you to dinner?" she whispered. "Because Ashanti dared me to. She said if you came and was civil towards Gavin for once in your life, she'd consider me making the squad but you ruined everything! Gavin was a test for you to pass so I could make the squad. Get it?"

I blinked at her. This... *this* Chessie, wasn't making sense. Nothing made any sense.

She stared at me as if I threw sand in her eyes. "I can handle Gavin and the cheerleaders on my own," she scowled. "Stop judging me like you know what's good for me." She wrenched away from me when I touched her hand.

"I can't freaking stand the way you look at me anymore," she shouted. "I'm not some kind of victim-stop trying to fix me, Seth! You're the damn problem. *You.* Not me!"

I wanted to say something. Anything.

She finally climbed out of the car and slipped out into the rain. I slowly tore my eyes from the empty seat to her face. Her eyes were dark.

"Don't call me again. I don't need you." Before I could think to stop her, she slammed the door shut.

It took another beat before I could gaze out the passenger window.

Chessie ran up her driveway, grating my heart under her heels as she left.

CHAPTER SIX

It was a long night, getting Eli's car back to his house and taking the bus home in the cold rain. Finally, lying warm in bed, body aching, and the constant migraine kept my brain from shutting off. The walls I had built in my mind around a specific memory came tumbling down.

I was late. Dropping Mom off at the supermarket took more time than I anticipated and I was rushing to pick up Chessie from volleyball practice.

Before sending a quick text to Chessie I told her that I was on my way and waved goodbye to Mom. I hurried down the express lane on the highway, hoping to cut down on traffic.

I parked in the Dormant's student parking lot and read the dashboard clock. It was more than twenty minutes since practice ended.

I hopped out of the truck and speed-dialed Chessie's number. No answer.

I glanced up and down the lot as I ran my fingers through my thick hair, growing more annoyed. Did she forget to tell me she hitched a ride again?

Time ticked by. I was making up my mind about heading to the girl's locker rooms when Chessie walked out of the building, looking disheveled. She was still in her volleyball uniform.

Why the hell did she take so long if she hadn't changed?

"Chessie, didn't volleyball practice end forty minutes ago?"

Chessie walked past me and stepped inside the truck.

"If anyone should be ticked, it's me," I grumbled. I hopped into the driver's seat. Chessie had her eyes unfocused out the window. I sighed. I guessed practice was brutal today.

I drove off school property and headed down the road. I turned on the radio, filling the uneasy silence. Two minutes into driving, Chessie started crying uncontrollably. I tore my eyes off the road, surprised.

"What's wrong?" I turned off the radio.

Chessie continued to cry as she rocked herself in her seat, clutching a hand to her chest. I started to grow more concerned.

"What's wrong?" I repeated. "Are you hurt?"

I pulled the truck on the side of the road and unfastened my seatbelt. "Is it your stomach? Do you need to go to the hospital? Chessie, what's wrong?"

I begged her over and over until she gazed up at me, her brown eyes filled with tears and despair.

"I-I tried; I couldn't," she shrieked. "I tried- I couldn't."

"What did you try to do? What happened?"

She was started shaking and hyperventilating. Wet, gagging sounds rattled her chest. She needed a doctor. I panicked. "Chessie, what's wrong? Whatever it is, it'll be okay. Talk to me."

She shook her head violently back and forth. "I-couldn't-tell-him-no," she wheezed. "I tried," she shook in her seat." I-couldn't-say-it-I-tried-I-wanted-to-say-stop-no," she shook harder. "I-was-so-scared."

"Who couldn't you tell 'stop', Chessie?" I asked, trying to understand while I held her cold hands. "What happened, Chessie? Please." And she did.

I don't know when I turned the truck back around- blind flurry was all I saw. I wanted to find Erving and crush him with my bare hands. I wanted to hurt him more than he ever hurt Chessie.

"Seth! Stop! Don't go back!" Chessie screamed as I flew by another red light. The sooner Erving was under my truck the better I'd feel.

"Seth, no, no, no, don't go back! Stop! Please!" Chessie cried as she wrenched my arm away from the steering wheel, causing us to swerve.

"Erving won't get away with it alive," I shouted as I jerked the truck back into the lane. Her body smacked against the passenger door and Chessie stared at me, shocked. I've never seen her so afraid of me. I realized I was the monster now.

I pulled the truck again on the side of the road.

Traffic whizzed by. I held her tightly against my chest as she cried and cried and cried.

"I'm sorry," I whispered. "You're okay, you're going to be okay," I told her over and over, stroking her hair.

Time stretched for an eternity, God knows, in that truck. "Don't go after him," she said between sobs. I nodded gravely. "We have to tell your parents." Chessie looked up from my chest. She was frightened. The look she gave me ripped my insides. I wished I could do more for her. "I'll be there for you all the way, okay? No matter what."

I witnessed her tell her parents. It was probably the hardest thing I had to see Chessie go through. The look on her mother's face when she heard what happened, I'd never forget. Mr. Jensen's face lost color. The police came after.

We were in the living room. Mrs. Jensen and Charlie embraced Chessie on the couch and her two younger brothers, Isaiah and Jonah, were upstairs on the landing, watching everything unfold. As Chessie later recounted to the police what happened, Mr. Jensen had joined them on the couch. Chessie explained when volleyball practice ended she was the last of the girls to leave the locker room when Erving stepped in her path. Earlier on the field before practice began, Erving cornered Chessie and asked her out. When Chessie denied him of any possibility of them going out, Gavin and the rest of his football teammates witnessed this. They laughed and put Erving down, saying he had lost his mojo.

When Erving met Chessie again outside the locker room alone, he was peeved. Before Chessie realized what was happening, Erving shoved her inside the locker room and started tearing her clothes off.

"Why didn't you pick her up?" Mr. Jensen said to me. The police officer glanced up from his notepad. Charlie and Mrs. Jensen turned from me to Mr. Jensen, bewildered. Mr. Jensen had stopped embracing his wife on the couch and stood up with his hands balled at his sides, shoulders raised. He spoke again, out for blood.

"Why didn't you pick her up on time?" he moaned. He was on me at an instant, grabbing my collar. "Why?" he shouted. "WHY?"

"It's not his fault, Daddy!" Chessie cried out. I believed it was. If Mr. Jensen punched me in the face I wouldn't feel it- I was too numb inside.

A police officer pried him off me and threw him in a corner with a fair warning. Mr. Jensen stayed down on the ground. Mr. Jensen jabbed a finger in my direction.

"Get him out of my house! I want him out!" Before I left, I heard Chessie's father cry for the first time.

After that night, police took care of the situation. Erving was pulled out of school and taken in handcuffs (he was legally an adult).

Gavin protested Chessie's story wasn't true. He and Erving's teammates denied Erving was involved in Chessie's rape but Erving's DNA in Chessie's panties and a rape kit was enough to put him behind bars. And with Erving's reputation after Matilda (The girl who was rumored doing the whole football team. She cried Erving raped her but no one believed her, even after she left Dormant) the case was solid.

Erving didn't have a corner to hide in now because he attacked Chessie, an honor student and star athlete. Gavin and his teammates were also questioned of their involvement but nothing came of it. Things spiraled out of control for Chessie. The entire junior football team was suspended until the matter with police were handled. The Jaguars football team was lost without their star quarterback and was suspended for the remaining season.

Gavin spread rumors Chessie blew all the guys on the team and Erving caught an STD from Chessie. The rest of Dormant High thought Chessie was the next Matilda and blamed her. Karin and Chessie were friends then, and Karin did her best to be there for her, but Chessie closed her off and said some hurtful things that pushed Karin away.

One day, Chessie stopped going to volleyball practice and skipped school for an entire week. When she returned, she was back to her bright, bubbly self as if nothing happened. I wanted to believe she was better. She began paying more attention to her makeup than her grades and ditched her volleyball friends for the cheerleaders. I started missing the girl I fell for in seventh grade.

I can't freaking stand the way you look at me anymore…

I bolted up in bed. The wind howled outside as rain fell like tiny rocks rhythmically hitting the window.

I listened to the storm outside but it didn't distract me from thoughts of last night. I couldn't stop seeing the fire as Chessie hid in that corner, afraid. The words she said to me after I dropped her off wouldn't shut up in my head.

There were a lot of things that changed between us, before we started dating. Things that, if you didn't look underneath the surface, you wouldn't have caught on. I couldn't joke how we used to because she became too serious and judgmental. We used to hang out on the patch of grass between the basketball court and the veranda at school. Now, it felt like she'd be embarrassed to sit and eat lunch there. I missed when she used to call me. We would talk for hours about everything and nothing. After school we'd hang out at her house with Karin and Eli while she argued with her sister Charlie or her brothers.

Chessie wasn't the only one who changed. I was messed up on the inside, too. Something broke inside me and those pieces could never be put back together again. I thought about going after Erving with my truck many times. I constantly beat myself up- I didn't head into the locker rooms- I could have stopped it. I also worried about the guys Chessie attracted with the outfits she wore and the way she acted in the halls when she passed a group of guys at school.

I wondered if she even knew what those guys called her behind her back. If I didn't have self-control, I would have bashed their brains in.

Stop acting like I'm some weak little girl who needs protecting! I'm not some kind of victim.

Victim. That word sliced right through my gut. Last thing I wanted was to remind Chessie of what happened to her, like she had this permanent label on her forehead. I didn't want her to feel that way at all.

It took both hands for me to lift the gallon of water off the desk. My hands were trembling so bad it took a couple tries to hold it steady. It was empty. Suddenly, the walls in my room felt like they were slowly caving in.

I shrugged off my sweaty sheets and flipped on the bedroom light. I found my running shoes and an irritated sound escaped from my throat.

The bottom of my left shoe was falling apart. I rummaged through my desk and found superglue. Quickly repairing it as best I could, I grabbed my soccer ball and sports bag, then made a beeline out the door.

The rain had let up during the night until it was a continuing light fall. The temperature had dipped lower and the sky was gray, matching my mood. When the sun barely peaked the sky and the roads were quiet, it was the perfect time for a run. There were no pedestrians, cars, or bikers that interrupted your flow of running through several blocks at a time.

Before the season started, Coach Wilkins ran our team hard every day, waking us up at the butt crack of dawn. It became a habit now, running at any hour of the day, long and hard. I picked up speed down the street, following the beat of my heart. I loved feeling alone on the road; just the sound of my sneakers pounding the asphalt usually comforted me.

You ruined everything!

God, why couldn't I shut off my brain?

Gavin was a test for you to pass so I could make the squad. Get it? I invited you to dinner... because Ashanti dared me to.

I started to laugh at myself. Sharp wind and rain whipped around me. Chessie used my soccer status for her popularity. Chessie only invited me to Black Tie not because she loved me, but because of a dare. She didn't love me. I couldn't pretend it didn't hurt knowing Karin was right.

Betrayal, a voice whispered.

Damn, damn, damn it all. I felt like the biggest idiot in the universe. More thoughts chased after me as my lungs begged for oxygen and my muscles began to strain.

...Civil towards Gavin for once in your damn life...

I started to get angry.

Don't call me again. I don't need you.

Sweat and rain tacked my clothes onto my skin as I flew down another five blocks.

I didn't believe Chessie knew how much I cared about her, how much it killed me when she said that. Did she really believe I was never there for her? Didn't I show her I loved her?

Worse of all, besides her shutting me out of her life, using me, and breaking up with me, was what I almost did to Gavin. I wanted him dead and my wish almost came true. All because of the way I loved Chessie.

My ankles and knees protested for rest but I kept pushing. I didn't want to think about anything. I didn't want to care anymore. I wanted to forget her. The wind blew harder and a stray leaf hit me in the eye.

I stopped. I couldn't see- my eyes were burning through the rain. I rubbed them until I could see again. From where I stood a vision started to play.

I crashed through a thicket of trees, sprinting over uplifted roots and dry leaves as the old man pursued me.

"Help!" I shouted, but I knew no one could save me here. Suddenly, bolts of lightning cracked open the earth, exploding dirt and wood everywhere. The explosion rocked me off my feet and flung me into a tree. I dropped straight down like a kite without wind, coughing out blood.

The dust cleared. There the old man stood in front of me, without speck of dirt on his coat, wearing a cold, lizard smile. I didn't blink- the old man had somehow closed the distance between us and his fingers clamped around my throat. They curled, cutting off my windpipe as fire lighted my skin. I choked out a cry as my lungs boiled in blood. Aside from the smell of my rotting, charred meat, another scent hit me. It was the scent of sulfur.

When I came out of the vision, I struggled to breathe.

No more visions, I pleaded with myself. I dropped and lay my back on the sidewalk, trying hard to push every thought, every feeling away. My eyes caught sight of my throbbing forearm.

The scars were brighter than before. Worse, they looked redder, sharper, almost alive. Intricate jagged lines carved into my skin, some of them twisting and shaping at odd angles between the welts on my arm. I shut my eyes and allowed the rain hit my face. It poured into my ears and into my nose.

At that very moment, I prayed for a sleep I couldn't wake up from.

CHAPTER SEVEN

I stayed out all morning and day playing soccer with teammates I called out after my run. At the park, Eric Nash, Victor Petit, and I played basketball on the court.

I trailed back home, tired and exhausted as the sun was starting to set. I bumped Logan's feet under his truck as I walked up the front door. Did this guy ever go home?

"Watch where you're going," he grunted. I ignored him and entered the house, calling out to Mom. She emerged from the kitchen, wiping her hands off her apron. "Nice to see you."

I greeted her. "I went to the park, caught up with friends."

She placed her hand on my cheek and frowned. "You should not overdo it; you just came from the hospital Friday, three days ago." She dropped her hand from my face. "Go to your room and change your wet clothes. Did you take your pills?"

"I feel fine, I promise," I said, checking the fridge. "I didn't need those pills after yesterday." I shook the carton of juice. It was less than a quarter full. "We ran out of juice." I twisted off the cap and ran the carton under the faucet. I shook the contents to mix well and drank it down.

"I will tell Logan to take us grocery shopping," she said.

I winced. "So what's the deal? Logan's rooming here so often he's your gopher now?"

"What do you mean 'gopher?'"

I took another swig before answering. "Means he goes and fetches things for you; your Nyquil, now your groceries."

"He means much more than a gopher to me," she smiled. "I wanted to make some homemade dinner from scratch."

I gulped before answering. "What do you plan on making?"

"Meat lasagna," she said, pointing to the open cookbook on the counter. "I wanted to make it authentic."

The carton of juice paused to my lips. It's not that Mom couldn't cook. Aside from the *arroz con pollo* and *arroz y frijoles* she made all the time if it didn't come from a premixed batter, canned, or sealed in a bag, she didn't make it.

When we were still speaking to Abuela Antonia and Abuelo Miguel, a good Cuban meal wasn't an issue then because we were always at their house and often went home with leftovers. My Tía Evangeline and Abuela Antonia would loudly crack jokes and make slick comments about Mom's cooking skills to whomever was within earshot of the kitchen.

It was typical Cuban mentality that the women were supposed to cook, as though the talent was infused in their DNA. Mom would smile, kneading the dough or stirring a pot, because that's the only job she could handle, they'd joke, and Mom would go on pretending nothing bothered her.

Mom was giddy with excitement. "*Mijo*, I saved so much at the store." She dug out the receipt from her pocket and unfolded it.

As she read it, I started for the dollar store plastic bags on the counter. I poked a finger inside one: ground beef, prepackaged lasagna noodles, and canned tomato sauce. "The tomato sauce was on sale for twenty-nine cents so I bought two more. And the cheese! Can you believe it cost two dollars for fifteen ounces in one bag? I was smart to buy three," she told me.

"Instead of ricotta cheese, I bought American cheddar. We have until January before it spoils so please remember to eat whatever is left after I make the lasagna."

I nodded. "Sounds good. I can make grilled cheese sandwiches for breakfast." I cracked a smile and turned to the kitchen sink to wash my hands. "I'll help you with the lasagna."

Mom beamed and gave me a side hug. *"Gracias, mi amor."* she thanked me. "Go change your clothes before you get sicker," she said.

I came back into the kitchen wearing warm, dry clothes. I had on my faded jeans and a long, baggy-sleeved shirt to hide my arms. I had bandaged my arm and chest with new dressings and my handiwork didn't look pretty. My chest was darker than my arm; the skin thin, grey, and red and it stung every moment I took a breath. Besides the fact it had the same freakish tattoo pattern on my forearm, it wasn't hurting as bad as it was yesterday.

My left arm was worse. It was too sensitive to touch and I couldn't look at it for too long. It bulged from my wrist to my elbows, and the angry purple and red welts didn't look like they were going to heal either. I had to get a doctor to check it out but not today. I wanted to have a normal night at least.

Mom and I listened to some Spanish oldies and Christmas songs on the ancient radio that sat on the kitchen table. We often used to do this when I was little. Mom would sing into cups as the microphone and my drumsticks were spoons. I remembered a time I banged on the countertop and "The Little Drummer Boy," chimed through the radio. Dad joined in on our concert, but he wouldn't sing because he hated the way his voice sounded. It used to make me laugh at how embarrassed he'd be when Mom would force him to sing.

Once we were done with the meat lasagna, with a bump of her hip, Mom shut the oven closed and set it to preheat. Mom worked on the salad while I rummaged the kitchen to make dessert. We had nothing but juice, milk, eggs, and near-expired bread in the fridge. I thought about making something from scratch. We had some leftover baking soda and flour, so that was good. I riffled through the cupboards until I finally settled on making homemade cinnamon biscotti. This was as authentic this Italian dinner was gonna get. I started kneading the dough. I loved the feeling of sticky flour beneath my fingernails and the texture between my fingers.

Cooking reminded me of soccer. You had this idea in your head how your opponent would kick the ball past you and you relied on your skills, talent, and luck to win.

Sometimes you didn't perform well. But cooking gave me something more; I created something out of nothing. It was the only thing I had any control over the outcome.

The rain started again, falling hard against the roof. It sounded relaxing. While we waited for the lasagna to bake, we scraped the remaining biscotti batter from the bowl with our fingers. The chill evening with Mom helped calmed a few storms in my head.

"Do you think we can put up a Christmas tree in the living room?" I said, recalling Eli's home. "We could buy a fake one instead of a real one because it'd be cheaper."

Mom licked her thumb. "I do not see why we can't." Her eyes drifted to the living room. A memory must have come to mind because her eyes had that faraway look. They were starting to get watery when the phone rang. She made a little jump and went to the phone on the counter. She wiped her hands on her apron before picking it up.

"Hello?" There was a murmur coming from the other line. Mom's face ashen. "Eve." She turned her body away from my direction.

Mom couldn't say she was busy, sick, out, or tired now. Mom spoke softly in rapid Spanish.

"No, Seth told me you called. I have been busy. I work overtime."

There was a slight pause.

"Yes, yes, how are you doing?" I could tell Mom was ready to put down the receiver. "I'm sorry to hear that-"

Another pause. "When?" Mom took a deep breath. "I don't know, Christmas day I was planning to do something with my son. "A long pause trailed off. Mom looked over her shoulder and her tone dipped low. "You know how I feel if Marco is there with his wife and son."

My hand formed a fist. That wasn't his son, I wanted to say. And who cared if Dad's new wife showed up? Why did Mom have to hide from the cheater?

"I understand." Another pause. "Yes. Take care of your health."

She hung up. Mom entered the kitchen looking worried. "That was your Aunt Evangeline. She says hello."

The oven timer chimed and she replaced the lasagna dish with the cinnamon biscotti. She did her best not to make eye contact. "She wants us to visit her before the New Years."

My guard was up. "Are we?"

Logan interrupted whatever she was about to say. He strolled into the kitchen, stinking of sweat and motor oil.

"When's dinner?" he said. I ignored him as I drunk out of my gallon of water.

"In ten minutes," Mom answered him. "What were you doing to that truck?" She wrapped her arms around his waist as she buried her head in his chest. I noticed it was an action for protection than comfort.

"I'm only tinkering with the motor. I think I may have to go to Ace and get a couple new parts," Logan said.

"That reminds me, the toaster is still not working. I think we need a new one," Mom told him.

"I told you we don't need a new one," Logan said. "I'll fix it after dinner." He pulled Mom closer and started nuzzling her neck.

I narrowed my eyes. "Get a room." Logan's smile fell. He frowned to Mom. "Did you tell him?"

Mom's eyes fleeted from Logan's face to mine. Mom looked back at Logan.

"Go wash up before you do anything else." She flicked him with a dishtowel at his rear. He grimaced.

"You have to do it tonight," he said and left.

"Is there something I'm missing here?" Mom looked at me, her smile wavering.

"I have something to tell you. "I couldn't believe I didn't see it before. The cooking, the singing and hanging out…she was buttering me up for her big announcement.

"Beth!" Logan called out, "Where's the hand soap?"

Mom gave me a pat on the shoulder before she went to Logan. A little while later, I was setting down forks and plates on the kitchen table. I paused at a seat. Dad's place at the table was always in the middle, in front of me. Logan came in half-naked in his faded jeans. He glanced at the table.

"Did you ever think about putting another plate out, or did you forget how to count?"

"Apparently not." I sat down, facing him. Mom came into the kitchen as Logan fetched his plate. He sat beside Mom who seated across the table from me.

"What is it you wanted to tell me?" I asked.

"Can you please wait until after we have food in our mouths?" Mom asked. She busied herself with the lasagna dish at the center of the table. I tore a piece of warm cinnamon biscotti and popped it into my mouth.

"I've got food in me," I said. "What's up?"

Mom sighed and let her fork drop on her plate.

"I waited long enough for you to tell him," Logan said.

"I was not ready to tell him," Mom argued.

Logan frowned. "He's practically a grown man. If you're worried he can't handle it, you're wrong."

"Seriously, go on. Pretend I'm not sitting right here," I said. Mom grabbed my hand from the table and squeezed. She peered deeply into my eyes. "Seth, you know I love you."

"Tell me you're not pregnant," I blurted.

"Mijo!" Mom sounded shocked. She shook her head, momentarily jaded. "I am not pregnant," she stuttered. She looked down at my left hand. She squeezed it again.

"About six months ago the nursing home started doing budget cuts. They finally let me go. That was two months ago."

"Wait- what?" I said, feeling upset. "Why'd you wait so long to tell me?"

On Mom's income, we barely had enough to stretch. She sacrificed fixing her bathroom shower that could only spout cold water, to pay for my soccer uniform and cleats alone. If she was out of a job, I don't think we could manage.

"I did not want you to worry, *mijo*," Mom said, rubbing the top of my hand with her thumb.

"This year was hard on us when they cut my hours and you stopped working at Don's Deli-"

"Because you told me to stop working and concentrate more on school," I finished. "I can always find another job." Mom shook her head. "That is not what I wanted to say."

"Then...what?"

Her wrinkles deepened around her frown lines and tired eyes. She aged in the last five years. "Since I stopped working I've been relying on Logan's income and it has not been enough for us."

I started speaking in Spanish. Granted, my Spanish sounded so Americanized and watered down I'd embarrass myself if any of my cousins heard me. Still, Logan wouldn't be able to tell the difference. "He's been supporting us this entire time?"

Spanish sometimes made the nicest words sound like curse words. I watched him as I rounded my words and raised my voice. Logan immediately looked offended.

No wonder Logan acted like he owned the house. He was paying for rent. All those times I told him it wasn't his house. All those times when I thought he was here too often and he never left. He already lived here and I never knew. I pulled my hand away.

"When did he move in?"

"That is not important."

"Two weeks? A month?"

"I don't like your tone," Logan said.

Just that line alone made my blood pressure rise again.

"Seth, he's been helping us," Mom said. She didn't want to answer me, but she pleaded with her eyes for me to understand.

"Logan had a promising job that was offered to him and he turned it down because of me." She sounded guilty. "He wanted to stay here with us, but now I've convinced him it is better for us to move," she explained. "He called the construction company that wanted to hire him a few months ago to see if their offer still stands, and thank God it is. The pay is good for us and I do not have to be in a hurry to find another job."

She was trying to convince me it was a great plan but I wasn't giving in. She lied to me.

I refused to switch back to English and stared dead at Logan. "We were fine on our own before he came along." Logan's feathers ruffled. I glared at him for good measure.

"Seth," Mom said. I leaned back in my seat, crossing my arms. It got real quiet. Mom spoke again, gently.

"We need money, Seth. It is good we have Logan here. I cannot afford not to have extra income in this house. I searched for jobs here in Miami. No one is looking for a CNA." I flinched when she leaned in closer. "I don't even have the money to pay for your medical bills." She knew that would make me feel guilty. It was her way of making me bend. My leg started to shake. "Logan can start work as soon as early next year. The work is in Washington, D.C."

I couldn't believe my ears. I stared at Logan who continued spearing his fork into his lasagna.

"You're saying," I repeated slowly in English, "The job is in Washington D.C."

"It's not a bad place," Mom said, trying again. "There are good people, and there is also the White House-"

"Beth," Logan interrupted her. "There's no use babying him."

He plugged his mouth with more food. I was tempted to chuck the entire lasagna from his plate into his face.

"How is he worth it?" I glared. "I have school to finish- I have friends, and you want me to start over?"

I couldn't think: Chessie, Mom, Aunt Eva, Logan, those nightmares- all of my pent up anger bubbled to the surface. Logan banged his hand on the table, rattling our plates.

"Enough!"

"Lay a hand on me, I swear," I threatened.

"Seth!" Mom started.

"This boy thinks he's man of the house now, huh?" Logan shoved his chair back, towering over the table.

"Logan, stop!" Mom said.

I stood and kicked back my chair. My nails bit into my fists. "This isn't your house!"

"Seth, sit!" Mom yelled. "Stop."

I wanted to jump over the table and kill him. I didn't get the chance with Gavin. Now I had someone just as good. Mom put a hand on my forearm and tugged. I was about to smack her hand away, but I caught myself. I gazed back at her pleading eyes.

Screw this.

I turned on my heel. Mom followed me to my room. I grabbed my empty soccer bag from the closet and started chucking clothes and underwear inside it.

"Where do you think you're going?" Mom demanded.

I whirled around. I glared at Logan who stood behind her. I held it all in because I wanted to spare us the pain. I was sick of pretending everything was okay between us.

"You lied. About working, him living here, and you're telling me we need to move?" I said. "You thought if you told me at the last minute, I'd agree to go with you, no questions asked?"

"Stop yelling, boy!" Logan roared.

"I'm not your boy, asshole!" I wasn't holding back now.

"Seth, do not disrespect him," Mom said.

Logan stared at me long and hard. He turned to Mom, putting up his hands. "You deal with him." He left.

"Why do you always take his side, huh?" I smacked a sweater and sock into the bag. "You think if you don't take his side, he'll leave you just like Dad?" I know it was a low blow when her face blanched. I couldn't stop.

"Why can't you just face things? Why couldn't you tell me you were going through money troubles?" I clenched a fist over a shirt. "You know I haven't been the same since Dad left, but do you ask what's going on with me? My soccer games, anything? Do you even care?" I threw the shirt as hard as I could against a wall. Mom made a noise.

"You keep thinking Logan is gonna protect you from talking to me? Talking to Aunt Evangeline?" I said. "He can't replace Dad. He can't even replace a toaster,"

"Shut up!" Mom exclaimed. I was surprised she was still standing here. Usually she'd be running for the hills by now. For one passing moment, I thought if she just admitted she chose to keep me at a distance, that she was trying to make Logan fill in the gap Dad left behind, I'd apologize.

Then I saw it in her eyes; fear.

Logan came back and stood right beside Mom. "That's enough out of you," he snapped.

I ignored him.

Mom quickly looked to Logan because she didn't know what to do, what to say to her own son. She wanted him to save her from dealing with me. I zipped up my bag, shoved past them, heading for the door.

"Get back here!" Logan bellowed. Mom wept in the background.

I ran outside in the cold rain, shaking all over. I shot a look at Logan's truck and my anger blew up. A dark part of me imagined taking a baseball bat to all four windows and slashing his tires. The darkness built up inside me, itching out from a pit I buried long ago.

Get rid of the vehicle. Now.

A rational part of my mind wondered why I would attack the truck; it never hurt me as much as Mom did.

They will never leave the city. The vehicle, a voice hissed.

A wave of dizziness took over as my legs gave out from under me. I fell on my side, smashing my ribs onto the pavement. Logan's truck went out of focus as my vision changed- one moment I was on the ground feeling like death. Then I was back in my nightmares.

The old man pursued another man who looked no older than thirty, with brown hair and a thick beard that grew under his obtuse nose. A hat hung low over his eyes. The old man and stranger were fighting not in hand-to-hand combat, but with power that soared from their fists. They disappeared and appeared faster than my eyes could follow.

"Seth, get out of here!" The bearded man boomed as the old man's blazing eyes shot a jet light- the bearded man countered it with a black column of smoke that filtered out his hand, missing his target.

The old man had vanished. The bearded man's head swiveled left and right - he didn't see the old man appear behind him. He struck him with blue electricity and the bearded man fell. Then the old man turned, facing me.

"You are next." Before he could hunt me down, a giant shadow stood protectively before me, snapping its jaws at the old man.

My senses came reeling back. I lay in the driveway- I don't know how long- screaming. A blazing heat settled in my stomach and it quickly grew. When I opened my eyes, my face was wet with tears and my nose was running with blood and snot. I blinked again. Logan's truck was on fire.

CHAPTER EIGHT

Mom knelt over me, calling out to Logan. Her voice amplified in my eardrums. Lights in the surrounding area had gone out. I saw a flash of Gavin's face in my mind.

Him screaming. Burning alive. The scent of charred flesh.

What happened at Black Tie was happening again.

Across the yard, two neighbors stood outside on their cell phones and some cars stopped in the middle of the street, surveying the scene. There was a man in a baseball cap standing in front of our sidewalk. The guy I saw at Black Tie.

A rush of power crackled my bones. My skin blazed against the rain- I must have yelled out again. Another surge built up into my chest and for a frightening moment, I thought I would simultaneously combust.

Peer into his eyes. Kill him; burn him, a cold voice echoed.

Stop, I begged. The scent of burning plastic and metal was replaced by a horrible scent of dirt and road kill- it filled up my nose until I choked and gagged.

A high pitch roar started in my ears. *Peer into his eyes, kill him.*

Stop, I moaned. I wanted the noise to stop.

There will be no future with him alive. Kill him, the voice hissed as the pitch grew deafening.

A pair of legs came into view. Fists yanked me up by the collar to my feet. "WHAT DID YOU DO?" Logan shook me.

"No!" I read Mom's lips. She managed to pull Logan off me. Once he let go, I stumbled and fell on one knee. Mom neared. Whispers strummed together into a high pitch command. *Kill the man across the street.*

I scrambled away from Mom and started to run. I didn't look back as I crashed into nosy onlookers on the sidewalk. I needed to put as much distance between me and the burning truck.

TURN. TURN BACK.

The entire world had gone silent except for the high pitch voice raging inside my head.

I staggered painfully up the wet road and crossed the Quik Mart parking lot. I was losing consciousness- my eyes followed my feet into the bathroom.

I collapsed on the toilet. The thick, visible grime on the seat encouraged me to throw up.

I must have blacked out at some point; I had no idea how much time ticked by. I lifted myself off the soiled floor and sat on the toilet seat.

I turned on the water faucet at the sink beside the toilet. I lay my head in the crook of my elbow and allowed the cool water to pour on my face.

I couldn't deny something was seriously wrong with me. I nearly torched down Black Tie and set Logan's truck on fire. I almost hurt Gavin. I was losing my mind.

I clenched my teeth together, trying not to vomit again.

I had marks branded on my arm. I had vivid dreams of a king from some far away land. I had nightmares of a psychotic man with a golden face and electric white eyes.

The voice in my head was faint now but I couldn't stop shaking.

Breathe. In and out, I coached myself. Everything was going to be okay.

Time trickled by until I could move again.

I wobbled to my feet, holding onto the sink for support. I caught a glimpse of my reflection in the mirror and froze.

My eyes were blazing red. I had no visible pupils.

Another wave of agony struck me in the gut and I automatically ripped away my shirt, crying Bloody Mary as I did, and glanced at the mirror again. My eyes were expressionless, watching. Yet here I was outside of the mirror, bellowing louder.

Ripples of crimson light traveled on the surface of my skin; from my face and to my chest it spread to my arms, and down to my feet. I was going insane.

The ripples grew brighter as my skin underneath bubbled, carving shapes and symbols from my chest to my left arm- I was vaguely aware strangers outside the bathroom were banging on the door, asking if I was okay.

I laid in fetal position on the dirty floor, praying the agony would end.

I was past getting a doctor. I needed to hear my Dad say it was going to be okay, even though it wasn't.

I was in and out of consciousness. I blinked and I was staring across the bathroom floor. In another blink, the bathroom door had slammed open.

A guy stood in the doorway. He wore a baseball cap low enough to hide his facial features, except for his brown hair that curled on the sides of his cap and his overgrown thick beard.

I went into a dream.

In my dream, the man suddenly lunged at me. I rose from the ground in quick reflex. I dodged him, hitting the sink against my side.

The man shouted something, but I couldn't hear. I think he called out my name.

I hissed as a distant power radiated past my bones to the surface of my skin, chilling me with its heat- the power was an uncontrolled geyser and it was spewing everywhere.

Distantly, my mind registered the room had become a sauna; the porcelain sink and toilet cracked. Overhead lights flickered in and out. The customers' shouts outside the gas station grew louder.

Still moving, something within me focused on that raw power: my muscles bulged, my hands strengthened and my fists tightened. I watched as my hands drew up and blocked the enemy's attack to my face.

He looked surprised. He didn't let that stop him- he pulled away and tried again, knocking his elbow into my jaw.

I flinched inside as I let him connect- a foreign part of me knew I couldn't dodge him in the cramped bathroom. I grabbed for him, leaping into the air at the last minute, misjudging the space.

I hit the corked ceiling panels and they crumbled as we fell. I felt my foot hit something hard and water splashed everywhere- I ignored this- and my hands locked around the man's throat.

I wanted to, needed to, remove his hat. I had to see his eyes, peer into his soul but my hands were preoccupied, choking the life out of him. Wet, sputtering sounds were coming from his lips and his eyes were losing focus. I enjoyed that.

The man pivoted his body around and slammed me against the bathroom mirror, catching me off guard. I felt the glass crack against my cheek.

He was too strong for me. I was limited in this body.

I saw he called out a name in the mirrored reflection: Seth.

I blinked. Was that my name? I watched my brow furrow. My ears felt like they were beginning to unclog; sound was returning.

Who was I?

"Look in the mirror!" the man boomed.

I started to panic.

NO. NEVER.

Why was looking in the mirror wrong?

"Seth, you're in there," he said. "Don't you want to see the face of the man who is about to kill you?"

I was going to die.

My eyes flew open.

I stared at my reflection in a daze.

Scrapes peppered my face. My jaw was swollen and a huge gash spread from my temple to my right brow- blood dripped in my eye. Sweat pooled down my back, armpits, and between my balls.

Still, that wasn't the reason I couldn't stop staring My eyes were fire, ruby red. My body glowed rainbow-like colors. I was a firefly on steroids.

I suddenly remembered comic book stories about mutants being hit with radiation or bitten by intergalactic bugs. It didn't matter; I was about to die in a woman's bathroom by some stranger. I looked inhuman. Scary.

"NO!" I shouted.

I don't know why I did. Strangely, my voice didn't sound attached to me. It sounded off. Dangerous.

In a split second, the crackling energy and power halted. I didn't glow anymore; my body went limp like a wet noodle and collapsed. My hand fell and hooked inside the toilet bowl, holding me upright. My head felt ready to split open and the world spun. I couldn't raise a finger.

A shadow loomed over me. Slowly and agonizingly, I lifted my head.

He crouched beside me. He leaned close enough for me to smell his lack of cologne and absence of breath mints.

"We need to talk Seth Castillo."

I must have blacked out again because I was on the bathroom floor.

My arm wasn't floating inside the toilet bowl. The man in the baseball cap was about to kill me. I swung at him.

Only, my fist didn't connect to anything but air. I lost my balance and clumsily fell forward and hit the ground, bewildered. The guy had disappeared.

"Put your sewage hand down, I'm not here to fight," he said in the corner. I whirled onto my back and scrambled to sit. The guy watched me as he stood with his feet apart, arms crossed over his Got Milk? T-shirt.

My migraine pulsed harder. I pressed myself against the garbage can.

'There will be no future with him alive. Kill him.'

I couldn't forget what the voice in my head said. I pushed myself off the floor. I clung to the wall behind me.

"We either do this the easy way or the hard way." He paused. "The hard way will get both of us killed."

I looked past him. He was blocking the only exit. He watched me.

"We have some things we need to discuss." His eyes remained hidden under his hat. If I escaped, I wouldn't have been able to give the police a detailed picture of him; most of his features were hidden under his hat. "I rather not do it here."

"What do you want?" I demanded. I puked my guts in the women's bathroom-I hardly seemed tough.

"To talk," the man said as if he were speaking to a five-year-old. "I hate repeating myself."

Suddenly he was a foot closer. He tightened a grip on my forearm.

"Do not struggle," he growled. "I will only break your sewage arm."

The world around me tilted and went dark- I momentarily felt weightless. With a jolt, my feet hit the ground and I tumbled and fell sideways- my bottom hit the wet ground again. Thunder and lightning flashed the sky. The man had materialized, standing above me.

"Get away from me," I rasped. He rubbed his hand against his noggin.

"Listen, you're in danger."

"Get away from me!" I rolled onto my stomach, fighting to stand. I launched into a run but my legs wouldn't hold me steady. I fell sideways, smarting my thigh on rocks.

"Did the voice inside your head stop?"

My fingers clawed the earth as the world shifted again.

"Get the hell away from me!"

A shimmer of a shadow appeared until it materialized into focus. The man was suddenly two feet in front of me. I nearly pissed my jeans.

He kneeled to meet my level. "I don't have time to waste. I'm definitely not going to spend it chasing after you." His voice grated against my ears. "Now answer me. Did the voice in your head stop?"

I swallowed. "Yeah."

His growl deepened. "Are you willing to get rid of the voice for good?"

My mouth moved on autopilot. "Yes," I said.

"Good."

"You're going to kill me," I mumbled.

"Why?"

"You attacked me in a woman's restroom."

"I was trying to save you." He sounded annoyed.

"You're in danger."

I looked up. "Yeah, I noticed."

"No, not because of me," the man said gruffly.

I stared.

"You received the Po'luxnann Gejruvhet a few nights ago when you were attacked. It's the power that's controlling you."

I started. What?

My face must have shown a reaction because he went on.

"Think back. Were you in complete control over yourself in that bathroom?"

I looked at him. Really looked. Chips of ceiling stuck to his cap and a black t-shirt. He had a red bruise on his neck. The fight in the bathroom wasn't a dream. He got that bruise from me.

"You know what the Po'luxnann was doing?" he asked. "Taking over your body," he growled. "Then it's going to get inside the center of your existence- your soul. You need to know that."

What did he say? What was getting *what* out of me?

"You're crazy." Yeah, he had to be crazy. I didn't have to hear this anymore. He massaged his temple again. "You hadn't had the Po'luxnann for three days. Three days," he repeated. "It's already begun controlling you."

I started feeling disgusted. "You're wrong."

"How would you know what I was talking about if you believe I'm wrong?" *No.* Nothing controlled me.

That mantra kept repeating in my head when I looked up at him again. I shook my head as though I could make it all go away.

"It can't be true." He thought I had a...thing inside me- a power. The thing inside me had a name? "Who are you?" I choked.

"I'm Laurenx. I sensed the Po'luxnann five nights ago and it led me to you." I could feel his eyes boring down on me. "The Po'luxnann allowed itself to join with you."

I snorted, surprising myself. Of all the things I thought I had, I never thought the voice in my head was some living thing. My heart drummed louder. It was better to pretend it was all a joke. "How can you sense," I trailed off.

The man abruptly craned his neck at the sky. I followed his gaze.

I must have imagined it; cloaked figures flew in the air. The man swiftly dove on top of me and landed us on the ground. I started wrestling him to get off. "I don't swing your way, buddy," I wheezed.

"Shut up," he growled, shoving my head deeper into the mud. "You saw that up there? If you move again I will knock you out before they spot us."

I stopped. It was a while before he let go. He stood. "You're a lit match in the dark for them." He peered down at me again. "Let's go."

"Those things- flying. Did you *see* that?"

"Let's go. Now," he commanded.

I sat up, shivering against the wind. Who was he to tell me what to do? I wanted to shout. I rubbed dirt off my mouth and spat. "I don't know who you are-"

"I told you, I'm Laurenx. That R'uttri," he thumbed up at the sky, "is after you. You are that unlucky human to possess the Po'luxnann."

This time I managed to stand. I started backing away.

"You humans lack common sense." He sounded revolted. "You are being hunted. I am *not* your enemy. The Po'luxnann isn't blaring in your mind and you are not lacking strength." He was losing his patience. "Check the pendants around your neck."

I didn't take my eyes off him as I inched my hand up to my throat.

Sure enough, I felt something hard against my chest.

My eyes shifted down to my bare chest- my shirt had burnt off in the bathroom. Around my neck were two separate twining, bronze ropes. Two pendants, one the color of sapphire and the other was the color of blood red, hung.

The sapphire pendant was as large as a lime, etched with symmetrical shapes and swirls in design. The blood red pendant was a simple coin with symbols etched on its surface. Both looked very old and well worn.

What's more was they felt alive on my skin. They had a sort of energy running through them, steady and constant.

The bloody red pendant had energy that ebbed and flowed, matching the beat of my heart. Shapes and swirls were moving on the sapphire pendant, mimicking the raging storm in my head.

"We need to go." In a blur, Laurenx was two inches from my nose, grabbing my arm. Stunned, I backpedaled. "Stop it!"

"I warned you about wasting my time," he snarled.

I flung the pendants over my head.

The moment I did, the air emptied out of my lungs and my body trembled. Then came a flood of pain.

"What did you do?" Laurenx's bellow cut short as an inhuman shrill pierced my ears.

Suddenly I was hurt everywhere. My back and my shoulders throbbed. My ribs weren't feeling too hot after knocking it against the toilet. The gash on my forehead and my bleeding cheek stung.

"Where is it?" Laurenx snapped angrily. He started searching for the pendants.

I couldn't answer him.

I WILL HAVE YOU. FIRST, I WILL DESTROY HIM, the Po'luxnann roared. It's screeching brought me to my knees- I cupped my hands over my ears.

"God, what's it doing in my head?" I gasped.

Laurenx grabbed my forearms and shook me. "Learn to control it, don't give in. Control yourself!"

My skin brightened like a beacon and my chest seized with pain.

He does not rule over you, the voice rumbled. *I will rid of him now. Peer into his eyes.*

My head hammered in agony. I felt myself slipping away. Laurenx shook me again. "Learn to control yourself," he demanded.

My limbs started to feel like they were being popped off like a plastic Ken doll, one by one. As it shrilled louder and louder, I watched as my hands, now glowing streetlight red, move towards Laurenx's hat.

I knew it was wrong, so very wrong, as the voice filled me up with its presence, its power. The pressure threatened to blow my head clean off.

"Get a hold of yourself." Laurenx slapped my hands away. "Don't give in and focus. Concentrate on who you are. What is your name?"

"God, it hurts," I whimpered.

"What is your name?" he repeated forcefully.

"Seth Castillo," I mumbled.

My hands jerked back up. I watched them catch on either side of his neck. I dug my nails into his flesh.

"Would Seth Castillo really want to kill me?" he barked. "Ask yourself!"

I shook my head.

"What is a memory that reminds you of yourself, huh?" he rasped. "Think of a happy memory."

What happy memory?

I was slowly crushing his windpipe like an accordion and he allowed it. I was going to kill him.

"Concentrate!"

My father's face tumbled into my mind's eye. I could just picture that day I kicked my first goal in a soccer match and how proud Dad was. There was so much joy in his eyes; he couldn't wait to buy me ice cream and pizza for a victory treat. I was seven, then. Soccer reminded me of who I once was.

"Do you still hear the Po'luxnann?" he wheezed.

"It's still in my head," I moaned.

"Will it to stop," Laurenx choked.

"Get out of my head!" Just as the words tumbled from my mouth, the pressure deflated. The power began to fade.

He is the enemy. The vision has not changed. Leave. You were happier on your own without interference. Safer. The voice stopped.

I opened my eyes. I was on the ground again.

My nose was dripping. I wiped it on the back of my hand. It was blood.

"Good. You're not tapping into the Po'luxnann."

"Shut up." I cupped my ears with my hands. He was adding to a colossal migraine.

"You should have never, ever removed the pendants!" His rage built again. He took another hard glance at me and began scouring the ground. I pointed a trembling finger in the opposite direction he should be looking.

"I threw them over there," I said weakly. My hand quickly fell back to my side.

I lay back in the mud, huffing and puffing. Laurenx muttered and barked to himself as he continued his search. I watched the stars twinkle in and out as the rain and wind beat harder.

Lightning flashed across the sky. I covered my eyes in the crook of my elbow.

"You're a stupid boy." Laurenx's voice carried through the whistling wind. "You allowed the Po'luxnann to control you again," he said. "It will eat your soul until you are nothing but a memory!"

Time had gone by. Footsteps crunched gravel and paused. My heavy eyelids gradually opened.

Laurenx crouched down beside me. He lifted my head and placed the pendants over my head and around my neck. He let go. My head hit the mud. The relief I felt when he put on the pendants were noticeable. The fog in my head calmed and the weariness in my limbs began to lift.

Laurenx didn't speak or move for some time. He loomed over me, watching and listening. For what, I didn't know.

The rain got colder. My fingers were growing numb.

"Do you want to live?" He suddenly asked.

My lips were chapped and my mouth was dry. I licked my lips and moistened my throat before I replied. "I do."

Laurenx uttered low. "Then get this through your thick head. Never take off the pendants." He didn't have to tell me twice. "The sapphire pendant keeps your mind intact. The Po'luxnann is able to worm its way into the mind of whoever it inhabits until you are but a shell of a person. Do you understand?" he snarled. "It's wearing you down until it can control you. The dark crimson pendant allows the wearer to block any outside forces from tampering with your soul, but it will only works temporarily. You have to stop feeding the Po'luxnann with your emotions. That's why you've been feeling out of control with your rage," he added.

"The Po'luxnann has the power to make you believe what it wants you to think. It has the power to make you believe eating ice cream will give you the power to fly over a cliff. *Do you understand?"* he said. "Or do we need to test that theory again by *flinging the pendants to Timbuktu?"*

"No, I'm good."

His upper lip curled. "The pendants are not strong enough to contain the Po'luxnann but it will provide some protection. You're human. You are weak," he spat. "The Po'luxnann will break through the pendant's barrier around your mind."

I slowly sat up, body aching. Besides my fingers, I lost feeling in my toes.

"The only way you can survive is if you have enough willpower against the Po'luxnann. We can return it to its original Bearer as long as you listen to me. Whatever *I* say, whatever *I* tell you to do from here on out, you follow. Understood?"

"Crystal," I mumbled.

Laurenx watched me. I didn't know if he was going to smack or kick me from the fury I felt around him. Laurenx shifted and my hands automatically shot up in front of my face. He stood.

"Pick up your backpack. Follow me."

I slowly lowered my arms. I watched as he started down the road.

I hesitated. What Laurenx said made me feel better about my sanity. I wasn't imagining voices in my head or seeing visions. It wasn't really me who set Gavin and Logan's truck on fire. Just knowing I wasn't crazy lifted a burden of weight I didn't know I carried.

I was feeling hopeful. Maybe Laurenx could help get my life back. No more visions, no more starting fires, no more excruciating stabs of pain. There was a light at the end of this tunnel.

I pulled out a new shirt from my backpack and chucked the old burnt one that clung onto my chest. I threw over my jacket and slowly rose to my feet. I swayed a little, watching the earth slip sideways. I bit down on my lip. I had to force my legs to walk a straight line.

Laurenx stopped to fumble in his pocket. "Here." He threw me a Snickers chocolate bar. "It'll help."

I tore off the wrapper and chewed off a bite. The moment I did, my weariness was beginning to wear off. I took a bigger bite, falling behind.

Twenty minutes later we climbed onto a heated bus. My sneakers squeaked as I traveled down the walkway. Laurenx found a seat in the back empty row. I sat my backpack between us and took a seat.

"Don't stare at anyone or out of the window; you'll see your reflection," he said.

"What will happen if I do?"

"After you destroyed the truck and ran into that bathroom, you looked into the mirror. Right? The eyes are windows," he said. "You don't want the Po'luxnann looking in." He cracked his neck, relieving tension.

"Forcing you to look into the mirror gave you the chance to see yourself as you truly are. If you want to survive, don't ever look into anything with a reflection. Don't think of looking into anyone's eyeballs, not even a watch. Got it?" He didn't wait for a response.

He leaned his head against the cool glass window, but he had his arms crossed in front of him, looking every bit agitated. I couldn't tell if his eyes were closed under the baseball cap.

My palms started to get clammy as the bus traveled further away from the road that led to my house. I forced myself not to look outside and shut my eyes.

I had to leave home, I told myself. I destroyed Logan's truck by fire. The similar sensation I felt when I set fire to Black Tie hadn't left.

I enjoyed it. The power I had in those moments made me feel I was invincible- that I was in control. Gavin would have been dead if I had given in to the Po'luxnann. If Mom hadn't been there I would have roasted Logan the moment I came to.

The intensity of power drummed into my veins and poured through every fiber of my body. It felt so good when I let go and gave into the power. That high was far better than running all day long.

I stopped myself.

Bottom line, I hurt people and there was nothing good about the Po'luxnann- I had to get rid of it. It was slowly killing my soul. The Po'luxnann wasn't something I could keep. I was being hunted for it.

I needed a smoke, bad. And probably three more Snickers bars.

CHAPTER NINE

Two bus transfers and nearly two hours later, Laurenx's head popped up. His shoulders visibly relaxed once he realized where he was. He pushed the red button and it chimed. We rolled to a full stop. Laurenx rounded to me.

"Let's go."

We stepped off the bus and were back out into the cold rain. I glanced down at my shoes submerged in water. I winced. These were my only good pair of sneakers and I just super glued the bottom.

I hitched up the neck of my jacket as Laurenx and I made a left down an uneven flooded sidewalk.

"You live here?" I said, glancing around. His neighborhood made mine look like the Sistine Chapel. We passed a park and in the dark. Visible paint sprayed all over benches, garbage cans were overturned, and the remaining swing on the set slanted to one side in the caked dirt. The houses themselves were so tiny and discolored it reminded me of a dull version of Candyland.

The way this night was going, half of me expected little gremlins to pop out singing, "It's A Small World."

We hadn't walked five minutes in the neighborhood when I heard three ambulances whirl by and several police sirens accompanied them. Cars riding on monster wheels raced down the flooded road with their music blaring, bass thumping. I was having doubts if the safest place was around Laurenx. He paused in front of a chain-linked fence. A dog barked.

"Come."

He unlocked his fence and led us up the short walkway towards his door. It was no different than many of the homes I saw here. It was puke green with a gray roof, I guessed, was white once upon a time.

Next door, Laurenx's neighbor was smoking outside his front porch, watching his dog go on the front lawn. The smell of weed and musty socks hit my nose. The neighbor whipped his head to us with a mean look. Laurenx shoved me past his front door. I ducked inside, shivering, happy to get out of the rain. "What did I tell you," he warned.

"Don't look anyone in the eye or I die," I responded under my breath. Laurenx had to shove his shoulder into his door to budge it closed. He switched on the kitchen light and it lazily flickered on. I zipped off my jacket and glanced around.

A mix-matched pattern of a brown couch and a black old leather recliner sat in the living room. The kitchen, painted yellow, had a small brown table and one wooden chair. Laurenx threw his keys on the living room table that had one short, broken leg. A few books held it on the bottom and balanced the table out.

There was a sound coming from the bedroom. A big black dog trotted out of the room towards Laurenx. The dog was ginormous. If I didn't know any better, I'd say the thing was a bear in its past life. It had intense blue eyes that reminded me of a wolf's, but its eyes were much bigger. Every time it jumped in excitement, the dog's weight rattled the entire house.

The giant animal stood on its hind legs, slobbering Laurenx with a tongue as long as my wrist was to my elbow. It's long thin ears, similar to a bat's, scraped the low ceiling.

"Dax, stop. I got it, I didn't forget." The animal bit him at his thigh and I was suddenly aware of the tight space.

Laurenx pulled out of his pocket a wrapper. I realized it was a Slim Jim sausage you'd get at a Quik Mart. I wondered if he paid for it.

The giant animal snatched the food with its teeth and swallowed it whole. Laurenx scratched under his neck then patted him on the head. "Good boy."

The animal dropped on his four legs and gave Laurenx a doggie grin- he revealed fangs that resembled a saber-tooth tiger's. His tail repeatedly thumped on the hardwood floor, causing the kitchen chair to hop at every beat.

"What kind of breed is that dog?" Laurenx opened the linen closet in the hall and threw me a towel. "It's a nighthound," he said. "No relation to any dog of your world."

He sat on the couch and threw the remaining Slim Jim on the floor. Dax-the-whatever finished his treat. I nodded slowly. "Right."

The animal's attention diverted to me. It took a step forward, growling.

On second thought, it was time for me to go.

"Dax trusts no one but me. You have to come and pet him on the head," Laurenx said. My back grazed against the doorknob and I fumbled behind me to open it. "He'll pounce on you in a second if you don't come. Run and he'll attack you like an enemy." He almost sounded bored.

"You're kidding, right?"

The animal growled louder as it inched its way toward me and sniffed. I heard fear was an animal's way of detecting prey.

In all its weight it moved swiftly towards my side and paused to lick my trembling hand.

"I'd pet him if I were you." Laurenx leaned forward in his seat as if he was watching a show.

I tapped it gently on its head. The animal's growl reduced.

I yelped as it suddenly rubbed its monstrous head against my waist, almost purring.

"He likes you," Laurenx said. That made me relax a little. "I was afraid he wouldn't," he told me.

I stopped petting. "If he didn't?"

"I'd be reattaching a body part right now," Laurenx said as-a-matter-of-factly.

"When you're done cooking your eyes at me, we can get down to business." Laurenx watched as I slipped away from the bear-wolf-bat hybrid. Dax followed instead and took his place right beside my feet as I took a seat in the old recliner. It bobbled as I sat.

Laurenx leaned back in his seat and carefully removed his hat. He took off his jacket and neatly folded it on the back of the couch. Although the kitchen light was on, it was barely enough to cast light into half the living room. Laurenx was covered in the shadows. I couldn't make out his face.

"Now we're all comfy," Laurenx started, "You nearly burned down your little girlfriend's family restaurant-"

"I didn't do it on purpose," I said offensively.

"And you burned down your stepfather's truck tonight-"

"He's not my step anything."

"It's clear the Po'luxnann Gejruvhet isn't yours. Who gave them to you?"

"I don't know how it happened," I said feeling angry.

"You don't know how it happened?" He repeated the question as if he questioned my intelligence.

I glowered. "I was standing outside a house and an old man came down from the sky," I shook my head, remembering how impossible I thought it was. "He comes after me, put his hands on me, and *electrocutes* me. Next thing I know I'm lying in a hospital bed."

He didn't flinch. "What did the man look like?"

I grounded my teeth together. I never told anyone this. "He has...glowing gold skin," I hesitated. I thought the old man had rubbed himself in gold glow-in-the-dark paint, the way he shined in the moonlight the night he attacked.

"Go on," Laurenx said.

"He's old, maybe fifty, short with black hair and brown eyes," I paused. "Maybe the eyes were white because they changed color."

He frowned. "That's it?"

I almost died and it didn't faze him. "It's not like I was trying to remember the curve of his face while I was getting electrocuted," I said coolly.

"Did he say anything?"

"No, I think he was too busy killing me, you know, to tell me what's on his mind."

Laurenx considered a moment. "He wasn't killing you. He was performing a Ggatgin, a process that transfers the Po'luxnann to another being." Laurenx leaned forward in his seat. "I'm surprised you, a human, survived the transfer," he said. "Has this man tried appearing before you again?"

Only in my nightmares, I thought. "Nope." I took that moment to rub my hair with the towel and kicked off my waterlogged sneakers.

"The R'uttri are also after you," he said to himself. "How has the Po'luxnann changed you?"

I frowned. He tried to explain. "Do you have strange cravings, experience supersensory senses?"

"What?"

"Are your senses heightened?" He said loudly and slowly. I spoke through my teeth. "I get migraines." I thought a second. "I smell weird things coming from places and people." I remembered Chessie's sour milk scent and how I could smell the cigarettes and musty socks off Laurenx's neighbor.

"That's all?"

"I burn things," I said coldly.

"Do you have visions?"

"I see visions," I told him.

"About what?"

"About this king. King Razhatlab."

He didn't say anything right away.

"Do you know him?"

"Yes." He didn't explain. "What did you see when you saw visions of him? What do you know?"

"His world is falling apart," I said. "The suns are going out and forests are dying because some power was stolen."

"It's not *some* power," he snapped. "It's the Po'luxnann Gejruvhet. The most powerful source in the universe is inside a child."

He was making it hard not to hit him.

"What is the old man's condition? What is he doing to get back the Po'luxnann?"

"He's dying. Someone poisoned him. I don't know."

I flung the towel and stood so abruptly the recliner knocked against the back of my legs. "I didn't come to answer your questions, I came to get rid of this thing inside of me. Can you get rid of them or not?"

The animal at my feet startled. He began to growl.

"Sit," Laurenx ordered *me*, not the animal.

My breathing became shallow- I couldn't think straight. He sat there while my entire world was crumbling to pieces.

"Don't unleash that temper around me," Laurenx said. "I will snap your neck before the Po'luxnann Gejruvhet overtakes you. Calm down or I will make you."

My fists clenched and I bit back my tongue, swallowing my words down like gravel. I finally sat. Satisfied, Dax lay back down. He folded his legs beneath his ragged fur.

Laurenx tried again. "I won't waste time convincing you I'm not human." He paused. "I'm from another world."

I snorted before I could stop myself. "You live on another planet too?"

His voice flattened. "Yes, on a different solar system that can be accessed through the Bror Gate."

"You don't look alien," I accused. "You look human."

"And you look Temcaltiafan," he grunted. "I don't have to look different to be inhuman," he added. "I'm from a world called D'uthne, where gods reside." He let the silence stretch on. "Reason I found you was because I sensed a D'uthnian's power spiking all over the city. As it turns out, it was a human." I gave him an annoyed look. "It was as though a newborn baby was trying to drive a car on a highway. Wasn't hard to track or see the disaster behind it." I didn't bother hiding my irritation.

"You have no control," he said bluntly. "Wherever you go, you cause and attract trouble."

"Hey, I didn't ask for powers-"

"You don't know how to gather your emotions," he snapped. "You're in distress; this I know. And yet, if you didn't throw a tantrum whenever something didn't go as planned you wouldn't have set anything on fire."

"You're blaming me for what the old man did to me?" I said defensively. "I didn't start those fires on purpose-"

"You are ultimately responsible," he continued without remorse. "I've observed you in the past few days. How do you confront your battles?" he inquired. "Do you wait to resolve conflict before it festers? Or do you take on the challenge by its roots and face them head on?"

My legs shook restlessly. "You bury your emotions until it spews over," he barked. "You don't face your problems, you avoid them."

"You don't know me," I glared. "You don't know me at all."

"I do," he said. "You harbor your emotions and the Po'luxnann confuses and controls you. Setting things aflame is a reaction to your bottled anger and fear. You also seek justice and vengeance," he hissed. "What is worrying you that you can't seem to resolve within yourself? What happened that made you go out of control in the restaurant?"

I got up from my seat. I didn't need to hear this.

In a blink of an eye he was standing in front of my face. "What is it that you are harboring inside?" He prodded a finger at my shoulder. "What is it, Seth?" He jabbed me in the shoulder again. "Tell me!"

"What is wrong with you?" I snapped. "Back the hell off."

"You see? That right there, what you're holding back? Tell me or I will make you."

He prodded me hard again and I nearly shouted. "I'm going to burn you if you do that again."

"You're waiting for anger to well up inside you," he said. "If you don't release that festering anger the Po'luxnann will control you. Start letting go."

I didn't answer.

"Now, what is bothering you? Is it that your little girlfriend hates your guts? Or that your mom didn't continue running after you?"

Rage welled up inside of me and I let it pool into my soul. Another foreign part of me awoke, biting at the chance to use my anger to release power. This realization hit me with surprise and frightened me.

He was right, my heart hammered bitterly. It's true the Po'luxnann gave me a reason to give into my feelings and lash out. I tried to convince myself I was okay, but the truth hurt like hell. I thought it was better to show anger than to admit my true feelings.

After my parents split, I got used to burying the pain. That tear in my soul was full of demons and it was overflowing like an ocean poured into a cup. I was angry with myself about how things ended with Chessie.

Truth is, I was angry because I was so hurt and so confused and afraid. How could someone I saw as a friend for so long just walk away? She threw me away like I didn't matter at all. I couldn't face that our relationship as boyfriend and girlfriend was over. Worse, I knew we could never be friends anymore. If I called her phone, I doubt she'd call me back- that hurt the most. I didn't know how to deal with it. How was I supposed to let this go?

Tonight was the first time I said out loud what I was afraid to admit for so long. Mom and I haven't been the same after Dad left. Mom didn't know who I was anymore, not for a long time. I couldn't believe I shouted her and told her she didn't want to face me. I was also afraid of facing the truth, too. I was such a hypocrite.

As my anger deflated I felt the Po'luxnann's power simmer down. My shoulders sagged as a knot in my stomach loosened. I fell back into my seat, drained. The yawning silence made me uncomfortable so I started to scratch Dax's ear. It gave me something to do.

Laurenx lingered for a moment before backing away. "That's better. You didn't tap into the Po'luxnann Gejruvhet. The more your anger and fear burns, the deeper you bury yourself and give into the Po'luxnann. Face your emotions. Get over yourself."

"I get what you're saying," I mumbled. He gave a firm nod. A few minutes had gone by. I changed the subject. "Where'd you say you're from?" He didn't move for another minute. The presence around him was stifling. "D'uthne," he said, moving back to his seat.

"So that's a solar system?"

"It's our Earth," he interjected. "D'uthne is separated into two kingdoms: Temcaltiaf and Imudmid. Natives from my homeland have abilities that generate power and energy."

"Uhuh." I humored him. "Gods like Persephone, Zeus, and Aphrodite?"

"You're thinking Greek mythology; gods who created nature and built the world around us. There is only one all-powerful Creator who is omnipotent. He created the heavens and the earth and moves outside of time and space. All of D'uthne know His Name. Your people call Him the Almighty One, Elohim, and many other variations." I nodded, assuming I knew the God he was talking about.

"Beings you believe are fairytales: Dax, ogres, zombies, witches, are smaller gods. We are gods, and I use this term to fit in general context because our abilities come from the evolution of nature and the environment itself. We cannot create things out of thin air; we only use what is already created by God." I let that sink in before I uttered a word.

"Okay," I started to say, "so you're telling me gods exist, sure, but are you telling me a," I tried to think of something outrageous, "A vampire is a god?"

His upper lip curled. "Yes. Humans believe anything wearing wings and pointy ears are fae and those who begin a lightning storm is Zeus," he grunted. "We have beings that can control lightning through their wings. Your people wouldn't know what to call us. Humans like to label your own people: black, white, Columbian, or African although they have no varying differences between them aside their appearance. D'uthnians are classified by their nature." Laurenx shifted in his seat. "You know what a werewolf is?"

"I do," I said.

"No you don't," he interjected. "You humans," I winced at the phrase, "believe a werewolf that mutilates a family of humans without reason can shift into a scantily dressed man with sex appeal."

"You talking about the movie that just came out?"

He grunted again. "I saw the movie poster at the bus stop. I told you-gods are classified by their nature. A werewolf is a god of appetite; what it wants, it hunts and kills. There is no other drive in him and once he is a werewolf, he is lost to his god. He cannot shift entirely into his original form. He will stand deformed, with rabid teeth, inhuman limbs, and glowing eyes, always scavenging for his next meal."

My throat went dry.

"They don't live very long; they're perpetually on a cycle of starvation. Eventually, their hunger kills them."

I shook my head. "There are werewolves walking on this planet. For real."

"Yes. There are few in existence on this side of the Gate," he said. I glanced up at him. "There are three Passages. Two of them, the Temcaltiaf and Imudmid, reside in D'uthne. D'uthne is set apart from your human world, the Bror Passage. Each Passage is locked behind Gates and Passagekeepers make sure of that."

Another world. Gods exist. Passages. How the heck humans didn't know anything about this? It would have been on CNN by now. Wait-

"You said the Passage people make sure we all live in our own Passages, right?"

"Passagekeepers. Yes."

"If that's true, someone sucks at his job," I said. "How come we know about you guys? Little kids know about vampires. Ever heard of Dracula?"

He made an irritated sound. "Some humans came across us on this side of the Passage and truths soon became myths as many D'uthne died off over the years."

"Why did we start believing vampires could burn in sunlight?"

A snarl escaped him. "If I could bring back Shelly from the dead and kill her again, I would," he said. "The author of Dracula was a vampire who used her artistic license to bend the truth about her nature. Would you reveal your weaknesses to a world of gullible humans if you could suck on their bone marrow like lollipops?" I flinched, feeling more offended. What did he have against humans?

"Vampires are gods of winter. They're dead without body heat, eternally cold, and are inherently born gloomy and insane. Have you met a Londoner during winter? Constant cold can make anyone bitter and insane."

"But the whole thing about burning in the sun,"

"Vampires don't burn, they melt," he snapped again, breathing heavily. These misconceptions clearly bothered him. "There is no sun on Imudmid so they are naturally attracted to the human world behind the Bror Passage." He tried to find the right words.

"Human blood is… hot chocolate on a cold winter night; it warms and feeds them. Temporarily," he added. "The smoke that rises off vampires when they step into the sun is the same reaction when you drop an ice cube into hot tea. Vampires adore sunlight but it eventually melts them if they bask in it for long.

"The Po'luxnann was the reason why we had Passages put into existence. It's a form of a peace treaty; it keeps us from ruling, maiming, or eating each other. The last Creature War nearly wiped off every being in our world," he explained. "There were rebels who decided against the Treaty of Peace, the Po'luxnann. Before the Gates could be established, some took the opportunity to hide and live within the Bror Passage among humans. Others saw humans as an all access, all-you-can-eat-buffet. The Gates are very hard to break through, near indestructible. Once you were behind them, you were in the Passage forever." He stopped. "Is this all a little too much for you?"

"No." He sounded too condescending for my benefit.

"Several nights ago I sensed a D'uthnian passing through. They don't exist on this side of the Bror Passage, period. And when I sensed R'uttri by a dozen? They're trouble in the worse way."

It almost hurt to ask. "What are they?"

"Obvious answer? They're human predators. Vampires don't need to feed on humans twenty-four seven because at some point, they get bored. But R'uttri?" He shook his head.

"That bad?"

"The R'uttri are undead flesh-eating hired assassins."

I allowed those words to absorb into my skull.

"They're dead things that hunt people and eat them."

I didn't answer.

"They're zombies," Laurenx said slowly.

"I get it," I glared.

He still appeared convinced he was dealing with a stupid kid. He watched my feet jiggle at my side as a fresh sheet of sweat made its way down my brow.

"You are now Bearer of the Po'luxrann. You have a power that goes beyond your limited ability of understanding. Calm yourself before you hurt yourself. Don't do stupid mistakes like taking off the pendants," he warned.

I stood again. I had to do something to keep myself steady. I swallowed a few times before I could speak. "These monsters are coming from your world because I have the Po'luxnann." The weight of my words settled on my chest like an elephant. Pieces started clicking together.

"Vampires. The R'uttri. And the old man after me- why couldn't you guys stay behind your stupid Gate?" I said. "Who's going to stop them from killing us?"

I could feel Laurenx's eyes boring into me. Dax looked at him, probably waiting for the signal to chomp my head off.

Laurenx answered. "The lines between D'uthne and the Bror Passage aren't going to disappear anytime soon. The Passagekeepers are holding the Gates together as long as they can. If they weren't, there'd be far more human bodies outside cemeteries."

"So if the Gates completely go, werewolves, the R'uttri, or whatever else can enter our Passage. Humans wouldn't be able to hide from them."

"Yes," Laurenx drawled.

A memory of a vision started to make sense.

"*'The Bror Gate has been under more attacks in the past four nights. Passagekeeper Emikrili has reported a dozen R'uttri and ghouls have entered the Passage,'*" Melwimik had reported.

I thought about it more. "*'Some nut job was digging graves in the local cemetery and left dead bodies on the highway,'*" Logan heard from the news.

"*'The body was missing an arm, a leg looked like it was chewed off like some dog got to it, and the eyes were gone,'*" Eli had explained.

The R'uttri ate humans.

The realization knocked me down harder than a running bull.

Oh God. Humans were really in danger.

"*'The forests are slowly dying as our suns are going out,'*" the king's advisor said to King Razhatlab. My stomach churned.

"*'News says there's a cold front moving in fast tonight. Coldest it's ever been in Florida in seventy-five years,*" Mom told me. "*'They say it's going to get colder.'*"

No one was immune. Both worlds were affected by odd weather

changes, too. "Why aren't we doing anything?"

"I'm glad you realized the gravity of this situation," he mocked. "The Po'luxnann is now in a human boy while Gates are crumbling apart as creatures are crawling through the Passage."

I snapped. "You think I meant for this to happen?"

None of this would have happened if the old man or people like Laurenx were around. The Po'luxnann was inside a seventeen-year-old guy way out of his league. I didn't bother keeping my voice low. "We need to give the Po'luxnann back to its owner."

"The R'uttri will assassinate you on the spot once they realize you are now the Bearer. Every time you use the Po'luxnann, it brings the R'uttri closer to your location. My house," he barked. "You're lucky if the king made a deal with the Imudmid Council to send R'uttri to retrieve the Po'luxnann from the thief."

I didn't get to hear him finish his sentence. I thought back.

"*'My king,'*" Melwimik had explained, *"our Passagekeepers are holding up the battle to safeguard our Passages, but they are losing in numbers. The R'uttri have been relentless.'"*

"King Razhatlab didn't send those R'uttri after the thief." I sat as I explained to Laurenx. "He's having a rough time getting the Imud," I said, trying to recall. "The Imud people to hold back the R'uttri. He didn't make any deal with them."

Laurenx didn't say anything for a while. "You had a vision."

"Yes."

"You saw it happen."

Didn't he hear what I said? "We have to get the Po'luxnann to the king, right? Then the Gates are going to stay up and close up the Passages for good, right?"

"Yes."

"How do we get past the R'uttri and Parp…Parp…?"

"What?" Laurenx said annoyed.

"I had another vision a few days ago. A girl was talking to her brother. They mentioned a name. I'm sure it's the thief who Ggatgin me."

"'How can you stand here after what Parpagg had done?'" Vaora said with rage. *"'That cockroach betrayed the kingdom, and stolen the Po'luxnann…'"*

"Parpagg," I said aloud.

I didn't expect Laurenx's reaction. He shot up to his feet. He was right in my face, invading my space.

"The thief is Parpagg?" he hissed. Dax whined in the corner.

Laurenx loomed above me. Energy emanated out of him in tiny, wispy threads. The kitchen light peppered into the living room, but the darkness that rose out of Laurenx swallowed it.

I slipped out of my seat and moved as far as I could away from him. The temperature in the house quickly dipped twenty degrees. His voice came out in a rasp.

"Are you sure it was him?" I backed away again but he was already on me in a blink, wrenching my arm. The black threads slithered against my skin. Ice crystallized my veins.

He shook me. *"Answer me!"*

Everywhere I turned was pitch dark. My limbs hardened into glaciers once my body started shutting down.

"Yessss," my teeth clattered.

"What else do you know?"

My mouth was slow to respond. "Say it!" he spat.

"I-I don't know anymore."

His breath on my neck prickled my skin. I was suddenly afraid he was a vampire. Or worse.

He pulled away and I went down like an ice pick.

"We'll get the Po'luxnann back to its owner. Parpagg will deal with me first," Laurenx promised. "Dax, come."

I heard the sound of paws trotting over to Laurenx. A gust of wind blew in the middle of the living room, blowing hair into my frozen eyes. The cold air expanded and collapsed, sucking the air out of the room. With a bang, Laurenx and Dax disappeared.

Air soon returned. I instantly clutched my throat, coughing and gasping, like a fish without water. No light had returned. I was left afraid and alone in the dark.

CHAPTER TEN

After I switched the breaker to turn the power back on in the house, I flipped on the kitchen light, the living room light, and the bathroom light. I came back to the couch and pulled off my wet socks. I unzipped my bag and replaced them with clean ones. I shivered under the pullover, drawing my legs close. I wrapped my arms around me as I watched the room with eyes wide open.

Feeling and warmth slowly returned to my fingers and toes. I wanted to bolt out the door. I wanted to blink and go back to a time when things were simple- a time where Mom and Dad were the people I looked up to. But I wasn't twelve anymore.

Everything would be okay. Things had to go back to normal soon. Laurenx was out hunting Parpagg, I convinced myself.

"Parpagg." I spat his name out like venom. That was the old man's name. My fingernails dug into my palms.

If Parpagg hadn't used me as a stowaway for the Po'luxnann, my life would have been different. I wouldn't be here, in this dark neighborhood. I would have never set Black Tie and Logan's truck on fire. Nightmares and visions wouldn't come haunting me every night.

If Laurenx didn't find him, I wanted to dish out more pain on him than he did me. The Gates were breaking and creatures were coming through the Passage killing humans. I'd be doing my world a favor if I got rid of him.

Gavin burning flashed in my mind again.

My thoughts made me shiver. In that moment, I was more afraid of myself than I was of Parpagg in my nightmares.

The silence in the house stretched for an eternity. Outside, the wind howled and thunder rumbled louder. Lying down on my back, I took out my phone and brought it up to my face. I hit the home button.

Several missed calls glared at me. There were several from Mom, Eli, and Karin, and four phone calls from Logan. I frowned. Why was he calling?

Down on the list was the fifth call I missed. I read over the number a few times but there was no mistaking it. Dad called. My heart skipped a beat.

Mom must have called him after I left. I deleted his number from my contact list three years ago but I remembered it. He still called me at least once a month to check on me. Sometimes I picked up. I thought about what I could tell him now and how it would go.

"Hey, Dad."

"Seth, how are you?"

"Nothing much, just that I burned Logan's truck because of this power I have. It occasionally talks in my head and I'm being hunted down like a dog at the moment so I'm hiding out. How's life?"

It's been so long since we had a decent conversation that lasted more than five minutes. The knife he stuck in our family twisted my gut. My soul still bled from the trauma.

I turned off my phone and chucked it aside. I didn't want to deal with anything right now.

I wasn't sure if I hadn't made myself clear enough or God had a sense of humor; I should have been more specific.

I drifted into ugly images of Parpagg every time I closed my eyes. Then I fell without a parachute into a vision.

A brown woman stood over me. She wanted power for so long, she didn't mind hearing me beg for my life or scream. My blood on her hands was a small price to pay. Her slender vines and pink petals darkened into deep crimson as they latched onto my chest, pulsating to the very beat of my heart. I couldn't move and I couldn't speak. I tried to fight, but my body didn't respond. She finished the Ggatgin and I was dead.

There was a thunderous roar in my head. I fought to wake but another vision assaulted me, pulling and twisting my body and soul into different directions. I became unglued and as quickly as it happened, I snapped back together into a shape. A vision came.

There were flashes of emotions of torture and destruction in a sea of darkness; there was no light, no joy. I saw a shadow of a face flashing by. Glowing dark and disembodied was Parpagg's head with wild piercing eyes. He circled around and around above me until he hovered away.

Another face came and circled me once before it flew away, too. It paused a few yards away in midair. The face contorted and limbs sprang in four different directions. Soon, a body sprouted. In moments was a figure, kneeled. His head was bowed.

I knew who it was without knowing. I wanted to call out his name, but in that moment I forgot what name to call; none of them fit. His head snapped up as though he heard my thoughts. Then I saw his face.

It wasn't a person anymore; the body had beetles, leeches, worms, maggots, and other crawling things eating at it. The corpse still had tendons and muscle hanging on the bones as blood oozed out of its remaining veins and arteries.

When it drew its attention to me, I was compelled to stab myself in the heart to know if it was still beating- that I was still alive and it hadn't obliterated me.

But I had died. My ghost peered down at my body, cold on the ground.

I woke up gasping for air, clutching around my ribs. My throat hurt from the sounds I was making; I couldn't calm down fast enough. I peeled off the pullover and stumbled into Laurenx's bathroom. Before I reached the toilet, whatever was left in my stomach spewed over the closed lid.

I quickly opened it and tossed the rest of my stomach's contents inside the bowl.

In both visions, I died. The corpse left me an empty shell, and the woman left me drowning in my own blood.

You have two roads. There are two possible outcomes of your death.

I nearly jumped out of my skin when I heard it.

He will become Death. She will be consumed with power and bring death, the Po'luxnann informed.

I wanted to scrub my skin raw and clean my brains out. I didn't want to know Death, I wanted to shout. I needed to tell the Po'luxnann to kick rocks, but even in my thoughts, my strength was gone. Any energy I had was left for throwing up. The Po'luxnann was wrong. It was the death of me.

The one you must fear most is the owner of the house you entered. You witnessed the vision.

My stomach heaved again. Was that corpse Laurenx?

Not Laurenx. It paused. *Xa'renul.*

Sh-are-ren-oohl. And there was the woman.

How many more enemies?

My left arm and chest burned deeper. The tingling soreness began to travel down to my forearms and to the very tips of my fingers. The crimson tattoo was glowing.

My right hand felt around my neck. The pendants weren't working against the Po'luxnann-

Did you enjoy his display of power earlier? I can do much worse.

I glimpsed down, confused. I was only wearing one pendant, the dark crimson pendant.

I panicked. "Shut up."

My eyes fell onto the sapphire pendant across the bathroom. It was lying on the side of the bathtub.

When I drifted into both visions, the Po'luxnann somehow had enough control to throw the pendant across the room.

An immediate wave of dread kicked straight to my balls. Laurenx mentioned the sapphire pendant blocked the Po'luxnann from my mind to keep it from taking control. I dove for the other side of the bathroom.

I fought to reach the pendant but my spine twisted- I watched as my fingers flinched away and I fell backwards on the linoleum floor. Something invisible locked my arms to my side and my legs glued themselves together. I couldn't move. Just like in my vision.

You may move if I should allow it, the Po'luxnann said.

My left hand suddenly shot out in front of me. I watched it, horrified. My body was moving without my say so. I started to shout. "Leave me alone."

It is not my goal to harm you. I want you to surrender your body and will.

"Let me go!"

For now, I release you.

The pressure that held my joints in place, deflated. I rolled to my side, gasping. I was never so afraid and angry in my life.

"I'm going to kill you," I vowed. I started crawling for the bathtub where the pendant landed.

Before or after death finds you?

I didn't respond. The Po'luxnann talking in my head went past my limit. When it controlled my body, it took away my freedom.

I have not wished you the same harm as others have. You seek to restore your Gate and rid your Passage of R'uttri and the like. I can save your world.

When pressure finally alleviated my skull, I pressed myself against the side of the bathroom wall. I let out a shaky breath, pendant in my fist. Was that thing supposed to save humans? It was evil.

Your enemies are my enemies. I serve a far greater purpose using your body.

"What do you want from me?"

The answer didn't come right away.

Before I entered the Bror Gate, Parpagg was in a vision of the future. His thirst for power would be the key to release me from my prison.

"Prison?"

I will explain it in such a way you will comprehend. After studying you these few days, I understand you appreciate explanations. Do you wish to remove the pendant?

"I'm not stupid." Laurenx's warnings were echoing through my head.

You will only gain knowledge. Allow me moments of your time. I will not control you.

"No deal."

It will be disadvantageous to be bare of knowledge. You seek answers and I am willing to provide them. I will not control you.

If I didn't know any better, that almost sounded genuine. My fingers clutched around the pendant again. I inched them over my ear as a test. Instead of controlling my fingers to throw it away again, the Po'luxnann went into its story.

You have been told I was originally created as a Bringer of Peace to maintain balance and order on both worlds. Yet, my history is littered with more wars and destruction than the purpose of my existence. Many of those who have had a hold of me have exchanged my purpose for death, domination, and thirst for power. Wars have been fought over my birth. I have come from many rulers. I have been with Razhatlab's line of descendants of kingship for thousands of years.

It stalled.

Millennia ago, there were two blood brothers, once the best of companions. When their father had perished, according to Second Law, I was to be passed down to the firstborn in the family. The youngest brother did not appreciate this law. The eldest brother, fueled by his new possession of power, eradicated laws his father the king, had placed long ago. He used me for his personal gain, his lust, and his greed. He compelled me to destroy whoever stood in his path. There once was a child who did not bow to him as he crossed his carriage on the road. That child soon became a dead child. It stopped. *I feel your anger. Why?*

"Some king killed a kid because the kid didn't bow to him?"

Those with power beyond their means destroy others before they destroy themselves.

I shook my head, disbelieving.

Bloodlust and power corrupt the mind. You have slowly come to realize this.

It did take a moment for the thought to settle in.

The Bearer of the Po'luxnann usually drowns in his own flesh, convinced he is to be celebrated and feared. He hungers to take reign of the universe; he longs to see the stars kneel at his feet. In the end, the eldest was slain by his younger brother for fear of what he had become. Yet the youngest brother's true intention for murdering his brother was for power. As for my existence, I have experienced it time and time again. It is all I see. I was not made for revenge. I was not created for blackmail and deceit.

I saw where it was going with this. "I never hurt anyone for power."

Ah, but you desire to control.

I grounded my teeth together. "No, I don't."

You desire for your mate, your mother and your father to love you as deeply as you do for them. You wanted to injure the competing male who is after your chosen mate.

"I never-"

You have set fire twice, as a result of your deep desires and need for control.

"You got the same script from Laurenx?" I sounded bitter. The Po'luxnann ignored the question.

Your father abandoned you for another family. Will you burn your father next? Is that the control you desire? It said. You are headed down the road to destruction. You are no different than the king who murdered the child.

"Shut up." It went quiet. I could feel it disagreed. My anger gave it the satisfaction.

Eventually, the thirst to gain power, wins.

"I don't want you for anything," I glared. "You're the one using me. You talked me out of my mind and took over."

Are you attempting to convince yourself this is true?

"You tried to control me," I shouted. "You used my body."

Certainly. You serve my purpose. I need a body with a mind that easily bends to my will. You are no god. You cannot fight me. You cannot use me. I use you.

"Get the hell out, you hear?"

It ignored me. *Fate and destiny chose you.*

"What is that supposed to mean? I didn't choose you!" It drowned out my voice as it thundered out its threat.

I have come to bring peace and order. I will establish a new kingdom among humankind where I will rule, not destroy them. I have no need for power; I am it. I will not go back to D'uthne, to King Razhatlab. For my purpose to come into fruition, all of Temcaltiaf and Imudmid will be decimated.

CHAPTER ELEVEN

It was a slow process, stripping off my shirt and jeans. I didn't bother removing my boxers.

The Po'luxnann had stopped sharing. True to its word, the Po'luxnann left me in control over my own body and mind again. I pulled the sapphire pendant over the crimson pendant and watched them glow against the scarred tattoos on my chest. Out of my jean pocket something light fell onto the floor.

I would have ignored it until I saw it was the chocolate bar Laurenx handed me earlier. I tore the wrapper with my teeth- my hands were too jittery. I bit off half of the Snickers bar and didn't bother chewing.

I turned the shower on hot. The heat relieved my screaming muscles, the cuts, and the bruises I had all over my skin. The water gradually became pink from crusted dry blood. I watched it wash away the dirt and grime that stuck to my hair and scalp as it went down the drain. Exhausted, I sat in the tub and the shower fell down freely.

Every time I closed my eyes I saw a flash glowing ember. Images of the burning truck stuck in my mind. I played yesterday over in my head, how it all started with an early morning run, the laughs Mom and I shared, and the corny jokes she said. Then there was the food we made for dinner I didn't get to finish. The fight that followed before the fire.

Fear and confusion crashed over me until I was tired of feeling wet.

Dressed, I returned to the bright living room and shrank back into the couch.

I lay there in a daze, thinking. The wind moaned and the rain pounded against the rickety house. Thunder and lightning clashed outside.

The Po'luxnann made sure I knew it could control me.

It's funny; I always thought control was when someone told you what to do, when to do it, where to go, but I realized those things didn't cost me my freedom.

The Po'luxnann showed me how precious freedom was. I wasn't safe in my thoughts or emotions; it used them against me. I was angry with Gavin, Chessie, Dad, Logan, my Mom- the world. I burned things down because of it. My body wasn't under my control anymore. I attacked Laurenx, a complete stranger, in a bathroom.

The thought of Parpagg and the R'uttri out there hunting was too much. The visions of me dying twice brought me close to my breaking point.

I didn't trust Laurenx. He could summon cold and darkness, disappear and appear when he wanted to, and wasn't afraid to kill anyone. He wasn't human- he was a monster from another world.

Something else he said bugged me. He said the Gates were hard to get through, and according to him, the Bror Passage had been locked until Parpagg broke through the Bror Gate. So how long had Laurenx been living among humans? Was he really a vampire? What was his god?

There were so many questions and so little answers. I didn't want to stay in this house and wait for Laurenx the potential vampire, but I didn't know what else to do. If I left, the R'uttri or Parpagg could find me. Laurenx didn't like either of them and he seemed eager to kill them off. The Po'luxnann said people always abused it for power. Did Laurenx keep me around because he wanted to Ggatgin me?

I felt trapped; caged. I wanted to get rid of the Po'luxnann and I was no match for it. It made sure I knew it wasn't going back to D'uthne.

The Gate to the Bror Passage was breaking, monsters were eating us, and the weather had gone haywire. Humans couldn't fight off zombies or gods. We were weaker. Defenseless.

The Po'luxnann mentioned it didn't want to kill humans; it wanted to save us. From what I've seen and heard so far, Temcaltiaf and Imudmid Passage weren't the nicest places in the universe.

There was a choice here; forfeit my soul and hope the Po'luxnann was willing to save my world, or force the Po'luxnann back to the king and repair the Temcaltiaf and Bror Gates. But if the R'uttri and Parpagg broke through the Gates once, what could stop these monsters from trying again?

Tired of stressing and overthinking, I swiped the phone screen unlocked. I checked the time: 4:34 A.M. Displayed on the home screen was a preview of phone calls I missed last night and texts I didn't answer. I couldn't ignore the fact none of them were from Chessie. Just when I thought I was numb to pain, the thought hurt more than I believed it would. I decided to text the easiest out of the bunch, Eli.

> Hey, I guess Mom called Karin who prob texted u.
> Bet u got an earful real sry bout that.
> I need a break frm everything rite now.
> I'll tell u da details wen I can.

My finger hovered over the screen.

Should I really tell him about what's been going on? Would he believe me?

I clicked send.

I had to be free of the Po'luxnann; I didn't care about its stupid plans or the other world. All I needed to do was hand over the Po'luxnann to its original Bearer and move on with my life. I tweaked Eli's message and sent it to Karin. I texted Mom next:

> Hey Mom. I really need some space.
> I know u don't understand why.
> I'm over @ one of my teammate's frm soccer.
> don't worry. I'm safe.

A dark thought settled long after I sent the message. I wondered if it was the last text my Mom would ever receive from me.

I didn't know how long it'd be until Laurenx would find Parpagg in time before he killed me. I didn't know when it would be safe to go home or if I'd be hunted all my life for the Po'luxnann. I wanted to call Mom and tell her everything. I wanted more than anything to go home.

I started texting Dad what I told Mom except I mentioned he should look after her. I hesitated.

It didn't seem right to ask him to watch over Mom; we were barely speaking. I doubted Mom spoke to him too. If I sent the text as is, he'd probably ask why he had to watch her and I'd have to go into telling him about Logan's truck and the fight I had with Mom. Of course, I could have ignored his messages. After ten minutes of erasing and rearranging, I finally sent a short text:

Hey Dad. Saw u called. Busy.

I'm at a friend's house. Talk soon.

It was better to let them think everything was alright. I didn't want to get them sucked into this.

I quickly glanced up. Something black moved from the corner of my eye in the edge of the room. My heart started beating hard as my eyes lingered at the corner. There was nothing.

I let out a breath I didn't realize I was holding. I was terrified of shadows now.

I played mindless games on my phone the rest of the night, killing time. Hours later, Laurenx appeared and I nearly jumped out of my bones.

"You're awake," he greeted. I glanced at the front door then back to him. I didn't hear him come in. I stood up uncomfortably. I didn't know how to be around him. He nearly froze me to death last night.

In the very same corner I was looking at earlier, a shadow grew into a giant form.

It was Dax. He trotted up to me and licked my hand. I gently patted him on the head.

"I didn't find Parpagg," Laurenx announced.

I stopped patting Dax and he regarded me with soulful eyes. Silence filled the room. I waited the whole night for good news and just like that, any ounce of hope I had split in two.

Laurenx entered the small kitchen, rummaging the cabinets. He seemed normal in his jeans and black t-shirt in his kitchen, not like the kind of guy who went out to murder someone. I stalked into the kitchen.

"Why couldn't you find Parpagg? I thought you said you can sense him."

"I'll find him," he threw his voice over his shoulder.

I stood in the kitchen doorway. Dax bumped me out of the way and sat in the middle of the kitchen floor between us.

"How are you going to find him? Where did you go looking for him?"

Laurenx slammed a cabinet door shut. "What did I tell you about flinging that anger around? Don't ask useless questions."

I glared at his back. "You didn't get Parpagg."

"You'll hand over the Po'luxnann to the king and he'll be able to kill Parpagg. It won't be a problem for you anymore."

"It's not that simple," I retorted. Dax's eye shifted from Laurenx to me as though a tennis match was taking place.

"You want to get rid of the Po'luxnann." He tapped a fingernail on the plastic cup he placed on the counter.

"You should know it's already attached itself to you like a stubborn tentacle. Unless you have the ability to Ggatgin me with them, I'd have to kill you to retrieve it." His words triggered the woman in the vision last night, standing over my bloody body.

"The Po'luxnann said it didn't want to go back to D'uthne."

Laurenx froze. "How did it speak to you?"

"It said that it wants to kill off the Imudmid and the Temcaltiaf race."

He started in a dangerous whisper. "You removed the pendants around your neck?"

It got quiet. After a few tense beats, he spoke again.

"You are stupid. That is what got the Po'luxnann controlling you. Your stupidity."

"You don't think the Po'luxnann wanting to wipe out the entire

D'uthnian race a big deal?"

He marched over. "Control your temper. Now."

Dax growled and Laurenx looked at him. Laurenx finally took a step back and moved towards his fridge instead. He opened it. "What the Po'luxnann wants won't change a thing." He shut his fridge again and remembered his cup on the counter. "Parpagg had you Ggatgin. Count your blessings. The R'uttri aren't targeting you yet."

I didn't want to wait until they did. "Take the Po'luxnann. You know about this better than me."

"King Razhatlab can do it without killing you."

"Then try not to kill me," I said.

"You wouldn't want the Po'luxnann in my hands," he uttered more to himself. I didn't say a word. I looked away.

"I know the king," he said.

I glared. "So?"

"I have a plan for getting the Po'luxnann to him. I have someone from the inside." I stared at him. "What's the plan? Who is it?"

He slammed his empty cup on the counter. "I won't tell you what the plan is because I don't want the Po'luxnann to know." He threw open another cabinet and then banged it shut. He rounded to me. "Here you go." He threw something across the kitchen and I caught it. "It's all I got." I looked at the wrapper. It was another Snickers bar. "I don't have any breakfast for you. Any human food," he emphasized.

"There's a drug store at that intersection we crossed after the bus stop. If you want to get fancy with a meal, try the Publix. Take a left at the bus stop and continue less than a mile down." He popped open the fridge and came out with a water cooler and began pouring himself a glass of black juice. He brought it to the microwave and began warming it up.

"You don't think anyone's going to attack in broad daylight?"

"Most Imudmidians avoid sunlight. If anything, Dax and I would sense them in the area before they could."

The microwave beeped. Laurenx pulled out his drink. "Go get your food. Be back in an hour or I hunt you down. Don't take off the pendants and don't stare into any mirrors- anything with a reflection. Got it?"

I gazed around. Laurenx's house contained nothing that reflected. His microwave had a plastic finish, his spoon to stir his black drink was plastic, the bowls in his sink were plastic and now that I thought about it, there wasn't a mirror in the bathroom.

I doubt Laurenx owned a silver chain or a cell phone. It dawned on me.

My cell phone had a reflective screen. The time I recently used my phone was this morning to text, but nothing happened.

"Grab the forty bucks off the table."

His baseball cap was lowered over his eyes so I couldn't tell from his expression if he was being nice.

"No, I'm good."

"Is dying of hunger a luxury to you? Take the money."

I shut my mouth and scraped the money off the table. I pocketed it. I made a mental note to repay him.

"Thanks." I slugged my backpack over my shoulder.

"Catch." Laurenx threw a candy bar at me. "Buy ten more; you better buy ten more," he grunted. "And buy extra food. You don't know how long you'll be here for."

I looked behind him. There was an ice chest against the wall. "You got any water?"

He followed my gaze. His shoulders tensed. "There's nothing in there."

I glanced back to the ice chest. There was a padded lock on the front. He already looked the part of a drunkard.

As I turned on my heel, the pendants rose six inches in front of my face; a flickering image jumped in front of my vision. The kitchen went dark. The only source of light peeked through the cracks of the ice chest. The padlock snapped as easily as a Popsicle stick and the door swung up.

There inside lay a decomposed body in rags, in midst of raw meat.

My eyes blinked against the harsh light. The pendants were glowing. I stared at the chest right in the kitchen, closed. Laurenx made an annoyed sound. "Why are you still here?"

I practically ran out the front door.

The sapphire pendant hovered off my chest as the Po'luxnann fought to enter my thoughts. I strained to listen through the static.

Why...rid of me...he wants to kill you. The pendant dropped again. It went silent.

The rain was gone and the sun was already high up in the sky, but the gloomy gray clouds and cold wind reduced any heat in the atmosphere.

Seeing a body decomposed with half of its flesh hanging off the bone and visibly green with rot was enough to institute myself into a psych ward. The body didn't look human. Gray leathery skin was pierced with gruesome teeth marks on the collarbone. Black goo spilt onto the cemented ice and dyed the unpackaged meat it laid upon, like thick black sauce. The corpse had to be there long before I arrived to Laurenx's place.

I fell on my knees doubled over onto the sidewalk and projectile vomit. I watched it go down the storm drain. I couldn't believe I slept less than twenty feet away from an R'uttri in the freezer.

I wiped the slobber off my chin and straightened up. I was starting to believe what the Po'luxnann said last night. I had to get far away from Laurenx.

I lifted the pendant halfway up my neck. "You don't control me," I told it. "If Laurenx finds me, you take care of him. Don't kill him. And you don't own my body," I added. It was the lesser of two evils, siding with the Po'luxnann. A cold presence wrapped around me.

I will rid of him.

"Don't kill him if he ever finds us."

What will you do if he doesn't extend the favor?

I hesitated. "We'll cross that bridge when we get to it."

There was a slight pause. Very well. You fulfill my purpose. You have use to me.

My voice shook. "You don't own me," I reminded it.

I've inhabited you less than one week. I have taken possession of a corner in your mind. I am adapting to your motor functions the longer I am in you. Our conversation is also allowing me access to your emotions. In time I will own you, it promised. I couldn't hide my fear now.

You have begun to trust me. You are in desperate need of my help. Every instance you use me, you lose your will to me.

The vision of my body cold and drained of blood on the ground played over again in my head.

"Just...whatever comes my way, you protect me." And I'll somehow survive long enough to find the king and dump you on his doorstep.

Before yesterday, my only problems were Chessie using me to get on the cheerleading squad and cheating with Gavin in front of me; it all seemed ages ago.

My phone suddenly rang. I hit the home button to answer the call.

"Where the hell are you? Do you realize how worried sick your mom is?" I let out a shaky breath.

"And what was that stupid text? You need a *break*?" she said sharply.

I tried to sift through the fog in my brain. "Hey, Karin." I was surprised I sounded normal.

"What did Chessie do to you now?" she asked.

"What makes you think I left my house because of Chessie?" I internally smacked myself. Maybe it was better if I didn't correct her. She ignored me.

"Where are you, Seth? I need to come and kill you." Normal conversation. Good. Some of the tension relieved from my back and shoulders.

"You're not going to tell me? Seth, I swear I am going to break your kneecaps if I find you myself."

I didn't want her involved but telling her what happened between mom and I could help me feel sane. "I'll text you the address to a park. I'll be at the front entrance."

"You better, Seth. Text me."

"Gotcha."

I hung up and texted the location. Replacing my cell back into my pocket, I stood in place.

The call with Karin reminded me how things used to make sense- it was a fight with Mom and a friend was trying to be there for me. Now things had changed. How could I go on pretending everything was alright?

I closed my eyes as the world around me left me breathless. I swayed on the spot; my ears rang and saliva weighed on my tongue.

I couldn't have a panic attack- not now, in the middle of the road. My feet shuffled to a tree on the corner a little ways away. My back found it for support and I forced myself to stand. I've been holding it together for so long, before Laurenx entered into my life, before Parpagg Ggatgin me. It took me a few deep breaths to shake that feeling of drowning from the inside. When I was calm enough I willed myself to move.

Rain started to fall as I headed for the convenience store. It was much closer to the park I saw last night. I grabbed ten Hershey's chocolate candy bars, two hot dogs, three ramen noodle cups, a pack of cigarettes, a lighter, and two microwaved bacon, egg, and cheese sandwiches to go.

The cashier was watching a small television screen on the counter.

"More than one foot of rain has fallen in the last twenty-four hours in Hialeah. Record flooding has occurred in seventeen locations, including Miramar, Okeechobee, and as far as Fort Worth. The city of Miami is alerting everyone to stay in their homes," the reporter stated.

"Tornadoes have inexplicably expanded in parts of North Florida, and in other states; Georgia, Alabama, Mississippi."

"Hello." I greeted the guy behind the glass. The cashier paused a glance at me and I stared passed him. Given how my life had changed drastically I was sure I had physically aged several years. I wore long black sleeves and a jacket today to go with my faded jeans. My thick hair probably looked wild since I hadn't combed it this morning. He started to scan my cigarettes without bothering to check for an ID.

I slowly traveled to Evergreen Park in a daze. I filled up my water jug and found a bench near the entrance in the rain. On the way, I had already eaten half of my soggy sandwich and went on to finish the rest.

The symbols of the Po'luxnann continued to throb from this morning, now a permanent scar on my torso and forearm. It was a reminder of what I had to get done. I needed to get to the king, but how? Laurenx had connections to the king, but I had to forget about his help. Had an hour passed before he came looking for me? How much longer was it before Parpagg or a live walking zombie found me?

I took another swig of water and tried to maintain calm. I sat as it got darker and windier. Except for one female walker, everyone else had already gone home. Soon, I was the only one left in the park. I pulled the hood of my waterproof jacket over my head and zipped up.

A Lexus came right when I was freezing my tail off. Karin parked next to the sidewalk, her emergency lights blinking. I opened her car door.

"Hey, Kar, how you been?" She scowled in response. I climbed into the passenger seat and pulled on my seatbelt. I was glad she had the heater on. I rubbed my hands together against the air vent. Karin pulled the car into drive and made a U-Turn.

"Are you going to explain to me why you're in the ghetto?"

I slicked the wet hair out of my eyes. "I'm staying with a friend."

"Who?"

"One of the soccer players. Doubt you would remember him," I lied. I stared past the wipers.

She didn't say anything else for a minute. I didn't want this silence. I was more than happy to see a familiar face and I'd be a hundred times happier if we spoke of anything normal.

"I thought I was going to be picking you up at Chessie's."

I scowled at myself. My heart still leapt when I heard her name.

"You thought I was having a one-night stand?"

Karin glared. "What was I supposed to think? I thought you were going to be a Romeo outside her house, reciting lovesick poems."

"You really think I'd do something stupidly unoriginal?"

"You haven't been acting like yourself and you look like crap," she told me. "Your mom called me. She was tearing up on the line. What happened?"

I didn't feel like speaking. I watched the windshield wipers go back and forth.

"Fine." Karin took the hint. "Next topic. I heard what happened between Gavin and Chessie at the restaurant."

Right now, I couldn't remember if it happened a day ago or two nights before. Time stopped moving for me. Karin pressed on. "Ashanti has a huge mouth. It was all over her Facebook. She and her friends reported the blow by blow."

I shook my head. Dad called women like that *radio bemba;* they gossiped like nobody's business. Not a couple days went by and now everyone knew. "It's the last thing I want to talk about. Why are we heading towards the highway?"

"I'm kidnapping you."

I snorted aloud. Kidnapping was too frequent in my life. "We're going to my house. And we're talking about it." I didn't reply. "What I'm going to say next might hurt but I'm letting you know because I care about you."

"That sounds comforting." We were under a red light before the highway ramp. Karin took the opportunity to face me, her brown eyes serious. I shifted to avoid them. "You have to let go of Chessie."

Damn my heartbeat. "That's a surprise."

Karin went on as if I hadn't spoken. "Last year Chessie and I hung out at my house one night watching a movie. A kissing scene came up and

Chessie said she wished guys were that passionate in real life. After she said it, I made a game over what guys in our school knew how to love a girl for more than sex and your name popped up." Karin drove up the highway ramp. By now I was hanging onto every word. I held my breath as the bottom of my stomach threatened to drop.

"Chessie said you understood how to treat a girl. She said," Karin paused before taking a breath herself. "'The only problem with Seth is he reminds me too much of my brothers. When I think of him, I think incest.'" Karin let that sink in.

"Chessie wasn't saying it to be mean," she added.

I did not want to hear this. "You're driving too fast in this rain," I pointed out. My voice sounded thick.

"She said it while she laughed at the idea of you and her," Karin said softly. That sinkhole widened and my heart crumbled inside it. "I'm sorry."

God, why'd she have to go and say that? "Why are you telling me this now?" I asked flatly.

"Because I never thought you two would get together," she answered bluntly. "I didn't think Chessie would pursue you after you won nationals. I didn't think Chessie would get raped either." Karin swiped the back of her hand furiously over her wet eyes.

"Things change," I said. Those words meant more than I thought it ever could. I gripped the armrest tighter and ignored the stinging pressure behind my eyes.

She went quiet again. She didn't speak until we arrived at her house. "You really think she loves you?" Karin twisted in her seat, waiting for an answer. I opened my mouth but words wouldn't come. "Seth," Karin started.

"What?" I said this louder than I anticipated. I didn't want to look in her direction. I didn't know what my expression would give away.

"I know you care about her, but do you really think you're the only one who does? What about her mother, her father, her brothers, and her sister Charlie?"

"I know that,"

"Chessie was my friend too, did that slip your mind? Have you ever asked why she stopped speaking to me?"

I never did. She shook her head as she bit her lip. "Do you remember when Chessie missed a whole week of school after it happened?"

I did. "Her sister Charlie and her mom took her to therapy that week. The first few days she went but after that she stopped going. She said all she wanted to do was leave it alone and get over it," Karin said. "That would have been fine if Chessie didn't convince herself it was her fault she was raped."

My jaw slacked open. "Why?"

"Because she couldn't say 'no' to Erving," Karin said angrily. "He was choking her while he… did what he did to her." She fought to control her tears. "Of course she couldn't tell him '*no*'." Karin didn't speak for a moment. Rain hit the windows, drowning the world outside.

Karin's words shortly cut through the silence. "No one could convince her it wasn't her fault she was raped. The counselor tried. Charlie and her mom tried. It didn't help the football guys and our whole grade called her a slut." Her tone sharpened. "I told her she wasn't supposed to blame herself and that she never deserved what happened to her. I told her she was special and there were people in her life that cared about her, but she didn't want to hear any of it. I wanted her to be better. I think I tried too hard and I ended up losing my best friend."

She wiped away a tear on her cheek and stared out her window. She didn't speak again after a minute. When she did, her voice sounded so small. "You can't save someone who doesn't believe they're worth saving."

Silence hung over us like a polluted raincloud. I reached out and placed a hand on Karin's shoulder but she shrugged it off. I took it as my cue to leave.

I wrenched off my seatbelt and climbed out of the car with my backpack, slamming the door behind me. I stalked down the dark road as Karin yelled after me.

"Ya! Eodiga!" Hey! Where are you going!

The cold wind and rain slapped at me as I sped down a flooded road and hit the sidewalk. I cut through overturned orange cones around sidewalks and sprinted through lawns. The night at Black Tie flashed in my mind and I clenched my fists. I remembered how Gavin pressed his body into Chessie's and she allowed it. My rage boiled into battery acid. I should have shoved Gavin's ass into the flame. I wanted to squeeze his throat with my bare hands like I did with Laurenx.

I was there when Chessie was crying on the couch in her living room. I watched her the day she told her parents. I saw how she cried in her mother's arms. Chessie lost more than her virginity to Erving; she lost herself.

I can save her if you would give in to me. I will personally wipe any memory of her pain. A memory hit.

Dad was pumping gas at a local gas station. I called him on the phone as I stood across the street. The traffic light hadn't changed for me to cross. I watched Dad dig into his pocket for his cellphone. He briefly looked at the screen and put it right back in his pocket and continued pumping his gas. His eyes happened to wander across the street. I turned around and bolted.

I can end your suffering. I can make it all go away for you, your father, and your chosen mate. My purpose of peace and order allows this. Give in to me, it coaxed. *I will erase your burden. Is it not a beautiful way to die?*

Yes, it would be better to erase all those memories; they were worthless. It'd be great if the Po'luxnann could erase Chessie's memories of misery. I would kill for a peace of mind. I wanted to be free.

Somehow, the pendants were high above my head. I forced the glowing pendants down my neck and squeezed them into my fist.

"Stop it!" I punted a lone tire wheel against a tree and watched it bounce and roll down the road.

It didn't make me feel any better but the shooting pain in my right leg gave me something else to focus on.

"You're going back to where you came from!" I was done.

"King Razhatlab!" I shouted at the gray sky, "I know you're out there!" I knew I looked stupid but I didn't care. I was going to do everything I could to get rid of the Po'luxnann. I was hoping I could somehow give the king a calling card. If I was seeing what was happening in his world then maybe he saw what was happening in mine.

"King Razhatlab, I need you to take the Po'luxnann back. How do I find you?" I shivered in the rain as the pendants glowed hot against my chest.

Maybe he could find me instead. "I live in the United States. My address is 12921 NW North Miami, Florida. You can get your stupid Po'luxnann back," I shouted at the wind. "I don't want it!"

The Po'luxnann rattled my bones as it pushed and shoved against my soul. My heart leaped. Maybe what I was doing was working. "Tell me what I need to do to get it to you," I said. "Tell me and I'll-"

The Po'luxnann erupted. I fell to my knees in the water as it screeched.

I dove headfirst into King Razhatlab's head.

"I have one final report," declared Melwimik.

"Continue."

Melwimik nodded sullenly. "It's Princess Vaora."

"King Razhatlab! I know you're out there!"

I stirred. My eyes were closed. Now I looked at Melwimik.

"What?" I told him.

He struggled to speak. "I...one of the guards from the east corridor watched as she left castle grounds without any of her attendants. Princess Vaora escaped her detainment," Melwimik said. "This occurred last night. Princess returned before morning, muddy and scathed."

Deafening silence constricted around us like a choking blanket. I stomached what Melwimik said. Rumors of Vaora's deception surfaced about a week ago. I recalled Melwimik's recount of the report of twelve witnesses that included two royal guards. They all claimed they heard Vaora's voice in the west wing library, expressing her sentiments at the top of her lungs.

"'He has been unfit to rule the last seventeen years; he's grown too soft against the people of Imudmid- when will he die? Why is it taking so long?'"

Vaora shortly appeared from the library, perplexed by all the shocked faces in the hall.

A voice, clearer this time, rang in my mind.

"I need you to take the Po'luxnann back. How do I find you?"

I was surprised. The human boy.

"I live in the United States. My address is 12921 NW North Miami, Florida. You can get your Po'luxnann back. I don't want it!"

Melwimik waited. I remained focused to the immediate matter at hand.

"Has she been secured?"

Melwimik nodded. "Yes, she is in Mirg Ega under strict confinement."

This information opened fresh wounds of hurt. My daughter was high risk; she was in one of the worst prisons we devised for infamous criminals awaiting trial.

"Chancellor Melwimik, be sure to express to Officer Carnede, the castle head advisor, to keep this matter under control. No more than our highest ranked officials need to know."

Melwimik looked severely troubled. "Yes, my king." He dared not meet my gaze. We equally knew we had no control over babbling lips; the news would eventually be tomorrow's scandal. I worried what the scandal may do to the kingdom and to the people's morale. But the human boy established a mental link. He was the key to ending the war.

Instead of answering him with words, I sent him a memory of the past.

CHAPTER TWELVE

The full moon overhead broke through the thicket of trees. Mag impatiently crouched less than three paces from me. She had removed her coat that lay a distance away and her gray skin shined under the moonlight. A fur tunic wrapped around her shoulders down to her ankles. Her totem etched fiery red on her torso.

"There is no need to be restless," I told her.

She straightened with a dignified scowl. "Razhatlab, do not patronize me. You brought me here without protection. No soldiers-"

"I will protect you," I said sternly, moving toward her. I placed a careful hand on her shoulder. "I am your protection."

Her eyes softened. "In your state?"

I was stripped of the Po'luxnann and my strength had diminished over recent years, but I was far stronger and wiser than most Temcaltiaf men in their prime. I would sustain in this life for a little longer and fiercely protect the ones I cherished. Words again formed on Mag's lips, but they were cut short.

Her legion spirit leapt off her forearm and sunk its claws into the earth. The shadow creature roared, black eyes darting to the left. I was at the ready, sensing four beings.

"Imiv, Ugud, Cheg, Savoris, reveal yourselves," I ordered. "We mean no harm."

A rustle in the distance cut through the trees. Soon, four figures circled us.

"My king, you startled us." Cheg, the squat old man boomed.

"My dear Council of D'uthne," I scorned, "who but you knew where we would hold our encounter? I made it clear to you there would be a meeting regarding the Passage of Bror and Temcaltiaf. Is there a reason for such an attack?"

There was no immediate response. The energies in the air swirled about us, signaling tension. Ugud, second in command on the Council, barbed his words. "Did you purposely come with this beast?" He gazed at Mag with hatred and malice. I quelled my own anger. "You will address her honor with the proper title."

Imiv sneered. He looked at Mag with ruthless disdain. "We are not among her people. She is but princess of the worms to us," he spat.

Savoris threw his head back and laughed. "You bring the enemy in our midst to discuss her execution before us?"

I maintained a steady outward composure but outwardly I feared the meeting was of poor judgment. If only the Councilmen could see Mag and her family maintained the side of good. They were not at fault for the recent attack against on the Bror and Temcaltiaf Gates. We need not go to war.

I spoke. "No one will dare touch another with violence. Mag Ghuhji Tr-io, Lady to Ghuhji House and Councilmember of Imudmidian Dreshne, has come to honor her good will. She is unarmed with a show of good faith that the Council of Temcaltiaf will favorably lend an ear to the plight we face. Her visit's purpose is to warn us. There is a traitor among our side. He allowed the R'uttri past the human's Gate and into the Bror

Passage." I carried on. "Mag has reason to suspect Frih Kio, a wanted Imudmidian, sent his servants into Bror and Temcaltiaf's Passage."

This was a grave matter for Temcaltiaf. Frih Kio was a notorious savage beast, once king of the R'uttri. If his intentions were to claim the Bror Passage as his territory, he would be able to turn R'uttri on the humans. The humans would then turn into R'uttri themselves and Frih Kio would have his vast army.

"Mag," I regarded her calmly, "please explain to the Council you and your family's allegiance remain on the side of peace."

Mag stood. She addressed no one in particular. "We do not partake in Frih Kio's plans. His soldiers breached the Bror Passage without our Court's knowledge. If you would please return the traitors you have not murdered, our people will make sure to use them as an example."

"Release them in your steed to breed more an ill fate toward us?" Savoris drew on his power and his eyes began to glow alight. The three men unleashed their power, a battle-ax ready to be thrown.

Imiv looked aghast. "We release them and they spread what they know within our Passage. We do not concede to your nightmarish wish, worm!"

Mag was familiar with the prejudice and hostility Temcaltiaf had towards Imudmidians. When the Councilmen unmasked their power Mag however, could no longer hide her own instinctive nature to kill. Her legion spirit roared as a whistling wind picked up around us. Mag's voice reverberated through the air, her god lingering to the surface.

"I will end you."

Twigs and leaves and branches flailed about. Mag did not recoil as a bolt of energy aimed for her chest. I went before the attack and released my power. Palms out, I absorbed the energy. Remnants of the

Po'luxnann's power allowed me to contain the blow; the attack surged through my bones and I held onto it until it snuffed out. Mag's totem, seeing Mag was safe, rounded to her attacker. It shifted in its shadow form before it lunged for Ugud's throat.

"Stop!" I commanded. "Mag, call back your totem."

"My king!" Savoris and Cheg exclaimed.

Imiv had a crackle of energy radiating from his shoulders. "Why must you defend her? Why must you believe we can reason with beasts?" he seethed.

Mag's legion spirit waited for Mag's command to react as she rounded to the Council. The wind whipped harder as her black hair rose about her like tentacles. She displayed her sharp teeth and her talons grew. A dark, guttural sound erupted from her throat before she spoke. Her voice was deep and lethal with power.

"You soon forget what we are. We will crush you."

The power in her voice carried a wave of promising terror. "Peace has not made us docile creatures. Cross our territory and we will relish in eating you alive."

Ugud, Cheg, Savoris, and Imiv simultaneously raised their arms. They had strategically surrounded us from four sides before our conversation began. They had well intended to kill us with the Hirtnim Baze, the Final Attack.

They were no ordinary Councilmen. They had power, both in politics and ability. But they were not the head; someone was their leader. It was the same creature from our Passage who opened the Bror Gate and permitted Frih Kio's soldiers inside.

"Who are you working for?" I demanded calmly.

Who was the real leader in all this betrayal? Ugud addressed me with a conniving smile. "One of your own. Your successor."

It could have meant many things. My true successor was my first-born, but he was no more. There was my second born, Sixa, followed by Vaora in line for the crown. Or could Ugud possibly describe someone else entirely?

The four men started the chant. The ground beneath us quaked as cyclone of power and debris flailed about. Mag was on all fours, calling up the dead to protect us. Before anyone could complete their attack, I closed my eyes. A tear momentarily escaped and rolled down my cheek. When I opened my eyes once more, they were dry and devoid of remorse. I became King Razhatlab, ex-Bearer of the Po'luxnann.

With a whisper of a thought, the four soldiers caught fire from where they stood. Screams erupted. The flames exploded and immersed all it licked. Soon, there was nothing but pits of fire licking from every side. The bodies halted all movement. They were nothing but charred corpses.

The remaining power of the Po'luxnann I contained vanished and I sagged inwardly at the intensity. The Po'luxnann was as natural as the air I breathed. For a time it was as familiar as a cloak worn on a winter's night.

I could no longer feel its light and its strength I heavily relied on all these centuries. Like a world without sun I had gone blind- I was alone inside myself; I had become a shell once lost an important piece of myself.

I acknowledged Mag's presence. "I have to report this to the remaining Council. They attacked the king and went against maintaining the treaty of peace with Imudmid. You may go." I paused.

"Remain well."

Mag's legion spirit had now returned to her forearm. She stared at me with her coal eyes, reflecting the red from the flames. She appeared sorrowful.

"Very well." She placed a cool hand on my cheek. "Until then."

I looked away before she departed. I lingered underneath the full moon, well after the burning corpses were but ashes.

Before I came out of it, I heard King Razhatlab whisper. *We lose the fight but we will win the battle.*

Freezing rain pelted my face. I was back in my own reality.

You cannot trust anyone, declared the Po'luxnann.

From my aching joints I could tell I was stuck in the same position for a while. I grunted when I stood. I crossed my arms against the cold and wheeled my head about, looking for shelter. I ran for the nearest house.

Everywhere I turned, gust of wind and rain blinded my vision. Palm trees bent over backwards, enduring the raging winds as the pendants whipped high above my ear, threatening to escape. I dove under the cowl of an abandoned house with a For Sale sign out in front. My teeth started clattering together as I shivered where I stood.

I made contact with the king but he didn't tell me how I could give him back the Po'luxnann. He didn't tell me what to do. Why would King Razhatlab show me a memory of him committing murder?

With Gavin, I almost burned him but I didn't know I had the power to do it. The king knew he had the power to burn and he did it without flinching. Everyone in Temcaltiaf and Imudmid were killers. All this death, I wanted it all to stop.

I warned you. Nothing good will come of lingering on to your soul as

Frih Kio's followers enter your world. Look around you. The weather is a testament to the war that lies ahead. Your world will soon be eviscerated the longer you withhold your will to me. You are leaving your world open to harm. Give your body to me. I will rid all of the R'uttri and the likes of Parpagg.

I wanted to believe it. It was tempting to think everyone who came in contact with the Po'luxnann was twisted. Everywhere I turned I saw death, destruction, and dark powers from the old man, R'uttri, Laurenx, the brown woman with petals, Xa'renul, and now Frih Kio. The story the Po'luxnann told me about the younger brother murdering his brother for power- and King Razhatlab killing Councilmen in the woods- proved it was easy for them to kill. It was easy to hate everyone from D'uthne.

The rumble of thunder clapped and lightning streaked the sky. Just like that night.

My phone vibrated in my jeans. I slipped it out. Rain pelted the screen and I wiped it off with my thumb. I missed call and a text, both from Mom. Suddenly I had to hear her voice. I clicked my phone open and read Mom's text message before I called her.

Emergency. I need to talk to you.

I speed dialed Mom's number and she answered on the first ring. There was a muffled voice. "Seth! Whatever you do, don't go home," she cried.

I pressed the phone close to my ear against the screaming wind. "Can you repeat what you said? Something wrong?"

She sounded panicked. "Seth, someone broke into the house."

"Wait, Mom, someone's in the house with you?"

"Seth, I am afraid," she whimpered.

Oh God. My heart raced.

"Where's Logan?" I shouted.

"He's at work. Oh no-"

The line cut off.

CHAPTER THIRTEEN

The old man found her or the R'uttri. Vomit rose up to my throat.

Oh God.

I sped up the road and washed up Karin's walkway. I knocked and rang her doorbell until she swung open the door.

"Are you insane?" Karin snapped. "My mother is sleeping! If you wanted to kill me-"

"I need your car," I said breathlessly. "I need to get to my house, now."

Karin's dark eyes narrowed. "Why? Didn't you hear the news? The cities are on tornado and flash flood warning."

"Please Karin, it's important."

She rolled her eyes. "Alright, but I'm driving."

Karin grabbed her umbrella and keys from the front table. She locked the house behind her and we ran for her car through the pounding rain.

Karin's umbrella nearly ripped out of her hands as the elements beat against it. She wrestled the umbrella inside the vehicle but it had broken; the metal ribs were bent. Karin swore and threw it in the backseat. I was already seated in the passenger seat when she started the ignition and turned on the heater. She shivered as she looked out the foggy window up at the sky. "It's starting to look like a hurricane."

She turned to me. "Don't think for one second we'll stop talking about Chessie and," she faltered. "What's wrong with you?"

"My Mom," I said feeling sick. "She called."

"Yeah? What'd she say?" We were out of her driveway and on the main road, heading for the highway. My house was more than fifteen minutes from where Karin lived but if we gunned it, we could reach there in no time at all.

"You're ruining my leather," she muttered at my wet clothes.

We entered the highway ramp and ran into traffic ahead. Rows and rows of cars were bumper to bumper. Two lanes had shut down because there was flooding, and police cars were detouring cars off the highway up ahead. I sat straighter in my seat.

"Stupid traffic jam," Karin mumbled. "It looks like an evacuation. We'll have to get off the next exit. When I was on my way to pick you up, it wasn't like this." Her expression changed when she glanced at me. "Seriously, what is wrong with you?"

I took a deep breath. Keep cool. "Nothing, Mom's just upset I didn't come home last night."

Karin relaxed. "Okay, just talk to her. Why do you look so stressed out? You're turning as white as my car."

My vision grew cloudy as guilt started eating at me.

I couldn't stand to be in this car right now. I had to get to Mom.

My fingers wrapped around the pendants. The Po'luxnann's whispers grew louder as I held them above my neck.

I can...save her. Give in...to me.

I clutched at the armrest. We were crawling at a slow pace. Cars were honking, everyone trying to get ahead of one another but no one was going anywhere.

I'm so sorry, Mom. It was my fault.

I wasn't protecting her. My fault... Would these cars get the hell out of the way?

"You were saying?"

I struggled to find something to say. "She said...she said she's going to marry Logan."

"What?" Karin exclaimed and pounded the steering wheel. "She serious? What the hell?" Karin went on and I tried to keep it together. The Po'luxnann's presence neared the surface as my heart pounded.

Remove...the pendants. We will...arrive...in a breath.

I had to believe anyone that had Mom only wanted the Po'luxnann. God, I hope she was safe. If they hurt her-

I can...save her. Remove...the pendants.

Karin looked at me expectantly.

"I-I totally agree. I'm going to...."

We were finally approaching the highway exit. There were more cars swerving off the highway causing more blockages. My legs shook restlessly.

"Why didn't the cops close off the ramp? They waited until after we got on to tell us to get off," she sounded irritated. She regarded me. "You have every right to kill Logan," Karin said. "You look miserable every time you mention that guy. Now he's going to be your stepfather? Geez."

I couldn't hold on anymore. "Karin I'm getting off."

"What?"

"I'm getting out of the car," I said.

Her voice rose. "In the middle of the highway?"

"Just drop me here." I was already pulling off my seatbelt.

"Are you out of your mind? *In this storm?*"

"I'll be fine," I told her. "By the time you get me home, I'd already be there."

"Your house is thirty blocks away!"

I didn't have time to argue. "Go home. Thanks, Karin."

I hopped out of the car and landed in water up to my shins. Before Karin could say another word, I slammed her door shut and broke into a run.

Tapping into my soccer skills, I sprinted in between the honking cars stuck in stop and go traffic. A sedan jerked and stopped after it saw me. It honked as I slid in front of his bumper to dodge another vehicle and hit the water once more.

I finally reached the end of the ramp. Once I turned the corner onto the open road I yanked the pendants high above my ear.

"My house, now!"

There was a rushing roar in my ears. With a jolt, my feet were off the ground and the world around me went out. My feet soon planted the earth again.

I faced my house across the street, daring to believe it. I made it.

The Po'luxnann made good on its word. My ears were ringing but I was still in control.

The front blinds to the house were closed. What was left of Logan's truck wasn't in the driveway and the rain washed off the scent of burnt metal. Black smudge marks on the driveway were the only visible signs of the fire last night.

There wasn't a cop car in sight. I told Mom to call 911 more than ten minutes ago.

Remove the pendants now or you will fight alone.

"Can you save my Mom?"

Yes. Give in to me.

My mind was whirring a mile a minute. I was trying to decide what to do next.

You hesitate. I have extended my patience to save one of your own. You have rejected me. I was alone again in my head.

I had to make a decision- I was running out of time.

I slipped on the right side of the house and paused by my window. I slung off my backpack and unzipped it. I found my pocketknife on my key ring and I flipped it open, wrapping my fingers around the slippery handle. It was my tiny weapon versus whatever psycho that had my Mom.

I started cutting the mesh over the window as fast as I was able. I ripped out the mesh piece and flung it behind me and peered through the gaping hole.

It was dark inside. As my eyes adjusted I noticed my room was the same as I left it.

My ears weren't picking up any sounds inside the rest of the house.

I slipped off my jacket and wrapped it to my arm. Once I fastened it around my elbow, I steadied my hand and aimed for the window. My fist went through it and glass fell. I slowly pulled my arm back from the pieces of glass that stuck in the frame. I inspected my arm. My fist throbbed but it wasn't bleeding. Less carefully this time, I punched the remaining glass and heard them thump onto my bed below. My ears weren't picking up any movement inside.

Did Mom run away?

I checked my phone. She didn't call or leave a message. My heart pounded harder but I was hopeful. Maybe whoever came here already gone. A nagging feeling of doubt crept in.

I hoisted myself up and through the window and tumbled into a somersault. The back of my neck cut on a glass as I hit the side of the bed and bounced ungracefully onto the ground with a crash. If there was anyone in the house they knew I was here now.

I clumsily jumped to my feet and slung on my backpack. I held out my pocketknife as my eyes darted through the darkness.

There was no use taking anyone by surprise after all the noise I made.

"Mom?" I called out. Silence met my ears as chills pricked up and down my arms.

"Hey, whoever has my Mom, let her go."

My hand grabbed a foot-tall brass trophy under my bed and held it backward, marble side ready to collide into a face or two. I replaced the blade in my back pocket.

"I'm the one you want, right? I have the Po'luxnann," I announced. I nudged the door open with my foot and it slowly swung wide open. When there was nothing amiss, I peered out into the dark hall. I couldn't tell, but I could feel there was someone else in the house.

My mouth had gone dry. "Mom, are you okay?"

I slowly made my way out of my bedroom. Every squeaking step sounded excruciatingly loud, while the rest of the house stood quiet. I couldn't shake the feeling I wasn't alone in the house. And that someone wasn't making a sound.

"Mom! Make some noise! Any noise!"

"I'm scared," someone whispered.

My heart shot up to my throat as my eyes narrowed to the end of the hallway. "Mom? Where are you? Are you okay?"

"He says you have to come closer," she whispered again. My trophy hand shook. "Whoever you are, let her go. You came for me, right? Leave her alone."

I stepped out into the living room.

Everything was turned upside down. The couches were split into two, the living room table was lying on the other side of the room missing a leg, and the curtains were drawn. The air behind my head blew as something hard smacked me from the side. The breath knocked out of me as I flew into a broken half of the couch. I tumbled onto the tile.

The rail holding up the curtains over the window shuddered and fell on top of me. Pain shot up to my elbow and I looked down. My left wrist bent at an awkward angle.

I barely had time to register fear- a hand found my right arm.

In one fluid motion, I was yanked forward; my head snapped back as my body tumbled and twisted until I hit the kitchen wall. Without waiting a breath, a force slammed between my shoulder blades and shoved me down. My forehead knocked against the tile and my stomach hit the ground. A heel dug into my spine.

"Hello, Seth." My mother said. "You have been very, very bad."

"Mom?" My voice muffled on the ground. I motioned to raise my head.

A hand latched my hair into a fist. "If you try to look at me, I will remove your eyeballs," my mother rasped. She shoved my head down again and my forehead bounced like a Ping-Pong ball.

My vision clouded. I tasted blood in my mouth. I willed my eyes to open.

A deep guttural hiss sounded in my ear. "You went and disappeared with my Po'luxnann Gejruvhet. Without my knowledge."

This time a male spoke and a hand yanked the back of my head again. "We will talk and you will answer."

My stomach made an abrupt jerk as the air around me shifted; the hairs off the back of my neck rose. In the next moment, I was freefalling. As quickly as the sensation came, I collided with the ground.

I rolled over to my side, groaning. My ribs weren't feeling too hot and my head was banging like heavy metal music in an auditorium.

I sat cradling my broken wrist in my hand and squinted through the cold, bitter rain.

I was sitting on grass that seemed to go on forever with holes and poles of red flags sticking out of them. In the distance was a pond and rough patches of sand and trees. I was on a golf course. I rubbed my eyes. My vision grew cloudy.

My attacker. The voice. I've heard it more times than I wanted to admit in my nightmares. I panicked. "Someone help me!"

I will.

Like tiny matches embedded in my skin my chest and arm burned horribly. I started to shout. The Po'luxnann's presence overpowered me- the first pendant went clear over my neck.

"No!" I caught myself before I threw the pendant across the clearing.

Suddenly, a whistle of a rocket sounded in the air. A bolt of lightning hammered into the earth.

The explosion lifted me off my feet and flung me to the ground. I dropped straight down like a kite without wind, coughing out blood. The noise nearly ruptured my eardrums and for a moment, my heart stopped.

I rolled to my side with the pendant still clutched in my hand, coughing and blinking through tears, dust, and rain. I pounded the ground with my good fist.

"Stop knocking me down, asshole!"

Once the dust cleared, a silhouette stood less than twenty feet away among the trees' shadows.

The pendant was high above my neck.

Relinquish control unto me. Remove the final pendant, the Po'luxnann pressed. *If you perish Parpagg will use me for his own selfish reasons. He hurt your mother. He will injure you far worse.*

The old man came out of the shadows in his trench coat, blazing blue with halo energy. He stood without a spec of dirt or water on him and wore a cold, lizard smile. He made sure to keep his sight line away from my face.

"What name did you call me?" he asked softly.

"ASS.HOLE."

"That does not sound very pleasant," he sniffed. "I am Parpagg. You should remember the name of the one who has come to kill you." He bowed, never shifting his predatory tone. I pocketed the sapphire pendant.

You are wounded. You are tired and slow to react. Remove the last pendant.

I hesitated. I didn't know if I could have full control over my body after I took off the pendant. I wondered what would be left of me. I couldn't think past my fear.

"Where's my Mom?"

"No!" Parpagg flared with anger. "You will answer my questions first."

His head swiveled around as if he was expecting something. It took all of five agonizing seconds before his composure relaxed. He turned to me, keeping his eyes diverted from my face. He put his hands behind his back and started stalking towards me. "Where were you hiding, Seth?"

I was paralyzed with fear.

"You will respect me."

Parpagg suddenly materialized in front of me. His fingers clamped around my throat. The bones bent in his fist as he picked me up a foot off the ground.

Something has changed. Your body has grown dramatically weaker.

I kicked and clawed at his face, but Parpagg appeared unfazed. In fact, he seemed fascinated to know how long I would last. His fingers tightened, cutting off my windpipe as my arms became useless, dead weight.

The Po'luxnann was right; something else was wrong. With every punch and kick I threw, my physical strength lessened dramatically.

In one swift movement, my body zipped across the field- I didn't have time to yell. I braced myself as I descended and skipped like a rock on a pond. I gasped through my teeth as pain registered quicker than my sense of direction. I didn't know which way was up, but I was sure I had broken a few ribs. I squinted. Thunder sounded overhead.

The answer has revealed itself to me. He has poisoned you.

Panic began to fill the fog in my brain.

He used the same poison to weaken the king. I recognize the sensation and your symptoms.

The Po'luxnann actually sounded concerned. My fear went up five full bars. I tried to drag myself off the ground.

Do not move.

I froze. The Po'luxnann never sounded like it had any care for my security. Heck, it wanted to eat my soul.

Heed my words. We can assume Parpagg knows humans are weaker than D'uthnians. He knows the poison will take less time to affect your system. Pretend the paralysis has overtaken you almost completely.

A pair of feet came into view. Parpagg squatted a foot from me. The halo of energy and heat rode off him. It was as though I stuck my head in an oven- the intense heat was unbearable.

Do not move. Do not blink. Allow him to assume you are immobilized. He knows if the host is physically injured I am also limited.

I nodded internally.

"This is no time to nap." Parpagg shoved his foot against my ribs and I rolled onto my back. An electric current zapped off him and hit me. My brain clocked out from the sharp pain; I convulsed on the ground.

Parpagg prodded me with his foot again and he managed not to shock me this time. I sucked in a sharp gasp. Breathing hurt.

"Where did you keep yourself hidden?"

He was at the back of my head, keeping out of sight. My heart was beating out of my chest like a trapped mouse. My muscles convulsed from the aftershock. I spoke in between wheezes. "I…met… guy…he knows… you."

Parpagg chuckled. "My dear human, I am of royal stature. There isn't a being on the other side of this Passage who do not know my name," he boasted. "After my brother dies and Bror Gate falls, your people will also come to know my name," he assured. "I have sensed there was another D'uthne in your city. It was an inconvenience," he added conversationally. "What is this parasite's name?"

It took a great effort for my lips to form words. "Dax."

Do not come on too strong.

I quickly extended Dax's name into a question as though I was convinced I had the wrong name.

"Dax? Are you sure?"

I made a sound in my throat. That worked for him. "What an unfortunate name. Is it the name of a filthy street squalor or pixie?" He sounded disgusted. "Where is this creature's location?"

"Yes," I answered his first question. I took my time to say a random address. I winced and frowned as my tongue roamed around in my mouth like a drunken tiger. "16765 NW 19th Ave in Opalocka."

That was an abandoned shipment yard where Logan once worked before it closed down. I extended the time between my eye blinks as I said him the full address. He could see my expressions but I couldn't see his.

Parpagg didn't speak for a moment. I lay there hoping I didn't make the biggest mistake protecting Laurenx. Maybe I should have given up his location. Laurenx could easily have killed this guy. Parpagg continued.

"Before I kill you, you will take me to him."

I was ten ways to Sunday screwed if he found out I lied.

"Your turn…my Mom."

"You show much concern," he mocked. He flipped me over with his foot like a pancake and kicked me until I flipped again on my back. He quickly covered my eyes. "You came too early. I was ready to scrape her heart out of her chest." I heard him lick his lips. "I mimic voices very well." His tone and inflection changed. *"When will King Razhatlab die? Why is it taking so long?'"* He laughed. That was the princess of Temcaltiaf," he whispered. "Easily took the fall for conspiring against the king."

On the last three words, his voice went high and I jerked. He sounded like my Mom. His voice shifted back to his. He leaned closer to my ear. "She begged and pleaded for me to spare you," he said.

Then, *"No! Please! Leave him alone!"* he called out in Mom's voice. He didn't hide his tone of amusement. A fire of rage overflowed the pit in my stomach. My fists rose as I moved to yank his eyeballs.

STOP!

My arms hovered an inch off the ground and fell back down.

"You have some fight in you, I see." He sounded impressed. Parpagg took my flinching as me trying to find the strength to move. I almost gave myself away.

He sighed again. "She was alive when I left her poisoned. Just as I have poisoned you." I could almost hear the jerk smile. "My friend is an expert cook. He worked with a poison maker," he said.

"Or was a great cook. He's probably dead now," he added flippantly. "The poison numbs and then slowly eats you from the inside. As for you I will show you mercy." He prodded me hard on the cheek with his finger.

Do not be tempted.

He poisoned her, I roared.

She may not have very long to live, it said, lacking remorse. *Keep your composure until it is time to act. We will be able to avenge her ill fate.*

The Po'luxnann's words struck me in the gut.

"Have you lost your sight?" Parpagg lifted his hand off my eyes and flicked me hard on the forehead. I tried my best to keep my face smooth. I kept my mind blank.

Parpagg flicked my forehead a few more times then ran a nail on the corner of my eyelid. A blurry hand moved in front of my face again. I pretended I didn't catch movement.

He stood and disappeared for a moment and returned with a flagpole. He squatted and brought it close to my head.

"Your mother was but a foot away from me when I called you." In a voice that sounded exactly like my mother's, *"Help me, Seth. Someone's after me!"* he cried.

"How I wish your face would move! Your expression would have matched your mother's. You have her eyes, you know," he told me. "Unfortunately for you, I will not permit you the same luxury I afforded her to scream."

NOW, the Po'luxnann boomed.

My eyes latched on to Parpagg's shocked bright eyes. I smiled in those milliseconds.

KILL!

I grabbed for Parpagg and gripped onto his cheeks and my nails dug into him, holding on for dear life.

Three things happened.

Parpagg, realizing I was staring back at him, bashed my head to the ground. I completely stopped moving. But it was already too late for him.

Raw, volcanic power flowed through my veins; it was as if I chugged a gallon of gasoline and lit myself on fire. I choked out a scream as my lungs boiled in blood. Parpagg bellowed, also feeling the burn.

It was strange what went on in my head in my final moments.

I thought about how the old man hunted me down the first time we met as my insides melted. I mourned my Mom who I would never see again. I regretted the words I never said to Dad. I thought about Eli and Karin, who would never know what really happened to me.

In real-time, I physically caught on fire. Aside from the smell of charred flesh, a second smell- the smell of sulfur- burned my nose hairs. Parpagg burned with me.

I was aware of a surreal night so cold and black it clung to the last of my senses, threatening to swallow me whole until I became nonexistent. Death marched around the corner and there was nothing else to do but wait.

CHAPTER FOURTEEN

A switch went off in my body as my spirit left Earth.

This will not kill me.

Where was that voice coming from?

This will not kill me, it repeated.

Would that annoying racket let me die in peace?

A sharp force tugged and I plummeted from a place unknown until my spirit collided back into my flesh. The force of impact hurt- it sent shockwaves through every nerve ending, vein, artery, joint, and limb I possessed. Numbness and heaviness stopped. I was feeling a little lightheaded.

I knew there was something important I was in the middle of before I took a short trip to the afterlife. The sudden disconnection with the Po'luxnann left me hurting, weak, and disoriented, like a power hangover.

Happy as I was to be alive, I made a quick body check. I wasn't missing any limbs and my bruises and small scrapes were gone. My broken ribs and wrist, were miraculously healed. The clothes I wore were less fortunate; my jeans were ripped and scorched, and my shirt had completely disintegrated. My exposed chest was glowing red with permanent tattoos- I bet my eyes were bloodshot. From the corner of my eye I sensed movement.

Parpagg crouched to one knee as he held the side of his disfigured mug, bewildered. His trench coat, his shirt, and pants were completely gone. He was naked.

Parpagg was still alive.

Death Lock was unsuccessful. You did not remove both pendants. You hindered my power.

Like a thing straight out of horror movie, Parpagg slowly lifted himself out of the mud. His face and limbs resembled a crispy patty left too long on a grill. The black and red welts that covered every inch of his skin carried the stench of rotting meat and sulfur. Parpagg's gaze fell on me. His bulging eyes were filled with unmistakable venomous rage.

Dax took his stance in front of me, his body a translucent image of darkness. It took my brain longer to realize what had happened earlier.

Dax smashed a thick tree branch into Parpagg so he could release his grip from my throat. I looked at Dax with gratitude. If I got out of this alive I would buy him a box of Slim Jims.

The great animal had become a literal shadow. Parpagg blinked at Dax. "You are this human's protector?" His focus rounded to me. "You dared to look at me." Charred pieces were chipping off him. I visibly saw the muscles in his jaw flex as he spoke. My stomach roiled. "You tapped into the Po'luxnann Gejruvhet." It was unreal. He was talking burnt flesh. "I will kill you after I dispose of the nighthound," Parpagg promised. He disappeared and quickly reappeared before Dax. Without warning, he knocked a fist into Dax's throat.

Dax silently went airborne across the clearing. There was no sound to be heard as Dax headed straight for a bunker. Instead of colliding, Dax phased through it, vanishing.

Parpagg fixed his attention on me and smiled. He was going to do more than steal the Po'luxnann.

"I need your help!" I snatched off the last pendant and stuffed it in my jeans.

Suddenly, a light turned on and my senses were sharper.

My eyes hurt- the stars were much too bright. My ears throbbed. The air around me stunk. A strong perfume permeated the air, followed by another scent, then another. Here, scents left colorful traces in the air like airbrushed smoke, clinging to my nostrils like Velcro. One gag atrocious smell of sulfur had a cloud of yellow tracing back to Parpagg.

You now possess the enhanced senses of a D'uthne and their basic strength. You are no longer a weak human.

I heard something coming fast in the distance. It sounded like it was coming from one direction and the sound broke off at another angle in the opposite direction. Before I could pinpoint its location it grew louder, heading towards us at a breakneck speed. I caught the scent of dirt and ash.

A thick column of smoke collided into Parpagg and sent him flying until he plunged into a water hazard. After a few seconds, water shot up like a geyser. Parpagg did a mid-twirl in the air and like a cat, landed on his feet in a low crouch.

"Greetings, Crispy."

Laurenx stood between Parpagg and I, his right palm steady out in front of him. Parpagg instantly stood, training his eyes on Laurenx. His eyes flamed. "You."

"Yes, me." Laurenx rumbled.

"I thought you died," Parpagg spat.

"Did you send R'uttri to my home?" Laurenx growled.

Parpagg looked disgusted. "You mourn the loss of your dwelling here among humans rather than the home you left in D'uthne?" His nostrils flared. "They are primitive and weak. As are you."

"Did you send R'uttri to my home?" Laurenx lethally repeated. More terrifying was the energy blazing off him: cold, dark, and deadly. He was a hurricane ready to be let loose.

"Your blood was the likely suspect."

"Are you working with him?" Laurenx demanded. Parpagg cocked his head to one side and smiled. "Come now, what makes you believe it wasn't your-"

"Are you working with him?" Laurenx repeated louder.

"Still sour." Parpagg's smile broadened. "I'm working with him less than more. We have…similar interests."

Laurenx's face shifted bronze and gaunt. Black smog rose out of him and clung to his body like a wetsuit. This darkness was tangible, more solid than Dax's smoke form. Laurenx's body transformed into someone who hadn't eaten for a month.

Parpagg's eyes hardened into blazing white flames.

"Kid, run!" Laurenx shouted.

"He will not leave!" Parpagg twisted around and disappeared- suddenly he was close enough to pull my teeth out. Laurenx was on him in a second and yanked him backwards, hurtling them on the opposite end of the golf course. Laurenx crashed, breaking through trees along the way. Parpagg had spun away from him in midair. I stumbled as broad branches fell overhead, somehow deflecting from me as I sprinted across the golf course. A shadow shifted under my soles then drifted a few feet away on the ground.

"Seth, get out of here!"

Laurenx's voice rattled the air as Parpagg's blazing eyes shot a jet blue light- Laurenx countered it with a black column of smoke filtering out his hand. The explosion of powers meeting echoed throughout the golf park. Parpagg dove out of the way and vanished with a snarl. Laurenx scanned the clearing. An earlier vision told me when Parpagg was going to attack.

I shouted as loud as I could. "Dax, save Laurenx!"

Parpagg materialized behind Laurenx before he could defend himself- Dax transformed from his shadow form to his solid monstrous form, bucking Parpagg in the spine- I heard it crack across the course like a dry pretzel. Parpagg slammed on the ground and bounced like a pebble several yards away.

Sand, dirt, and grass sprayed in every direction. Laurenx appeared- he yanked me by the neck and in a second my body was weightless. My feet found solid ground again. My knees wobbled from the shock of impact.

Laurenx took me up by my forearms and attempted to shove me. I sensed his movement before he completed it. I caught him by the wrist and reflexively balled my right fist in my other hand. I met it with the bridge of his nose. His neck snapped back as his body reeled away in surprise.

His nighthound had joined in, snapping its jaws at me. "Dax, stay back," he commanded.

He was momentarily distracted.

I sent a spinning kick to his solar plexus. He trapped my attack in the palm of his hand as I drew backwards- exactly what he anticipated. He matched my speed and lifted my leg high enough to keep me unbalanced.

He lunged forward and shoved me to the ground. His elbow lodged in my throat as the weight of his body pinned me down. He backhanded a slap across my face.

"Take control, boy. Dax, keep still!"

I head butted him- his head snapped backward and I rolled off to the side, already in mid-crouch. I was too focused on him I hadn't realized the nighthound appeared again. It lunged forward and hit my chest. It drove me to the ground and sat on top of me. The air swooshed out of my lungs and my limbs convulsed furiously. "Dax, I command you to stay! Seth is not himself. Stay. Back." I heard the nighthound's growl simmer. A presence leaned over me. "Let go of the boy. Now," it demanded.

"Curse this body," I hissed.

He grabbed the pendants from the pocket and placed them around his neck. "Seth, take control. Happy thoughts, remember?"

I addressed the abomination with much revulsion. "Remember this; I will destroy you. Every moment your back is turned, be overcome with fear," I told it. "It is a matter of time before I have his body and consume his soul." In a gradual pace, my power receded.

"You have trouble holding onto his mind," the beast uttered. "You won't be able to overtake him. Not when I'm around."

"I will not return to D'uthne. I vow to dispose of you." My hold was loosening. "You and the entire Imudmid and Temcaltiaf race."

I blinked.

"Dax, you can climb off him." Dax did as he was told. He stood right beside Laurenx, growling low and tense. I sat up dizzily as the tattoos of the Po'luxnann flared on both arms and my chest. My entire body glowed in swirling vivid colors of red.

"You gave the Po'luxnann control." Laurenx sounded grave. I could feel the murderous intent I had a moment ago. I wanted to fry him. I still wanted to.

"Get up!" Laurenx boomed.

I couldn't.

"Now!"

I struggled to my knees and slumped to one side. The glowing pendants around my neck throbbed. They formed a powerful vortex, blocking out the Po'luxnann. Every part of my body was bruised and beaten blue. I wanted to lie down and sleep a hundred years. My body gradually stopped glowing and the lights in both pendants went out.

Laurenx pulled me upright. I stumbled, trying to maintain my balance. "You gave him control over your mind, body, and soul." I closed my eyes as his breath hit my face. He needed to control his breath with mouthwash. He shook me. I managed to crack open an eyelid. "It almost killed you."

"It helped me," I mumbled.

"Help?" Laurenx asked incredulously. "It wants to consume your soul. It doesn't care about you or anything else but self-preservation," he said. "You're stupid to believe-"

I shoved him back but he wouldn't budge. "Parpagg was going to kill me." My arms fell to my sides. Adrenaline was fading now. "What the hell was I supposed to do?" my voice cracked. "He hurt my Mom."

"There is always another choice, and you chose the wrong one." He looked ready for round two. "Don't you dare tap into the Po'luxnann, you hear me? You have no idea what it will do once it has full control!"

"The old man was going to kill me," I pounded at my chest. "You have powers you understand. You. Wouldn't. Die." A low growl caught my attention. Dax appeared in a giant black form. He barked loudly at Laurenx.

"What?" Laurenx told him. Dax's growl grew louder until he let out a resounding bark.

Laurenx finally let me go and I seesawed on my legs. I glanced at Dax. He looked back at me with his blue intelligent eyes. I turned to Laurenx. "We need to get to my Mom. We need to take her to a hospital."

Laurenx hesitated. "She is under the Cazrem's care."

"What?"

His tone soured. "Three R'uttri showed up at my door after you didn't come back from the store." The energy around him rose and darkened. That power was enough to have me stumble into Dax and I held onto him for support. Dax slowly lowered me to the ground. Laurenx went on. "I suppose Parpagg was so desperate to distract me; R'uttri are useless dry bones in daylight. After I killed the R'uttri who ambushed and set my house on fire, I went out looking for you." I could feel his eyes boring down on me beneath his hat. "Dax couldn't get a good whiff of you through the storm. I doubled back to your house. Inside was a mess. I found your mother on the kitchen floor."

I froze. Laurenx scratched under his throat. "Her hands and feet were bound and there was a gash on her forehead. I alerted the Cazrem's. They are D'uthnian doctors. Be grateful Parpagg did not torture her physically."

My head dropped. It took a minute before I could speak. "Be grateful?" I rasped.

"Listen," he barked, "she isn't dead. Parpagg did not kill her."

A sharp throb stabbed in my chest. My mind tried to understand. "She was alive when you saw her."

"Yes."

I shook with relief. "Parpagg said...he said he poisoned her. Like he did King Razhatlab. He poisoned me too. I feel okay now." I looked up at Laurenx expectantly. He had his back turned away. "You think the poison wore off her too?"

"The Po'luxnann has the ability to use its own power to heal itself. You're healed because the Po'luxnann wanted to preserve your body."

"They found her in time, right? Your doctors." I gripped the earth, holding onto hope. "They can stop the poison."

"I'm no doctor."

"I'm not asking you anything hard," I snapped. "Did she look like she was going to make it?"

Laurenx hesitated. "Her body was cold when I found her. Her heart was still beating."

His words echoed through my mind. Her body was cold…

I should have listened to the Po'luxnann when I had the chance. I should have gotten to her sooner. Tears pricked my eyes.

"Sorry, kid."

Suddenly, killing Parpagg didn't matter. I had to see her. I needed to see if my Mom was alright.

I looked around. I didn't know where I was. I began to stand.

We were in the middle of a giant field of grass that stretched out in the middle of nowhere. There were no landmarks, only gloomy sky, and dry grass. I shivered. There wasn't any rain here. Laurenx was moving around the field in circles. "Where are we?"

I watched him as he started hopping into place. "What are you doing?"

He ignored me as he raised his hands over his head and started to sway them back and forth. This guy was crazy for Fruit Loops. He stopped. I watched him for another minute until black smoke flooded out his palms.

His eyes narrowed to a spot in the grass. "There it is."

"Okay, I don't care what you're doing, just get me to my Mom."

He bent to the ground, palms face down. Black smoke solidified and spread in several directions into the earth like a spider's web. Suddenly, vibrations shook the field. Dax curled his body protectively around me. My hand caught into his fur, holding on.

"What are you doing?" I shouted.

The tremor suddenly halted.

A gust of heat blew, tossing my hair back until the atmosphere around us warmed the brisk air. Pressure and vapor collided, shifting the atmosphere into a fog. Dax's ears twitched. He looked up at the hazy sky, focused at a particular point. A deep, lethal sound vibrated from his throat until a loud bark carried in the distance. I winced and ducked my head into his fur.

Dax's fur stood on end; his chest raised, paws extended with his claws digging into the earth. I felt his muscles tense as power stirred and pulsed through him. I heard the sounds of buzzing. It was coming near.

"Dax, come," Laurenx called. Dax turned his head and gave me a lick. With a jerk of his head that looked like a nod, his fur and vivid blue eyes darkened. Dax became entirely pitch black.

I stumbled as my hand went right through him. Dax wasn't just getting darker; he was becoming less solid.

The buzzing noise grew. Dax, now completely a shadow, jumped into Laurenx's outstretched hand and vanished. Laurenx's arm blackened. I peered up at the sky and finally saw what was making that buzzing noise.

Thousands upon thousands of bees hailed down towards the field, darkening the foggy sky. They were about a hundred feet away and began moving around us in quick formation; we were in the middle of a tornado of bees.

I put my hands over my ears again; it was *loud*. The sight of them bunched together made my skin crawl and my stomach sick. They circled us in a violent swarm until an invisible signal cued them to fan out.

They flew back to accommodate the five men who now had joined the bee circle. Bees covered the men in full armor and formed into bee shields and helmets; even their giant maces were covered in insects.

The Bee Men were at least eight feet tall. Their hairy, grasshopper legs bent backwards and their bulbous brown eyes covered half their bloated faces. They each wore a permanent scowl. Their tough brown skin were covered in vibrant green petals that tucked between their shoulder blades; they reminded me of dragonfly wings. A strong stench of dead bugs rode off them.

Laurenx stood. His face was darker and grew smoother, almost gunmetal bronze; silver streaks ran from his temple down to his neck. His shaggy brown hair and beard grayed as though he was stuck inside a meat locker for days.

"What is happening to you?"

He didn't answer me. Instead he gave me a command. "Don't answer any unnecessary questions they ask, got it?" He said this without turning to me.

"Who are they?" I motioned to the scene in front of us. I couldn't help but also ask, "What are they?"

"Himak Juivs, or Himaks. They're your saviors," he said. Their name sounded too gentle and unimposing for what I saw. One of the soldiers, who stood at the center, pointed his bee-covered staff at us.

"They'll take you to King Razhatlab," Laurenx said from the corner of his mouth. He kept his eye on the closest Himak. "Whatever happens from this moment on, remember I'm on your side," he said. "Don't forget."

"Golinta si ko!" Bells chimed in the Himak. He sounded too friendly to be threatening.

"Dochec su tima. Speak in Everyman language," Laurenx rasped.

A second raised his staff. *"Golinta si ko! Magresh, taki!"* He sounded more melodic than the other.

If they weren't looking lethally dangerous with their staffs pointed at us, you would have thought they were serenading us.

Laurenx pointed to the one in the center. The veins in his arm dimmed until they became a stark contrast from his sallow skin. "Speak in Everyman. I'm not singing your tune."

"Lower your guard!" The first one snapped in Everyman. "You have called us. State your purpose." The singsong voice sounded less pleasant now I knew what he was saying.

"Where's Emily?" Laurenx demanded.

That statement alone made them raise their staffs in unison. The bees around us buzzed louder. Laurenx shifted his stance; feet apart, arm still outstretched. A cold wind whipped around him, steadily driving back the bees. It made them buzz louder, angrily. "Address her authority by proper name and title," the second screeched.

"Emily would want to see me." On his last word, the bee circle snapped- the built up pressure around Laurenx diffused into a bomb.

The bees were caught by Laurenx's power. Bees started to rain in pellets, frozen to death. I shivered as they fell on top of my head and all around us. The ones left alive laid immobilized on the ground, trapped in ice.

The Bee Men screams were sharp sounds of metal snapping. The vibrations in the air shocked my body- my bones felt as if a buzz saw had gone through them.

I went weak at the knees. I fell to the ground, paralyzed in fear and pain. One of my ears trickled something warm and moist down my neck; blood. The Himaks shrilled louder and louder in a chorus of claws clicking and heels stomping.

The remaining bees swooped down and immediately began freeing some of their fallen comrades from the ice. And they began eating their friends.

Chips of ice cracked all around us as the bees buzzed wildly. My stomach grew queasy until I couldn't hold it together. I threw up again.

"Is there any reason you've come out of hiding?" one of them screeched to Laurenx.

A ripple of vibrations split through the air like a whip. A woman materialized in the contortion of the sound. The screams and buzzing around us lowered.

The lady was shorter than the men and was a much darker complexion. Slender vines of pink petals with purple thorns wrapped her arm. Her hair was pixie cut with a dark hue of sea green. I noticed she wasn't dressed in bees.

Upon closer look, I realized her hair were leaves of different shapes and sizes that framed her face and hung above her shoulders. Her eyes reminded me of acorns: brown, rough, and oblong in shape. She looked anything but human, but there was something familiar about her that made my bones quiver.

"The boy," Laurenx said gruffly. "He has the Po'luxnann," he informed her. "I cannot take him to King Razhaǝlab myself." He never removed his sights from the Himaks. Black tendrils began marching up to his neck.

"You may stand down," the woman told her men. They immediately stood back. The remaining bees that weren't caught in Laurenx shockwave also receded.

"You're going to need them," said Laurenx. "I'm about to go unconscious."

The woman's eyebrows knitted. "I will murder you before you change form." She shifted her stance.

From where I lay, I watched Laurenx drop down on all fours, head bowed. "That is a far sweeter sentence." He peered up at the woman. "If you're going to kill me, do it. Stop stalling."

The woman didn't hesitate on the offer. She stalked towards Laurenx and leaned over him. I couldn't see anything but her back. I saw Laurenx's expression. He was ready for death.

There was a type of coldness in the air that felt dangerous, like a snake ready to strike. The Himaks ascended and joined the giant bee cloud, crowding the sky. I couldn't stop feeling a rolling current of fear and dread as the atmosphere grew thicker and colder. I wanted to shout at Laurenx to run.

"I will not kill you," I heard the woman say. "I have other plans. A cell awaits you." The Himaks and bees beat their wings furiously and eagerly, sweeping in the cold wind.

My lungs constricted as the air became frigid and tight. The power pouring out the Himaks and bees dulled the grass beneath my feet- the Po'luxnann snapped with anger. It realized what I had too late. The bees were eating power. And they had drained the Po'luxnann dry.

After the battle took most of the Po'luxnann's strength to deliver the Death Lock, it became less of itself.

In one week, the Po'luxnann Gejruvhet experienced the Ggatgin and that process alone took power to release itself from its Bearer. Then, the Po'luxnann healed and saved me from dying in the hands of Parpagg. That also took a lot of power to protect itself from internalizing the damages the Gates succumbed to.

To go against its nature to protect and provide peace and order was slowly killing itself. Every blow the Bror and Temcaltiaf Gate was struck with was one step closer to its ultimate demise.

The reserve of power the Po'luxnann used to barricade itself from feeling any of the Gates' destruction, vanished. The Po'luxnann buckled to its knees.

The Po'luxnann didn't have any power to shield itself from me anymore. I was inside its head now.

Like an avalanche, the Po'luxnann poured itself into me for refuge. I sourly tasted its own thoughts now, a wave of fear and anger.

I mentally stabbed it back before I felt it swimming in my soul. Unfortunately, most of the Po'luxnann's essence fell within of me. When Laurenx spoke again. He sounded calm.

"Before you do me away, promise you will do whatever it takes to protect the boy." The woman leaned in closer. "I will do whatever is necessary to survive."

Laurenx's face fell between anger and disappointment. The woman blew a breath in his face. Laurenx let out a gut-wrenching scream.

I watched helplessly as a black shadow eased out beneath him and hid behind one of the Bee Men. After one endless moment, Laurenx collapsed on the dry grass. The woman resolutely turned and marched toward me. She paused when she was less than ten feet away.

Very carefully, she measured her steps, less confident to approach me. As soon as the hovering Himaks chimed a song in unison, the woman smiled and continued her forward march. She halted when her boot was a breath away from my head. She made sure to look down at my chest, her eyes eagerly measuring my broken state.

She didn't need to bother avoiding my eyes; the Po'luxnann ran out of power necessary for the Death Lock. She must have known it was out of juice, because her smile broadened. She revealed sharp, spiky teeth that crisscrossed into four rows of gray. It was like looking into the mouth of a shark. I was a wounded lamb, staring at a hungry predator's eager mouth. Then I remembered.

She was the woman in my vision. The one who was going to kill me. My panicked eyes found Laurenx crumpled on the ground. There was no one who would come to my rescue now.

"I am Emikrili," she announced. Emikrili bent down and laid a palm against my cheek. I rasped a surprised yelp. The blistering cold traveled down my neck, spine, and toes until it bounced back to my brain.

My body rocked and buckled in agony; I didn't know I soiled myself or the gagging sounds were squeezing out of my own throat. I didn't hear the Po'luxnann's own silent screams.

I must have been used to pain; I didn't acknowledge it as something that hurt or threatened my life. It soon became familiar, like a welcomed friend. Just when I started to embrace this new idea, the line to my brain went dead.

CHAPTER FIFTEEN

The enchanted ring shielded me from sight but I cautiously slipped down the flagstone steps, much slower than I intended. Sweat brimmed my vision as my breath came out in short gasps. My knees creaked as my foot reached the bottom stair.

I leaned against the stonewall for support. My sickness dared to overcome me but now was no time for rest. The Council had removed Vaora from Mirg Ega hours earlier.

Once my heartbeat maintained a steady pace, I veered right and entered the dungeon.

Vaora lay unmoving on the hay bed. She was immobile. Her gaze stretched out beyond her barred window. Her body was covered in black orbs with long spindles that crawled against her skin, shifting themselves every so often as they fed on her power and life force.

I swayed where I stood, overcome with anguish.

My daughter, I wanted to cry out. Any self-control I possessed momentarily wavered. Many members of the Council would be hanged for this. After a clear resolution, I came to her. I whispered her name through the bars. "Vaora."

Her shoulders flinched, but her hollowed eyes remained where they were. I called again. Her eyes were filled with life again. She turned her head. I quickly removed the invisibility ring and appeared before her.

She started. Her mouth slowly formed words. "F-father?"

Her voice sounded stripped of strength, her throat bone dry. I fought to think what horror she faced in the Mirg Ega, what forced her to lose her precious voice. Did she scream from the terror she witnessed in her time imprisoned? Or was she tortured to the point her vocal chords severed?

Vaora licked her cracked lips to speak again. I placed the ring back on my finger and became invisible once more.

Vaora fell to the ground and slowly dragged herself toward the bars of her cell. "Why can't I see you?" she whispered. She stuck her hand through them and her fingers caught the hem of my robe. I slid down the bars and openly looked at her in anguish.

"I should not be found down here," I responded. Her fingers traveled to my face and began working an outline of my jaw, my mouth, and then my eyes.

"You know that is not the answer I want from you."

A power leech crawled over the tips of her fingers and began feeding on her strength. Immediately she lost feeling and her arm dropped to her side. With a painful grunt, Vaora shifted against the mildewed walls to prop herself.

I silently cleared my throat. "I am wearing an Invisibility ring."

"It is Imudmidian made. Black arts," she stated.

"Yes."

The prisoner a cell down on the right gazed upward. His head collapsed back to his chest until he fell right back to his slumber.

"The Imudmidian princess bestowed it as a gift," I informed. My words did not surprise her.

Her tone rose. "They started a war with us."

I shook my head. "It was a planned attack from our Passage. Traitorous Passagekeepers from our side unlocked the Temcaltiaf Gate and led Imudmidian rogues in. This is also the case for the Bror Passage. It is safe to assume it was the same creature who planned alongside Parpagg to perform the Ggatgin on me."

Vaora did not answer. Her lack of response left me troubled.

"What are you doing here and not in bed?" she asked. "You should be resting."

How could I not see my daughter?

"I had to ask you a few questions."

Her head lolled on her neck. She could hardly keep upright. "What questions?"

I wanted to hold her in my arms. She needed her father to console her. "What were your reasons to leave your imprisonment? What business did you have on the outside?"

Vaora forced herself to gaze upwards. I saw the pain before her words form. "The Extractor got enough out of me in Mirg Ega."

"I need to hear it from you, Vaora."

"You believe me a traitor to the kingdom, Your Majesty?"

The title cut me far deeper than her narrowed eyes. She still held onto her spirit. I raised her to become a strong, capable woman.

"You disappeared from castle grounds for several hours, ignoring the lockdown I commanded. In those hours you were gone there have been reports of R'uttri, Parpagg, and many Imudmidians escaping into the human world. Are you involved?" I demanded. She slumped to one side. She didn't have enough strength to move again.

"Rora," I called out.

She closed her eyes. "You... once called me that...in time of comfort." I watched a tear escape under one eyelid. She found her voice once more.

"I am not involved, my king. I was in the rose garden outside Semlish waiting for a meeting with Ugud of Aichord and Denisse of Batisfir from our Council. We were to speak of gathering armies to save D'uthne. The suns are going out, haven't you noticed? It has become colder." She turned to look out her tiny barred window. "I planned to speak to them about Frih Kio and my suspicions about an enemy within our Passage. I believed it was someone within the castle walls, hence the reason for my meeting planned outside. They never showed."

I killed Ugud and he was very much a traitor. I suspect Denisse was a conspirator as well. My daughter was telling the truth about her meeting.

"You believe you were framed."

"Yes."

"You are aware they will deny ever planning a meeting with you."

"Yes."

I would sacrifice my heart for you, if I could, I wanted to say. I never intended for her to be faced with a dilemma that befell me. I was sorry for the fool I had been.

"That is all the information I needed."

She sniffed. "Do the best you can for the kingdom, long after I perish."

Rage and grief tossed my stomach.

I will free you, my daughter. I will never forsake you, I wanted to say.

"You will not die for false imprisonment. Stay strong. I will find the truth."

She said nothing. Her shoulders shook as she silently cried. "I will go now," I told her and began to rise.

"I love you," I heard her whisper.

"As I for you." I responded. "Remain well."

I headed towards the stone steps. I dared not a tear to fall. I would not allow myself the luxury.

Melwimik later caught me in an abandoned room, several doors before my chambers.

"Did it work, my king?" he asked anxiously. I gave a solid nod. I revealed a tiny pink seashell, no larger than my thumb. This was another gift from Mag. It had the ability to detect lies and reveal the truth. They were also excellent sound recorders. Had I revealed to Vaora what I planned, the shell would take it as me deceiving it to believe a truth. The truth told would have to be pure, coming from the heart. The little shell glowed ember in the palm of my hand.

I cautiously placed the precious device in Melwimik's open palm.

"Guard it with your life. Instruct Zenras the mage to make duplicates. Produce this in the capital as well. Play it in every hometown of all Councilmen, including Abdul and Lord Rangdal. Scatter them in rose beds and hedges, on windowsills, wherever they are not simple to find to remove but are easy to hear. Once we reveal the princess is falsely imprisoned, it will spare us some time before she can be executed. The people will not permit it."

Melwimik bowed his head. "Yes, my king."

The Council did not want anyone to know the Po'luxnann was not in my possession. They claimed they were attempting to keep chaos at a minimum, but I suspected they had vindictive intentions to keep the truth silent. I had to expose them.

I placed a hand on his shoulder. "You are dismissed." Melwimik nodded. He bowed once more and took his leave. He suddenly stopped. He turned around again. "We will save Princess Vaora. We will save Temcaltiaf and Bror."

It was my turn to nod. "Of course. I have failed as a father, but I am a victorious king."

I drew to my chambers. My body cried for rest, but there was one more task to be completed. I laid on my back and gazed upwards at my ceiling.

It was a comfort to me, the cluster of stars. Every star formed all those galaxies above. Small as they were, together, they brought light to a dark universe. My breathing labored, then my heart. Soon, my restless spirit subdued and my eyes grew weary. I could still feel the Po'luxnann, as distant as it was, potent; alive. I dug deeper into it and found a connecting line. Like a butterfly breaking out of a cocoon, I left my body and entered young Seth's mind.

The Po'luxnann flared, causing my body to ache in all sorts of places in my subconscious. Another presence pushed into my mind and the Po'luxnann's presence decreased until it was a shadow in my mind.

Seth Castillo, it is King Razhatlab. I need to speak with you.

He startled me.

King Razhatlab?

Wasn't I dead?

I heard him breathe a sigh of relief.

I have finally met the owner of the Po'luxnann, he said lightly. I am sure we do not need formal introductions.

I nodded in agreement.

If you hadn't made contact with me before, I wouldn't have discovered the link to speak with you.

"Right," I said, not fully understanding.

You merged a connecting link between us from the previous occurrence you attempted my audience.

You knew the entire time I was in your head?

Not at first. I have caught glimpses of your life in moments of distress. I have seen the two fire incidents. Your meeting with Laurenx and fleeing Parpagg. Your capture.

I'm in trouble now, I told him. Somewhere outside my head, I knew I wasn't in good shape. I could feel some of the Po'luxnann's injuries outside my own. It was barely holding on.

I felt the king's overwhelming sadness and it hit my heart in surprise. Now that I was more aware of him and the Po'luxnann, my own emotions were running an all-time high.

I am sorry, young Seth.

His words were a fuse to a bomb that exploded. I couldn't contain my anger in anymore.

He was a spectator. He watched when I was confused and felt afraid, and saw what I had done. He watched me search for answers as to why I had the Po'luxnann and knew how much I wanted to get rid of it. If he looked through my eyes, he saw when Parpagg completed the Ggatgin and what it did to me. My anger lashed out with burning fire.

You didn't stop Parpagg, I shouted.

After Parpagg's deceit, I called Passagekeepers from your side of the Bror Passage to find him and return the Po'luxnann. I have done what I could to protect you and your world.

I felt his guilt and sorrow but all of it were excuses.

You're the king, I snapped. The Po'luxnann is yours.

Yes, that is correct.

I felt the Po'luxnann stirring. The angrier and fearful I became, the more it scratched against the mental walls I locked it in.

Just call it or come find me. I'll give it back to you. That's all you have to do, I stressed.

I have attempted to call the Po'luxnann, but it has rejected me. I cannot simply take the Po'luxnann from you. I am no longer its Bearer.

So what? Just take it from me!

I am well aware of your anguish. This has been a burden to you, the king said solemnly.

So that's it? Are you forfeiting the Po'luxnann? I don't want these stupid powers. My Mom got hurt. If I never had these powers she wouldn't- I choked up.

He didn't speak right away. He gave me a few minutes to sob.

I am deeply sorry. Do not despair. She has a chance to live.

Hot tears fell from my eyes.

Do not allow the Ggatgin with Emikrili. I must warn you. The Po'luxnann also does not want to detach itself from you. It limits your chance of survival. Do not allow the Po'luxnann to consume you. You still have power over it.

What power do I have over it? I fumed. Parpagg wiped my face with my living room floor.

The Po'luxnann took control of me and I fought Laurenx, I told him. If Laurenx hadn't come around and smacked some sense into me, I wouldn't have a soul. I might as well be dead walking around with no memory of my Mom, my Dad, my friends, I shouted. You seriously think I can stop these monsters and keep the Gates from tearing apart?

I know Seth but you must bear it. You can save your world-

Why should I save anyone when no one came for my Mom and I? Choose someone who cares, I said coldly.

With the Po'luxnann you can save my world as well.

He wasn't listening. No one ever listened.

Why should I? I snapped. Your people start wars and eat humans.

I thought about the two-year-old girl's corpse that was found half eaten and grew angrier. King Razhatlab couldn't convince me his world was worth saving. They were all monsters.

You cannot sit idly in a corner. Chaos will continue the longer the Po'luxnann is inactive. This will go beyond the physical cold and dark skies and R'uttri are filtering through your world. More creatures of Imudmid will follow.

TAKE IT FROM ME, THEN!

This is nothing you can escape by wishing away, King Razhatlab strictly insisted. *If I could take your place, I would, but this is your fight. Your journey.*

Take the Po'luxnann from me. Please, I begged him.

The Po'luxnann took it upon itself to send a battering ram of power into my body and pummeled a sledgehammer to my groin. The startling attack immobilized me until I could mentally open my eyes.

King Razhatlab voice rose sharply. *What is wrong?*

Like a rabid dog, the Po'luxnann chewed through another barrier. Laurenx explained it was only a matter of time until the Po'luxnann could break out of its cage.

Give in to me. You do not have to prolong your suffering, it roared. *I am granting you an opportunity.*

I clamped my jaw on my tongue and tasted blood.

You have an opportunity to go into the light towards the Great Beyond.

I could feel the Po'luxnann's desperation. It was getting weaker. I hung on and thought of a memory that reminded me of myself.

Karin jumped onto Denny Battistelli from the top of the school stairs and landed on top of him on the bottom stair; she looked like Wonder Woman flying. Denny had called her chink-eyed witch and she didn't take it lightly. Karin's friendship reminded me a part of who I was.

Warmth and peace washed over me until I was submerged from the inside out. The Po'luxnann's stronghold lessened. Its power ebbed away.

Seth!

I wasn't sure how long King Razhatlab went on shouting my name. Somewhere in my unconsciousness, I came to myself.

Yeah, I'm here, I said, gasping for a mental breath.

King Razhatlab's power simmered down. *Are you alright?* He sounded concerned.

No, I answered. Nothing is alright, I said. The Po'luxnann is going to kill me anyway. There was no point in fighting it anymore.

Just as I spoke, King Razhatlab's power dramatically fell. As it did, his physical body weakened. He used his power to hold back the Po'luxnann at the expense of his own failing health.

Do not give in, Seth. Yes, the Po'luxnann has the potential to kill you, his voice strengthened. *You are simply a vessel to it, a weak human. You are not a god, lesser than a gremlin, and wasp.* I struggled to laugh.

For thousands of years, the Po'luxnann has been in the possession of gods, passed down from king to king for Temcaltiaf. It relished its existence as the sole power D'uthne relied on. It is a god all on its own, yearning for beings that are able to use its intellect so it can perform what it was created to do. To live in its purpose. It is not a god that is content inhabiting fools or drunkards. The Po'luxnann is also the power that maintains the Gates and maintains the three Passages from breaking apart. It holds the balance between worlds. He carried on.

Yet you have come this far, despite the odds, despite the Po'luxnann's immense power. What has happened in the past, your experiences, your wins and your losses, they do not matter at this very moment.

I couldn't save Chessie from herself. I thought. I couldn't help my Mom get over Dad. What world could I save?

You have done what most D'uthnians fail to do; you haven't given in to your god. Humans are prone to fall because they are driven by many of their idols: greed, power, lust, envy to name a few. But you, Seth, you are far from perfect but you strive to be better. You haven't given up. Believe an old man when I say this; you have overcome. He spoke in reverence.

You may have lost your father to his selfishness but you did not let it drown you. There remains your mother who has relied on you, and despite her unjust decisions against you, you've been a pillar of strength for her. You have also fought against a god that has outlived you more than a thousand times over and yet, here you remain in possession of your mind. You are fiercely strong and courageous, Seth. You do not need outward power to be powerful. Your strength lies in your hope to fight, to live, to love. It is not over for you. You overcame your struggles because simply, you did not give up.

He was king to a foreign land and Bearer to the Po'luxnann for centuries. He's faced battles I've never seen. He killed four powerful

Councilmen without batting an eye and survived long after being poisoned by Parpagg. Yet he believed I could survive the Po'luxnann Gejruvhet, the greatest power in D'uthne that was able to keep the Gates from all worlds from crumbling. King Razhatlab believe in me. I didn't know what to say.

I finally asked the question I feared the most. I knew it would change my life forever. I asked anyway.

What do I have to do?

First, you must know the Po'luxnann preys upon your weaknesses. It feeds on your emotions of anger, restlessness, and resentment because it reveals your inner scars. It recognizes the very memories that haunt you. It perceives your fears. Use what the Po'luxnann has exploited against you. Find its own weakness and discover your strength.

I didn't really understand what that meant, but I internally nodded.

Thanks for not sugar-coating the situation.

Sugar coating?

It means you don't paint the situation with false hope. You tell me how it is up front with honesty.

He mentally smiled.

I will try to remember that.

His presence lifted and the mind link severed.

CHAPTER SIXTEEN

"That is him? Rotcekt Emikrili, he doesn't look like much."

"I know, child."

"He looks deformed. No flower petals, pointy ears, and you see the lack of color to his skin? He looks strange."

"Bromir, that's an insult to his race. Evolution hasn't been kind to them, the little beasts."

"Your words aren't considered insulting?" she squeaked.

"Of course. Now go place my cup on the table. I will drink it later."

"Yes, Rotcekt." Then, "You know, he stopped shouting. Do you believe he is awake?"

Something hard jabbed me in the ribs. I automatically yelped.

"Awaken."

The fog of unconsciousness left and a tugging ache and heat brought a deep groan in my throat. I made a cruel search with my fingers, seeking a pillow to cover my burning eyes. Something heavy restricted my arm from moving. I opened my eyes and stared at the black heavy object clasped around my wrist, confused.

Attached to my wrist were black chains at my sides and another chain brought my legs firmly together. The air was hot and stifling, with a mixture of dirt of something oily burning- it smelled like exhaust fumes. A gas lamp burned against rugged black and gray walls, dimly lighting the room.

I didn't like the look of those rugged black and gray walls and gas lamps. I lay on something rough and caked, like moist, lumpy clay. My gaze traveled up to Emikrili. I made an aggressive noise as I fought to sit up and fell back down, panting.

She had little holes on the side of her head for ears and her eyes were a little too round on her face.

Emikrili didn't appear threatening in this light. Her vibrant petals freckled her skin. The vines entwined around her arms were thin and slender, not the prickly thorns I thought I saw earlier. Her hair, which was a sprout of vibrant green leaves, was pixie cut, framing her oval face. I avoided her eyes and looked away.

Standing beside her was a girl. She had pointy ears, dark brown hair with eyes darker than her complexion. Her emerald grassy hair was cropped short to frame her face. I would have mistaken her for a toddler if I didn't hear her speak. If I was sitting down I doubt she would come past my shoulders. She gazed at me curiously.

I swallowed to relax my dry throat. "Where am I?"

"*Agviget et na Thewhyr*," the little girl said. "The Place of the Unforgiven is a tear that lies within the damaged Gate."

That didn't sound very good.

I noticed what I heard her say in Everyman was breaking into garbled words. It was as if the Po'luxnann was having trouble dubbing her speech in English in my mind. If I was noticing it now, it probably meant the Po'luxnann was weaker than it ever was.

The little girl ran to the other side of the cell and hurried back with a cup. She propped my head up and forced my lips to the mouth of the cup.

"Drink. You're going to need it. It is honey water," she nodded encouragingly. I noticed she took great care not to look me in the eye. I sipped the drink cautiously. It smoothly went down my throat, spreading warmth and feeling to my tired muscles. The haze in my head lessened. The temporary relief bought enough energy to think clearly.

Without a warning, Emikrili backhanded the little girl in the face. She flew on the other side of the room and landed with a crash. She skidded and rolled to a stop, cup still in hand. She didn't move.

"What did you do?" I said hoarsely.

"I did not command her to give you my cup of honey water." As if on cue, the girl flinched on the ground. She moaned, coming to.

Emikrili's tone sharpened. "You should be more concerned for your own self-preservation. You are my prisoner." Her voice chimed like cut glass.

I glared. "Why?"

Emikrili slightly cocked her head. "You are the Bearer of the Po'luxnann Gejruvhet." She said answered as-a-matter-of-factly.

"Where's Laurenx?" Her expression never changed.

I asked again "Where is Laurenx?" Was she hard of hearing?

She spoke after a couple of beats. "He is detained."

"My apologies, Rotcekt." A voice mumbled in the corner. The girl struggled to sit. "Is there anything else you need me to do?"

Emikrili ignored her. "Are you hungry?" she asked politely. "The servant may go and bring you food. It will be your final meal." Her words promised death.

"No," I said.

She rounded to the girl. "You stay for now."

The girl groaned as she rose to her feet as she held her face where she was struck. Tears had formed in her eyes, but she didn't let them fall. "I will stay, Rotcekt."

I shifted slightly, feeling the restraints grip my wrists. The clay bed was uncomfortable, setting my neck and back in protest. I peered down at the lady's mouth. "What do you want?"

There was a ghost of a smile. "I want the Po'luxnann."

"You want to help me get the Po'luxnann to King Razhatlab, you mean."

"No."

Fear jumpstarted my heart. If she was going to perform the Ggatgin, I knew I wasn't going to survive. There was a strong possibility the Po'luxnann wouldn't either.

"How long have you known Xa'renul?" she asked.

My frown faltered a little. "Who?"

"Xa'renul, the convict you accompanied. When did you meet him?"

I frowned. "Are you talking about Laurenx?"

"Xa'renul," she repeated crossly.

I tensed. Xa'renul.

"'Was that Laurenx in the vision?'" I had asked the Po'luxnann.

"'Not Laurenx.'" It paused. *"'Xa'renul.'"*

My jaw set tightly. Laurenx *was* Xa'renul. He was the one the Po'luxnann warned would kill me. Not unless Emikrili did it first.

"You are under the suspicion of stealing the Po'luxnann Gejruvhet from King Razhatlab. You are a wanted felon."

My fists balled at my sides. I wish my hands were at least free so I could sit. Glaring from a chained clay bed was a waste of effort.

"Parpagg is the one who did the Ggatgin on me. I didn't steal the Po'luxnann."

"Yes, that is true. Prince Parpagg did."

So she knew. "Why did Laurenx think he could trust you?"

"He doesn't. He assumed I would do as he asked. Protect you."

"Why did he think you would?"

"I am a Passagekeeper of the Bror Passage."

I frowned. "I thought you looked after the Passage and its Gates. It's your job to keep monsters from coming through."

"Yes, but my master needed the Bror Gate to be kept open."

"You let the monsters get past the Gate on purpose?"

"Yes," she smiled. "My favorite Imudmidian are ghouls, gods of parasites. Have you ever heard of them?" she smiled. "These creatures can eat anything from the inside. A young child was found in Kentucky, missing her lungs and lower intestine. She could not scream for help as a ghoul ate her alive."

Her hand clenched into the clay bed until it molded into her fist. A chill crawled up my arm as my tattoos flared and throbbed.

"You let them through," I said. "You're the traitor who let the R'uttri past the Bror Gate," I said, remembering King Razhatlab's conversation with the Councilmen in the forest.

"I sought an opportunity." she objected. "I was not born of high social class. I am a Bukol, an enslaved race," she sneered. "The entire royal family is unfit to rule with the Po'luxnann. My own people will finally have a leader who understands their needs. *I* am fit to rule. Don't you agree, Bromir?" The girl startled at the mention of her name.

"Y-yes."

Emikrili went on. "A poor child like you, a Jackle, lost a family, and your brother was also enslaved by another family. How better would it be if a Bukol, was to rule over your race? Bukols would not judge you as harshly as Temcaltiaf has towards your race," she said, turning to the girl.

The way I saw how she treated Bromir I knew that was a load of crap.

"The Po'luxnann is passed down by King Razhatlab's bloodline. You wouldn't have the Po'luxnann." She looked back at me. I quickly averted her eyes.

"Until you, it hasn't been in the hands of any other bloodline for eons. You have changed history. You altered the future." I heard something in her tone aside from hatred and anger. I heard hope. "You have proven even the lowest of races, the human race, is capable of immense power." Her tone softened.

"King Razhatlab has his faults but he has ruled with the heart of a lion and the gentleness of a butterfly. Next to rule is Prince Sixa. He regards only himself and seeks to retain his family's power over the throne." Her expression soured. "He would not care about the children of Bukol who go hungry. He treats us as though we are equally of the Jackle race," she snapped. Bromir flinched. "We are slain every day because of what we are," she spat.

"Xa'renul is no better. A formal royal who stole from the king's treasury thirty years ago! The loss of wealth was intended for a poor village in need of ration. They perished because of Xa'renul's treachery. He is a traitor to the king and a menace to Temcaltiaf," she declared.

Although her method sucked, what she said made me realize she and the Po'luxnann had much in common. They wanted to kill off every Imudmid and believed they had the right to rule over everyone and everything. Emikrili didn't care about humans even though she was a Passagekeeper for the human race. She only cared about getting even and protecting her own people. Both swore what they were doing was for the best and didn't care who suffered or who died. As long as their plan was put into motion, they were golden.

Emikrili hovered above my clay bed. "I will not kill you immediately," she chimed. "If you can make contact with King Razhatlab."

She sensed my hesitation. Her upper lip curled and twisted into a snarl. "You will make contact with King Razhatlab. I owe King Razhatlab peace of mind. I must tell him I will rule in his stead and he need not worry once he passes."

I tried to stall. "Do you really think you should be the ruler of Temcaltiaf?"

"I will say it again; *I* am fit to rule."

She grabbed my wrists and squeezed. My headache mounted as the tattooed symbols reddened on my arms.

"Po'luxnann Gejruvhet!" she shouted. "I call upon you. Come forth!" She searched my face eagerly. I shifted away from her, perplexed. She waited for…I don't know.

"It's not going to work," I said haughtily. I would never let her get the Po'luxnann. If it fell into her hands humans wouldn't have a chance of survival.

"I need more power. What was loaned to me by the Imudmidian was not enough," she hissed. "Are you not ashamed, Po'luxnann? What purpose are you to gain if D'uthne collapses?"

My back suddenly jerked and I bit my tongue, holding back a surprise yelp. The Po'luxnann was going to have to stay down. I wasn't going to let it control me either- not without a fight.

"Rotcekt," the girl shrieked, "I can feel its power. You're making it angry," she warned. Her hands cupped the sides of her ears. She looked like she was ready to throw up.

"Quiet!" Emikrili snarled. She rounded to me. "I will succeed."

I set my jaw. No way would I let her Ggatgin me. No way would the Po'luxnann control me. *No way.*

Emikrili whirled to Bromir who cowered on the other side of the cell.

"Hand me the cloth bag," Emikrili demanded. "At once!"

Her vines began to transform. Sharp spikes started to spring completely covering her arms.

Bromir scrambled to her feet. She grabbed an old brown sack sitting on the table and brought it back to Emikrili came to her with a plain old brown sack. Emikrili snatched it from Bromir's shaky hand, opened the bag and frantically rummaged inside it. With a triumphant cry her hand came out clutching...dandelions?

"They are for you," she announced.

I stared. "Um, no thanks."

Emikrili glared. "These were a gift I handed to Debnard the head chef, Prince Sixa, and Prince Parpagg," she counted off. "It's my poison that ailed the king." She said this while she threw the dandelion-looking flowers at me. "This is how Parpagg was able to extract the Po'luxnann. I will have to do the same. Unfortunately, you will not survive the Ggatgin."

Emikrili's slender vines and pink petals darkened deep crimson as they latched onto my bare chest, pulsating to the beat of my heart. I tried to move but I couldn't. No words would come out of my mouth. The feeling of numbness, started to overtake me.

Emikrili's smiled with pleasure. It was obvious she had been wanting power for so long. She didn't mind hearing me beg for my life or scream. My blood on her hands was a small price to pay.

A wave of pain burned through my scalp; my brain felt like it was melting. The woman pulled me up by my shoulders.

"Stop it," I tried to speak. No sound came out. My eyelids grew heavy and the pit of my stomach burned like lava. I started screaming silently.

Emikrili's eyes rolled in the back of her head as her whole body trembled. She started to chant. Then she did the worse thing she could possibly do. She opened her eyes and locked onto mine.

"Po'luxnann, come forth!"

She hadn't finished her words when a black orb of energy hit her square in the face. She screamed in surprise and terror- she fell to the ground.

I was breathing like I had run a 5k race. Emikrili was down on the floor, her face frozen with absolute horror. Her attention shifted across the room. There was a woman.

She was tall and slender with straight jet black hair and gray. Her skin illuminated in the dim cove and a totem animal rested on her chest. I saw her once in one of my visions, the night she met King Razhatlab in the forest.

Standing beside her was Dax, growling in rabid fury. Bromir was on the opposite side of the cell, weeping silently. Emikrili's fear turned into anger. She crawled on all fours, clutching at her chest.

"You vile beast!"

The woman didn't respond. Before Emikrili could think to speak again, Dax transformed into a shadow. It leaped at Emikrili and phased inside her. Emikrili let out an ear-splitting scream.

Her pitch rose as her eyes bulged out of their sockets. Her cries echoed and resounded off the walls long after Dax landed behind her and her body crumpled to the ground. A beating heart clamped between Dax's jaws. Emikrili died with her eyes wide open with a look of agonizing shock.

The woman silently moved to the table in the middle of the room, towards me. My muscles clenched in horror. "King Razhatlab sent me." She introduced herself. "I am Mag."

She looked over at the girl crying on the ground. "Who is your master?"

"Y-you are now my master," she squeaked.

"No," Mag said firmly. "Who was Emikrili's master?"

"Prince Sixa," Bromir squealed.

Mag's nostrils flared. "When will he arrive to check on his merchandise?" she pointed at me.

"He is expected at dusk."

"What else? Does he want the boy half dead? Alive?"

Bromir gulped. "He wanted the boy chained alive, in the Gud Cave. There he will perform the Ggatgin."

Mag did not waste another second. "Hand me the antidote to this boy's paralysis."

Bromir jumped to her feet. She was at Mag's side in a moment and gave Mag a small glass bottle. Mag unscrewed the cork and tipped the blue liquid into my mouth. It tasted like sawdust. I couldn't swallow and my gag reflex didn't work, so it quickly went down the hatch.

Mag's black pupils focused. "I haven't got much time to explain. But you need to see." She held my face in place and forced me to peer into her eyes.

A deafening roar rushed into my ears as I entered Mag's mind.

"I had a vision of what's to come."

King Razhatlab called Mag for a private meeting in Alchord. He was troubled. "The Po'luxnann will be taken from me and I will die. There will be a mortal who will soon become Bearer of the Po'luxnann and he will be my successor. Watch him well but do not intervene until after I die. He must go through the trials and tribulations for this battle to be won."

I watched when he met Mag for a second time in Alchord, worried his knowledge of the future would end up in the wrong hands. I watched as he told her what he expected of her.

He grabbed a bottled potion from Mag, the size of a classic coke bottle, and downed it in one shot. He wouldn't remember the vision or ever meeting with Mag. Neither would the Po'luxnann because he kept it from his thoughts and memories. But Mag would know it all.

I saw when she transformed into Daniel O'Keeffe, my snoring roommate at Saint Mary's hospital.

Mag was one of the firefighters that night at Black Tie. She convinced them and the police the fire originated from a lighter.

She was a bystander on the sidewalk the night I torched Laurenx's truck.

Mag transformed into a shadow in my house. She also posed as a shadow at Laurenx's place. I watched as she took on the form of a woman. It was the same lady I saw when I sat on the park bench this morning.

Mag attached her shadow form to Karin's car and followed us down the highway.

She was one of the Bee Men who took me in as a prisoner.

It was her who spotted Dax leave Laurenx's arm before Emikrili knocked him unconscious. I saw when Dax's shadow leapt into Mag's arm. I watched as she transformed into a tree's shadow in this room, watching and waiting for the right time.

I blinked, my mind jumbled. I was staring back at Mag in the present.

I trembled as I stared back into her coal eyes. "King Razhatlab sent me to you. I could only come to you like this at the time of his death."

I found my voice. "He's not dead."

She ignored the statement. "Sixa will be here soon. You must pretend you do not know the truth. Soon, he will die by my hands." Before I could ask her what she meant, the lights went out.

* * *

I don't know how long I was out. I slowly pried my eyes open as my vision adjusted in the light. The stench of dirt and manure reached my nostrils. There was another lingering smell that mixed with something copper; blood.

The only source of light was a gaslight. As feeble as it was, I could barely make out anything farther than a few feet.

I groaned, feeling more and more aches and pains towards my back and arms. I was sweating all over. Heat locked in the room without a way out. The air was so thin here it was hard to breathe.

On my wrist wound a manacle that weighed as much as a car tire. The manacle attached to the short black chains were bolted to the wall. I wore a matching set on my other arm and around my throat was another chain.

Something black and slender wound around my torso. At first I thought it was another chain attached to the wall- until it shifted and expanded to my neck like a wad of gum. I yelped.

"About time you woke up," someone said.

I was too preoccupied with the black thing around me. I wanted to fling it as far as I could but I was limited in these stupid chains.

"Stop moving, hold still."

The black thing felt heavy and cold against my bare chest, despite the damp and suffocating atmosphere in the room. I wanted it off.

"Seth, if you don't stop moving you will fall to your death, you hear me?"

I stopped and glanced up. This was the first time I saw him without his hat. Or naked.

Laurenx was chained the same way I was on the other side of the wall. His slippery skin dulled gold and his lips were charred. All of his hair, even his beard and facial hair, had shed. To say he was skin and bones was an understatement- he looked like a decaying mummy covered in a sheet of sweat. Heavy black smoke emoted out of him in tendrils. Shadows covered him like a dark, moving cloud. When the cloud shifted I noticed his skin was peeling off. It's then I realized some of that awful smell was coming from him.

"Look down," he rasped. "You're in a cave hovering over a pit." He had his eyes closed as he spoke.

I peered down. The pit was deep and wide. It was a fifty-foot vertical drop down into black sand. Everywhere I looked were rocky smooth walls with a few crags here and there. The message was clear; once you fell in the pit you weren't supposed to climb out.

Something caught my eye. There was something long moving underneath the sand. My foot nearly slipped off the crag in surprise.

"What is that?"

"Stop moving," Laurenx ordered. "I'm the reason why you're not falling to your death. That's my power holding you steady." I looked down at the black thing at my chest.

"Down there is the Zafferg, or flesh-eating worm. I counted five of them." His voice cracked mid-sentence. It sounded like it took too much energy for him to speak.

"You see the chains you're attached to? It isn't to keep you from falling. The more your body shifts, the more it loosens." He took a sharp breath of air and steadied himself. "You wouldn't want to fall in."

He demonstrated with the chain on his right wrist. Sure enough, the chains began sliding out of the wall like butter. "I've been holding you up by my power." The black, cold restraint loosened around me. I looked up at Laurenx again. "It was an hour ago when Emikrili bought you in."

I slowly inspected my chains on both arms. My right chain was longer than the one on the left. I looked down at the pit, this time with unwelcomed fear.

The sand shifted again. It rolled up clear white sand as the Zafferg roamed underneath. There was a reason why the sand was white underneath and black on top; the black was dried blood that colored the sand. I pressed my body against the rugged wall behind me. My sneakers were right on the edge.

"Why are we here?" I panted. The heat, lack of air, and the pain in my legs were making it harder to stay focused.

"We're prisoners."

"Prison," I muttered. Never thought I'd end up here. "Where's," I hesitated. "Emikrili?"

Laurenx's body shook. "Somewhere bidding her time." He changed the subject. "I can still smell your blood," he said slowly. "The Po'luxnann isn't healing you?"

Sweat dripped into my eyes. "It's tapped out of power."

Laurenx understood. "Emily's men and the bees. Did you feel that power?"

I winced. "Yeah."

"That was no ordinary power. It was Imudmidian," he said. I didn't understand where he was getting at.

"Emily is a Bukol god of vegetation," he explained. "The power she and her army possessed when they sucked my power dry weren't of Temcaltiaf. It reeked of Imudmidian power."

I frowned. "Emikrili said she was working with an Imudmidian." I inhaled the thin air. "Said he gave her power that wasn't enough."

I heard a weak whisper of thought. *Frih Kio.*

Laurenx jerked against his chains. He was freaking out like he was possessed.

"What's wrong with you, Xa'renul?" I asked.

Laurenx stopped convulsing after a while. There was nothing but the sound of shifting sand beneath us. "I am holding a leash around my god." He considered me for a moment. "You know my name."

"What else have you been hiding?" I huffed. I gripped the chains to steady myself and control my temper. "You want the Po'luxnann for yourself?"

He gave a dry laugh. "Not at all."

I didn't believe him. It took me much longer to form my words. "How is it a coincidence that you, a D'uthnian, lives in the same city as me?"

Laurenx spoke into his chest. "I lived in Miami longer than you've been alive."

"She said you were a convict," I said. I was starting to get a little lightheaded. "You stole from the king once before. You gonna deny that?"

"No, Emily was telling the truth."

If I wasn't feeling so weak and helplessly chained to the wall I'd probably bash his face in.

"When Parpagg and you were at the golf park he acted like he knew you." My tone sunk low. "Do you know him?"

"Yes, I do."

The bottom of my stomach dropped. "The Po'luxnann was right," I said. My thoughts spun wildly. "You were going to kill me after you killed Parpagg." I can't believe I almost trusted him. "That's why you didn't want me using the Po'luxnann." I started to shake. "You didn't want me alerting the R'uttri and Parpagg. You wanted to Ggatgin the Po'luxnann out of me."

A rumbling groan came of his lips. He trembled against the wall. With a loud moan, his body violently contorted against his chains. It took him a while to speak again. His voice came out hoarse. "I had every intention to return the Po'luxnann to King Razhatlab." His voice pained. "Yes I know Parpagg, and no, I didn't work with him. I never had the intent to kill you."

"Why were you ready to risk your life? Don't say you did it for me," I scowled.

Laurenx raised his head. From the distance, I saw he opened his eyes a tiny crack. I immediately looked away. His tone grew somber.

"Because…because King Razhatlab is my father."

CHAPTER SEVENTEEN

"Your Dad is King Razhatlab?"

"Yes."

"Then that means Parpagg is related to you. That's how he knows you."

"He's my uncle." There was a silent pause.

"I thought my family had issues," I muttered. "Why aren't you in your world?"

He didn't answer right away. "I'm an escaped convict."

My eyebrows rose. I remembered what Emikrili said. "You stole from King Razhatlab?"

He let out a deep guttural sound. Thick black smoke thickened and coiled around him. The building pressure in the small space choked out the thin air.

"Stop it," I wheezed.

"I did not steal from my father," he whispered. "Parpagg framed me. I was young. I was naïve to trust in him. He knew I would one day be a successor to the throne. My father is first born, as I am among my siblings. I did not want to rule. I couldn't rule, because of what I am." His body began to spasm.

"What… do you mean?" I panted. My vision started to swim.

"I am not full blood Temcaltiaf and I am also an Imudmid. I am considered an abomination to my people. Among all worlds."

I recalled the Po'luxnann called him that; an abomination. The Po'luxnann especially didn't like anyone who was Imudmidian. It wanted to exterminate them, after all.

"Father didn't care what I was but I didn't want the title of king, so I trusted Parpagg to help me escape Temcaltiaf. And I did. But Parpagg betrayed me and sold me into slavery, then hid the treasury he stole from my father. I was framed for the theft and my people assumed I was a traitor. I'm sure my family thought I was dead after so many years. In reality, after my enslavement I ended up in your world."

"Returning the Po'luxnann was a way for you to make things right with your people and King Razhatlab?" I concluded.

"Yes."

"What type of Imudmidian are you? Vampire?"

A garbled laugh rattled his chest. His breathing was cut short when his body twisted again. I heard a crack of bones. Laurenx panted harder until his face winced with pain. "You will wish you didn't know but you will. Very soon."

"What do you mean?"

"You haven't worked out why you're in a cage trapped here alone with me?" he asked. "Emily wants the Po'luxnann. She is using me to get it out of you," he gasped. "I will go through the change. I'll be overcome by my god."

I heard the rustling sand beneath us. "What is your god?"

Laurenx never looked so fragile. His shoulders sagged. "My god is Death."

"Death?"

"*Death.*"

Neither of us spoke for a while. I couldn't bring myself to ask what he meant. He eventually broke the silence.

"My mother and father, King Razhatlab, are Temcaltiafan. The king's god was the Po'luxnann; righteous fire." He wheezed before taking another pained breath. "With the Po'luxnann's power, my father could kill whomever he believes is guilty with a single thought. My mother's god was the healer. When she bore me, a dozen R'uttri and Imudmidians attacked her, poisoned her womb. She later died but she healed me. I survived, born cursed. My father said I was too stubborn to die, and that was a trait I received from him." He shuddered against his chains. "I possess the same diet as any R'uttri; hunger for the living. But every now and then I get the munchies for a R'uttri."

He said it so casually it made my skin crawl. My thoughts went back to the vision of the R'uttri I saw in his ice chest.

"The pendants I handed you were a loan. The king gave them to me as a gift on my first birthday. It didn't cure me of wanting to eat my own father but it gave me control over my hunger." A sudden hiss poured out of his lips and his body writhed in agony. For a split moment the black gob on my chest loosened and I quickly caught my balance.

Laurenx howled in anguish. In a choking spasm, he expelled vomit. It streamed out of his mouth and nose as he continued to rock against his chains. This time it took him a while longer to recover. The black goo around me disappeared.

Laurenx was completely gray now. Drool dangled from his chin and dripped to his chest. He could hardly lift his head now. "I haven't had much control over myself since I lent the pendants to you," he coughed. "You need to understand you have to kill me."

A shiver went down my spine. I didn't like this side of Laurenx. He was tougher than this. He was the kind of guy who could hold his own against Parpagg. He was a royal prince who escaped slavery, for goodness sake. Why should he give up now?

"Why?"

"Emily is betting on me to kill you," he rasped. My knees almost gave out. "Once I kill you, the Po'luxnann will have no choice but to jump into the next available vessel. Emily will make sure she'll be there when it does."

My pulse quickened. "You said you didn't come to kill me for the Po'luxnann."

"I did. But I cannot change the nature of what I am."

"Just don't kill me," I said.

His body and teeth rattled as he spoke. "I am going to kill you and there is nothing you can do about it. Kill me before I kill you."

"No."

A cry erupted from his lips. His body jerked harder, threatening to throw him off the ledge. "You don't have much of a choice, Seth," he moaned. "Kill me before I kill you. Before Emily possesses the Po'luxnann. Command the Po'luxnann to kill me then take control of it. You can save yourself. Save your world and mine."

"No," I said. "You can fight."

"KILL ME!" The tendrils around Laurenx struck the rock beside my head. I watched it crumble down into the pit.

"I can't control it anymore," Laurenx quivered. "Seth, I never told you what god my mother was after the attack. She was a healer who became legion. She turned into a monster, do you understand? A legion of spirits all rolled up in flesh. When I was born, I inherited her god."

Laurenx's head rose again. His brown eyes sank deep within their sockets. They were full of regret and remorse. He struggled to keep his gaze locked to mine. "You don't have much time."

I heard the Po'luxnann suddenly speak. I shifted the pendants up my neck as I bowed my head.

Let me in. We will not survive if he loses to his god.

The Po'luxnann sounded panicked. Had it also given up?

"What are you doing? Praying?"

I slightly rose my head.

"God wouldn't want to save me," Laurenx told me. "Of what I am. What I've done."

His words struck me. It's what Karin told me Chessie felt about her rape. They both believed they weren't worth saving. A foreign sound rumbled. My heart drummed out of my chest as it grew louder.

Something above us creaked- the ceiling door flew open and light fell through the cell. Emikrili dropped through the hole and stood onto a crag across me. Two Himaks hovered behind, their dragonfly wings buzzing.

The sight of them sent my heart racing. It wasn't so long ago I forgot how she tried to rip the Po'luxnann out of me.

I shook my head as a way to shake off the dread and fear. It wasn't Emikrili. Dax killed her.

"Hello again," Mag greeted. "Today is a day for a funeral and celebration," she announced. "Your death and my time to rule."

Laurenx sneered. "You don't deserve the Po'luxnann."

"And yet you do?" she said. "Temcaltiaf will finally have a new order where royals will be slaves."

If I hadn't known better, I would have believed Mag was Emikrili. She leaped from her crag only to land next to me. "You humans wouldn't fare well with them around." She jerked her head to Laurenx. "The R'uttri appreciate a good feast. They enjoy the hunt."

An index finger lightly touched my hand and flinched. Her touch was the equivalent of getting pricked by a cold metal poker. I hissed in pain.

Laurenx reacted. He sounded like a wild animal. Mag was selling her performance so well the Himaks looked pleased.

"The R'uttri enjoy savoring their meals. They may eat the human fingers first." She raised my limp hand and gently placed it back down. She traced a line with her index finger down my pant leg above the manacle. Her nails left a scorching cold trail over the fabric of my jeans and burned right through my skin. I shouted as blood trickled down my leg. I was slowly losing focus.

"They love watching their food squirm and cry. The R'uttri would snap their jaws around the knee joint. They're very careful not to burst a major artery for fear of draining their prey too soon," she murmured.

"The artery is what they devour last to savor the warmth. I fancy them." She cupped a hand under my chin and raised my head. She smiled.

I gazed back with dull apprehension. If she wanted to kill me she should get it over with.

Emikrili once said an Imudmidian gave her power and it crossed my mind once or twice since Mag had given King Razhatlab gifts: the seashell, the memory loss potion, and the invisibility ring- Frih Kio wasn't the real enemy. It was possible Mag killed Emikrili before Emikrili could reveal Mag's real plan; to keep the Po'luxnann for herself.

"King Razhatlab, the peace treaty between the Imudmid, Temcaltiaf and Bror Passage will be eradicated." She gripped a manacled wrist.

"Time for a new world order." She slashed her sharp nails over my wrist. I screamed until my throat went raw. Blood streamed down my elbow.

I must have blacked out.

I no longer held Mag's attention. She was on the other side of the cave, caressing Laurenx's face. His jaw extended and his mouth twisted into a snarl. His limbs were growing out long, thin, and spiny.

"It won't be long until he kills you," Mag said to me. "He hasn't eaten anything for very long, I can tell." She rose an eyebrow at Laurenx again. "You've sworn off eating humans, haven't you?"

Laurenx bucked against his chains and Mag took a cautious step back

The Po'luxnann beat against the barriers of my mind with one giant blow. Before I lost total control over my body, my last thought was I wasn't going to die alone.

I wish I remembered how to smile. I knew it was the end for us, and I wanted Laurenx to know I was cool about dying- it was going to be okay.

I already had an experience with death today and it wasn't all that bad. Laurenx could give in to his god and I could give in to the Po'luxnann. I was tired of fighting and maybe it was time to exit this life.

Mag screeched, interrupting my thoughts. Three figures flashed into the cave. I rocked my head off my chest and squinted.

Their presence permeated the air. The R'uttri I saw dead in Laurenx's freezer was nothing compared to these guys. Their faces were skeletal and slimy black, as though oil dripped from the pores of their skin. They possessed no visible eyeballs but the depth of their eye sockets flickered. I shuddered. With eyes so black you wouldn't notice them until they blinked. The R'uttri's arms were spiny. Long talons went from their elbows and bent out at an awkward angle.

The black rags they wore only gave them the illusion of a body when there was none. The black energy and oil that clung to them were heavy and empty at the same time. In one second, they were formless and present but a second later they were shimmering out of focus. It was as if reality couldn't bend to maintain their presence. They were nightmares, something that wasn't supposed to exist in the Bror Passage but were. I slowly blinked.

Standing a few yards was a man wearing a dignified scowl.

"M-my prince," Mag stuttered. She couldn't have been surprised. She knew Sixa was coming.

The man regarded her coldly. "You betrayed me."

His long velvet and black cape widened around him like a bat's wings. The power around him expanded and Mag took a frightful step back.

"W-what? Why?" Himaks took their stance to protect Mag. Bee maces rose. "You will not threaten her," one proclaimed.

Before another word was spoken, a R'uttri ghosted in front of him. A rotting talon plunged into his throat like a razor. The Himak was dead before he knew it.

The last Himak shifted for an attack far too late. Two R'uttri killed them in moments, the same way their friend did with the first.

Their bodies' twitched, brown blood gushing. The R'uttri made guttural sounds in unison, looking at the writhing bodies with clicking talons. Sixa gave them a brief nod. Faster than my eyes could follow, three R'uttri were on the dead Himaks like vultures.

I heard a snarl of teeth, the crushing of bone and tendon. The feasting took all of one minute. I thought I was ready for death. I was wrong. Once again, fear held me captive. My bladder emptied itself.

"I know you performed the Ggatgin," Sixa said smoothly to Mag. "I can smell the power in the air." He sniffed for emphasis. I wasn't so sure he sniffed my piss.

He marched toward Mag then fastened his hand around her throat. Her eyes enlarged as he cut off her air supply. He watched as she clawed his arms, trying to pry him off. She stopped moving. Sixa flung her against the cave wall and she fell like a discarded rag, toppling into the pit.

The man regarded Laurenx. "Of all the places to find you!" He caught sight of the movement below. "Give me a moment." He casually stepped off a crag then landed in the pit next to Mag.

As soon as he landed, the ground trembled and five heads rose out of the sand. The heads shrilled in unison, extending their mouths wide, revealing vicious sharp teeth.

Sixa didn't blink. He centered himself, extending his arms above him as sparks spit out of his fingers until they formed a truck-sized fireball. The fireball split into five and aimed for the creatures simultaneously.

The Zafferg never stood a chance. They all screeched, jumped, and crashed into one another as they scorched to death.

Sixa casually shook the soot from his coat then peered down at Mag who was still as stone. "I want to be the one to kill her slowly." Sixa stared up at Laurenx from below. "You are right where I want to gut you." He turned to me. "We finally meet." He didn't mind looking into my eyes.

Inside this musky prison, Sixa held a dignified composure in his black tunic and velvet coat that wrapped around his black pants and boots. His black hair pulled back into a red ribbon from his round golden face.

His face, especially his dark brown eyes, reminded me of King Razhatlab's- it was like I was staring at a younger version of the king.

The Po'luxnann whispered an emotion of terror. It didn't believe Prince Sixa was anything like King Razhatlab. Not even close.

"Sixa," Laurenx roared.

He took a few steps closer until he was directly in La09urenx's line of sight. "Xa'renul. But I hear you don't go by that name," he cocked his head. "Your new alias is Laurenx, I presume?"

"Are you working for Parpagg?" Laurenx bellowed.

"Certainly. Only, he worked for me." The prince's eyes darkened to black stars. They were glowing. "The fool betrayed me. We agreed he would retrieve the Po'luxnann and I would later pry open the Imudmid Gate."

"He betrayed you. Then you sent the R'uttri after him into the Bror Passage to get the Po'luxnann back. I'm sure you killed him by now."

"I can't take all the credit, but yes he's dead."

Laurenx didn't seem to care. "Why break open the Imudmid Gate?"

"To combine all territories then rule them as one. I would destroy the undesirables of the Imudmidian race as well," he narrowed his glowing eyes. "I am doing what the king taught me; to do whatever it takes to get on top." He paused for dramatic effect. "The king grew soft. He allowed you to *live*. An abomination permitted to dwell in the same house our ancestors built. They would weep in their graves." Prince Sixa's fists sparked a flame.

"To answer your following question, yes, I planned to murder the king. Yes, I work with Frih Kio." He pointed a finger up in the air. "Yes, I hired Emikrili to create the poison, and hired the chef to give it to the king. But don't you worry about Father coming to the party," he said.

Sixa suddenly flashed before me. He dwarfed me by at least two feet. Aside from his great height, his radiating power loomed over me like a tsunami. I cowered in his presence.

"I should run the boy's blood faster, wouldn't you say Xa'renul?" he called out. I had his undivided attention now. "It's going to be an excruciating death for you." I believed him.

The Po'luxnann attacked against my force of will, threatening to bury me into unconsciousness. If I was going to die, I was going to experience it in my own mind.

I pictured an image of Chessie crying beside Laurenx. I knew she wasn't weeping because of me.

Razhatlab was wrong. I couldn't save the world.

"I tried to help you. You kept pushing me away," I told Chessie and Mom. "I did what I could." I saw Dad pacing up and down the pit.

I replayed the day he left for the last of his bags. Mom was on her knees begging from the floor of the pit, wailing for him to stay.

"You suck. You cheated on Mom and left us," I muttered. Sixa's eyebrows rose. To him, I probably looked like a lunatic.

Let me in. You have had your trust betrayed time and time again. I want to create a utopia. There will never be sadness. No more betrayal. I will bring order and peace.

Sixa was still speaking. I closed my eyes again.

You thought that was going to hurt me, I told the Po'luxnann. With those memories.

The Po'luxnann sounded frustrated and in panic. *You are a chained prisoner to a wall. You are dying. You have no hope of freedom. You will die here alone, covered in your human waste.*

King Razhatlab once said I should use what the Po'luxnann exploited against my fears and my anger. I now found its own weakness.

You're afraid of your own failures, I said. You said you were created for peace and order. You think you failed that.

I do not have human emotions of failure. I am simply turning back to what I was created to do.

You don't have to be human to be ashamed of failing and you do care about Imudmidians killing and Temcaltiaf falling apart. You wanted peace and order but everyone used you for their own selfishness and rejected you. It made you feel bad about who you are, I said, connecting the dots.

But the truth is, you feel guilty for what you couldn't control. You let Parpagg make his plans with Sixa to steal you because you gave up. I get it. You only wanted to start the world all over again because things haven't worked out the way you wanted it to.

Well, guess what? That's life. Sometimes it doesn't go as planned. It doesn't mean we give up. We try again. Make a fresh start.

Without words, I let it see into my memories. They still hurt, being vulnerable by showing someone else my scars. But I allowed it to see when Chessie broke up with me in the truck.

I lost my best friend, I told it.

I wanted the Po'luxnann to relive the look my mother gave when I left the house. Or the look she gave Logan because she didn't know how to talk to me. That look also revealed how much she feared losing Logan over me. She betrayed me.

People let us down but we love them anyway, I said.

The Po'luxnann saw the day Dad packed the last of his bags and Mom clutched at his shins, begging for him not to go. The look of pity he gave her will never erase from my mind.

I allowed the Po'luxnann to feel those moments that showed the amount of guilt I carried and never let go. I felt responsible for what happened to Chessie and I blamed myself for it. Dad pushed Mom away and I wasn't there for her when she needed me, too.

The shame I felt threatened to drown me. The Po'luxnann tremored under the weight of my emotions. I went on to explain.

For a long time I was angry because what I had in mind for my life and how it turned out left me feeling jaded. My Dad threw away a future I saw with him, with my Mom, and I. I have to accept things as they are. Dad moved on and built a life for himself with another family. Chessie didn't want me to be a boyfriend or a friend to her- I just don't fit into her world anymore. It sucks, it really does. But I'll survive. I got to start living for myself.

You can't control everything, no matter how far you can see into the future, I told the Po'luxnann. So let the past go. I can't keep living from back then, I declared. You need to do the same.

The Po'luxnann didn't speak right away.

Very well.

Very well, what?

You are right and I agree.

Do you?

I will also test your theory.

What does that mean?

I will try again. I will succumb to you as Bearer for now.

I breathed a mental sigh of relief.

It should be clear to you I cannot overcome you, no matter my efforts. The human will is a definite powerful force.

The Po'luxnann didn't mention it, but I knew it was dying and I was its only chance for survival; it was giving in on a technicality. We wouldn't be celebrating being buddies just yet.

I cauterized your wounds before Sixa made his appearance.

The Po'luxnann used most of its dwindling power to save me from bleeding to death under Mag's claws. If I died, it also died, and saving me was more of a self-preservation thing than a sacrifice of good intentions.

During our mental conversation, the beast Xa'renul has been losing the battle against his god. The scent of your blood and his antagonistic brother have overwhelmed him.

We need to get past Sixa and get the Gates patched up, I said. But how? I asked. We were running out of time.

Are you prepared to do what must be done?

Yes.

You may not survive this. Myself as well. To close the Gates would take my entire conduit of power. If you live, your former life will be no more. I have accepted you as my Bearer. You are made a king.

That didn't matter. We needed to get the Gates shut and Passages sealed. No matter what.

Like a knock on the door, my mind opened up to a visitor. He had been waiting.

Razhatlab appeared and we exchanged a few words; I couldn't remember them now.

"What have you done, son?" King Razhatlab had taken over my body and used me as a mouthpiece. Sixa blinked. It didn't take him long to figure it out.

He sneered. "Even in death you haunt me." Sixa turned away from us. He placed his hands behind him, back stretched with his head held high. "Relax, Father, I didn't come for a fight in the sandbox," he announced cordially.

"You can't bear to face me, son? You murdered me," King Razhatlab said. "Why?"

Sixa quickly rounded at us. "To ensure the crown would be mine."

"Why, Sixa?"

Sixa countered. "Why must the suns burn bright? Why was Xa'renul born first? *Why did you murder my mother?"* he seethed.

"You know very well your mother did not die by my hands," King Razhatlab said.

"You banished her!" Sixa lost his temper. The energy he harbored coiled around him and hissed like a viper, ready to strike. His mouth thinned as his eyes glowed brighter. "I am what I am, as you are what you are, Father. Dead."

He neared and I could feel the charge of his power pricking against my skin. "No quicker than the snap of my fingers you would gladly give this rat," he scorned at Laurenx, "the Po'luxnann Gejruvhet." Sixa wasn't holding back his power.

"It's the same old story with Xa'renul. He left the kingdom and instead of punishing him, he'll get off with a demerit." His expression soured. "You were hopeful all these years, waiting for him to show up to take over the kingdom while me, your loyal son who has been by your side like a dog, isn't acknowledged once."

"You're a fool, son," King Razhatlab whispered. "To plot with Frih Kio and Parpagg to rid of me. Your intentions towards the crown prove you were never worthy of the throne." King Razhatlab faded into the background of my mind. I was now in control.

"You killed him," Laurenx said. The cave's temperature had dropped dramatically and the lanterns feebly flickered.

"You murdered my father!"

Black smoke flew out of Laurenx and at Sixa who held his ground. Faces of what looked like people with long open mouths and hollow eyes, built into the smoke. An emotional current of torture, wrath, and destruction hit Sixa square in the chest. It drove him straight into the pit onto his back.

Before Sixa could gather his feet from under him, the smoke funneled around him until he was covered in a sea of darkness. I felt emotions of emptiness. There was no light, no joy, and no hope.

Laurenx once mentioned he was a legion and those faces were spirits trapped inside of him.

The R'uttri didn't seem to be so happy about Laurenx's transformation. They also were in no hurry to help Sixa.

With one final jerk of his body, the chains that held Laurenx released from the rocks. In one swipe, Laurenx unclasped the manacles and threw them aside and they fell, clattering down below. Sixa managed to burst himself into flames and the spirits burned in the light. Sixa tore himself free from the consuming smoke and whirled around. It was the first time I saw him look surprised.

"Leave at once, Seth!" Mag shouted from the pit below.

The Po'luxnann drummed up its power, filling me up like a reservoir. I yanked my wrists free from the wall. That caught Laurenx's attention. He watched me through gaunt black irises. With his knees bent he lunged over the cavern, clearing the distance between us. Mag shadowed before Sixa in her original form.

"Go, boy!" she yelled as she pulled him back.

I shouted the first place I could think of. "Napoleon Park!"

My body rose. Very quickly I disappeared through a funnel of darkness. My shoes hit concrete and I stumbled on the pavement. The cemetery was the only place I was sure there wouldn't be an audience.

The moon was full and high in the sky. The wind and rain slapped hard on headstones and grass.

Laurenx had crouched down and an inhuman noise came out of him. I clasped my hands over my ears, drowning out the Song of Death.

I wanted to call out his name, but in that moment I forgot which name to call- Laurenx wasn't Laurenx anymore. His bowed head snapped up as though he heard my thoughts.

Then I saw his face.

It wasn't a person. The body was a black spiny, gray creature. Leeches, worms, and maggots ate at the rotting corpse. Tendon and muscle hung off its bones as blood visibly squeezed out of its remaining flesh.

When I held its full gaze, I was compelled to stab myself in the heart to know if it was still beating, that I was still alive and it hadn't obliterated me.

Death came to me in a cloud of ashes and smoke- the Po'luxnann and I caught his momentum. I stepped into the background in my body and allowed the Po'luxnann handle the fight.

Don't kill him, I warned the Po'luxnann.

The Po'luxnann flinched- Death's fingertips were centimeters from my face- I deflected his attack with a green barrier and his attack hit against it. I flashed and a black haze trailed behind.

He will kill us, the Po'luxnann feared.

My fingers tingled, then my right hand shook. With a raging sound, the Po'luxnann called out its power. The trees swayed and the grass beneath my feet quaked. The Po'luxnann Gejruvhet called up for their life to surrender to it.

The call was short and immediate- the grass around us withered and the nearby oak tree shrieked. I held in my palm the power of light and life.

He is an Imudmidian and he is Death. He will exterminate us without thought.

I threw a green energy ball at Laurenx but Death smoothly evaded and slashed his claws into my shoulder. Death followed with another extended hand and I dodged it in time, flashing away. My shoulder hissed where Death struck- it didn't slow down to gloat or bask in his attack.

With Death's back turned, I shot out my own jet ray. A black haze settled around it and my attack slid off Death like oil. It spun to face me.

I looked past the monster. From the short time I've known Laurenx, he wasn't the most easygoing guy and he was definitely a jackass. But Laurenx tried to protect me from Parpagg. He wanted to do the right thing by helping me deliver the Po'luxnann to King Razhatlab. That had to count for something.

Laurenx was born Death, but he's choosing not to be evil, I told the Po'luxnann. He has the power to say no to himself. I bet he fights with himself every day to be normal.

Another green energy bolt released from my palms but Death dodged it again without losing speed. It wasn't stopping to land a blow as it rushed at me again. I released an energy barrier from the attack- Death's blow blasted hard against my shield, rattling my teeth. The Po'luxnann screeched in agony.

Death came at us and struck against my barrier. It shimmered and hit the barrier again and again. The attack bounced off headstones and trees, instantly setting them ablaze. Every blow I blocked knocked the wind out of my sails. I knew I couldn't keep this up for very long.

If you intend to save him act now, the Po'luxnann urged.

I eased down the barrier and Death latched onto my throat. I flung the pendants over its head and Death immediately reacted.

It shrieked in pain but it never lessened its grip around my throat. I bit my tongue and forced the Death Lock on Death.

We both fell into the same vision.

We witnessed how Death would not be killed for an indescribable amount of time until its final battle in the End of Days. Instead of waiting for Death to see its own demise, I showed it mine. We saw my death by his hands in the next few moments. I tasted some of Death's power as it tried to consume me.

Darkness: empty and cold, filled me. I couldn't deflect its power without tasting some of its bitterness and hatred Laurenx had within him. Before I could succumb to it, I absorbed half its attack and allowed Laurenx to feel what he was doing to me, how he was torturing me. The Po'luxnann emptied the power of light and life into him.

Death's resounding shriek echoed throughout the cemetery.

I forced Laurenx to see himself through my eyes. The eyes were the mirror to his soul and I was showing his. I had to prove he wasn't the monster he thought he was. He wasn't his god; he was Laurenx.

We entered far deeper into the Death Lock until King Razhatlab showed us his very own death.

Sixa appeared before him in his chambers. King Razhatlab had expected him. He calmly sat in his chair. The fireplace crackled with light.

"Hello, son."

"Father." King Razhatlab's face was drawn.

A white ball of magnificent power engulfed from Sixa's palm until it expanded itself, swallowing everything it touched. The power hesitated at King Razhatlab's feet, sizzling the hem of his robes. King Razhatlab looked past the shining light and directly into his son's eyes.

"I love you, son."

Without another word, King Razhatlab rose to his feet, touching the toxic, scorching light.

When he stood full height, he beamed brighter than any moon until he disintegrated at Sixa's feet.

Sixa's arm fell to his side and the raging ball of light was gone. It was as though it was never there.

Sixa went over to inspect his handiwork in the glow of the fireplace. He leaned over his father's bones and placed a hand into the ashes. He grounded them in his fist, whispering a final word.

His head bowed. "Goodbye."

A pressure drew into the room. His jaw tensed. Visitors.

The king's guards were flashing in.

Sixa quickly flashed out of sight.

Death fell to its knees.

"Come back to me, son."

I whirled around. King Razhatlab was now standing beside me, looking very healthy and alive. Death immediately rose. Its face peeled away like a mask until Laurenx's face returned.

"Father."

Devastation etched on King's Razhatlab's features. "I am so very sorry, my son." Laurenx struggled to speak.

"Why?"

"For letting you go."

Laurenx stepped closer to his father. "It is I who disappointed you, my king" he lowered his head. King Razhatlab shook his head.

"Stop, my son." He motioned him to straighten. "You did not allow your god become your master. I am most proud of you."

Laurenx appeared to be at a loss for words. He cleared his throat. "How much time do we have?"

King Razhatlab smiled. "Enough."

The Po'luxnann interrupted. "King Razhatlab, we need to seal the Gates now." The king slowly tore his eyes away from his son and sternly nodded. He held out his hands.

"If you may." I placed my hands in his. He nodded again.

The air around us chilled and in front of us materialized a giant hole.

Bright gold and white light whirled in between it; it was like getting caught in a lightning storm. It buzzed my teeth and rose the hairs on my skin. I didn't dare look into the portal. For one, it was too *bright*, and two, the power transferring between the king and I was able to tear me apart like a bug on a windshield.

I held on as three Passage Gates appeared as tall and grand as the Eiffel tower.

The first Gate to the Bror Passage was the first to close. The walls of the Passage mended itself, block by block as I thought of Chessie, my Mom, my friends.

We turned to the Imudmid Gate. It was dark crimson and highly detailed carvings etched on its surface. It was then I started to realize the carvings were creatures. And they were alive.

My nose started to bleed and my knees began to buckle. Creatures clawed and kicked and sent their rage towards the walls I attempted to mend. I could feel their resistance. Some tried to make a run for the Bror Gate and its Passage. I blasted them with righteous fire and many scurried inside their Gate for refuge.

I willed the Imudmid Gate to close, same as I did with the Bror Gate. The Po'luxnann resisted.

"What are you doing?" I shouted.

"Po'luxnann, you should be wise," King Razhatlab warned. "Think with your heart, not your head."

They are the vilest of all gods, the Po'luxnann said. *Their powers and purpose are tied to destruction. They need to burn.*

"Don't lump all of Imudmid or Temcaltiaf evil," I said.

"Laurenx didn't give in to his god. I can't close those Gates if you don't help us," I said. "Po'luxnann. Please."

I looked at King Razhatlab. He nodded gravely. "Po'luxnann Gejruvhet, we can change all worlds. Mass genocide is not the way. To change the world, we must change first," the king explained.

"We can start again. The right way," I added.

King Razhatlab continued. "This boy has chosen to give up his life for strangers and creatures that have torn into his world and attacked his people. Seth sees into the hearts of beasts rather than what they are. He saw you for what you truly are. Believe in this boy," King Razhatlab strongly urged.

Razhatlab, the Po'luxnann uttered. I felt its power reverberate through my bones. Instead of the dark, foreboding presence I've felt since I was its Bearer, its power now felt lighter, brighter, and gentler, like a glow of sunshine floating in an autumn breeze. As its power swelled through us, the Po'luxnann embraced the king and I.

It wasn't enough to will the Gates closed. I allowed the Po'luxnann take full control over my body. I let go of my fears and doubts. As the creatures roared and the Gates patched up, I gave in my heart. I thought about King Razhatlab and the life he sacrificed. I thought about Laurenx, Vaora, and Bromir. Every single one of those lives were worth saving.

The doors to the Temcaltiaf and Imudmid Gate closed with a loud BANG. All three Passages were officially sealed. All three Gates vanished and the wind calmed.

The Po'luxnann's power receded until my own strength left me.

Before I hit the ground, arms held me. "You did well, Seth Castillo. No sugar coating."

CHAPTER EIGHTEEN

A bright light beamed before my face. I turned my head away from it, groaning. I opened my eyes.

I was in a familiar room. I recognized the picture frames sitting on the table. I motioned to sit and the darkroom swayed.

"Take it easy." I felt a hand push me down. I winced up at Laurenx. My mouth moved to say something but his appearance stopped me. He wasn't wearing his hat.

His face lost weight and his lips were cut and swollen. A deep cut spread from his left cheek and was bandaged haphazardly. As far as I could tell, the cuts that zigzagged across his face, arms, and neck looked freshly inflicted. He looked a mess, but he was Laurenx. Only thinner and grayer.

"You look horrible."

One emotion flooded out of him and I felt it: a mix of sadness and humor; bittersweet. "I'll live."

I scrutinized him. "I'm under control," he insisted. He thumbed at his neck and pulled out the pendants. They shined under the table lamp. "I have them back because of you." His lips twitched. Was that almost a smile?

"You don't need them anymore. You have control over your god."

I smiled. "Not bad for a weak human, right?"

He winced. "Don't push it. You have to keep your mind and soul fortified. It only takes one slip up before the Po'luxnann overtakes you."

"Yeah. I can't look at mirrors or people straight in the eye anymore."

"I'm glad you remember."

His mouth twitched again."

"Thanks for not killing me," I said.

"You, too." He didn't say anything else. He didn't have to.

I looked around. I was lying on my bed, in my room. My tiny, small, cramped room. Never had I been so thrilled to be on my creaky bed. I gazed out my window into the night. My ears picked up the crickets chirping happily outside. I was really home.

"You've been out a couple days," Laurenx informed. "They brought you here."

"They?"

"Mag. The Awcers."

"Awcers?"

"Temcaltiaf's Secret Service."

I nodded. "Where's my mom?"

"Your mother is sleeping in her bedroom. She came out of the Reznem's Care, full recovery."

My spirit soared. Mom was okay.

I wanted to leap out of bed but Laurenx stopped me. "She doesn't remember what happened to her and neither does that man. The only memory they will have when they wake up is the night you destroyed that truck."

I settled back in bed, frowning. "How long ago was that night?"

"A week ago. Temcaltiaf's cleanup crew patched up the living room and anything else Parpagg might have destroyed," he said. "Just so you're clear, in about a week things will continue like nothing happened. The mess Parpagg left behind in the living room is all tidy. The trance your mother is experiencing will fade." I nodded again. All that mattered to me was mom. She was safe.

"You're not curious about the Passages?"

"I was getting to that," I said.

He grunted. "The Passages are all sealed and the Gates are fortified. I give it another thousand years before we need to worry about them chipping apart," he said. "You saved all worlds. Everyone."

"So everything's back to the way it was."

We both knew that wasn't true. I guess it was the thing to say. One noticeable difference was that a part of my mind that connected me to King Razhatlab was gone.

My hands formed a fist. Green sparks suddenly began flying out of my left hand. This new power surprised me.

Laurenx gave an inquisitive look and I unclenched my fist and shook my hand to put it out. When it was gone, I inspected my fingers and wiggled. This power was pretty cool. "Where's Sixa?"

I could feel a twister roaring in Laurenx's mind now. "Disappeared."

I looked away.

"We'll find him," he swore.

It went quiet. All that was heard was the shuffling of feet outside the room. "What about Princess Vaora, your sister?" I asked.

"Still in prison. Mag's trying to get her out. Only a matter of time, she says. All guilty parties who framed her and sided with Sixa are either arrested or on the run." His tone turned sour. "I would be careful around

Mag." Before I could ask, Laurenx shot me a glare. "There are ears outside of this room."

We looked at each other. We both didn't trust Mag. It seemed like for the first time we actually agreed on something. "Your job is finally over, right?"

"You mean babysitting a pain in my rear? " he said.

"Something like that."

His lip managed to twitch again.

"What's next for you?"

He lifted his hands. Green glowing vines intertwined and weaved into thin bracelets, locking his wrists in place. Red and black orbs of light snaked within the vines. The energy pulsating through them didn't look too friendly.

The door to my room opened and Mag appeared. She stood at the threshold. I sat up in surprise.

Behind her stood five men in the hallway, covered in deep blue robes and hoods. They were so tall they had to bend their necks to keep from touching the ceiling. Each carried a metal pole as long as a baton and as thick as a baseball bat. Suppressed energy, broad and invisible as a heat wave in summer, drifted into the room. The Po'luxnann stirred, already on guard. Its cool energy, like a breeze, brushed against my skin, cooling me off.

Mag stepped inside. "Your time has ended." She looked directly at Laurenx. "You have exceeded your five minutes from when he awoke."

"I know, a deal's a deal," Laurenx said. Before he lifted himself from the bed two men had already joined inside the cramped space. They held Laurenx firmly on each side of him and yanked him forward by his forearms. Laurenx gave me a sidelong glance.

"See you around, kid."

Aside from the handcuffs around Laurenx's wrists, he had cuffs wrapped around his ankles. The men started half dragging him out. I stood.

"Wait a second." More heat rolled into the room. The men purposely ignored me and continued out into the hall.

I wanted them to listen. "I'm trying to talk," I shouted. I siphoned a wind in the hall, blowing their hoods back. "What is going on?" I looked at the men. They rounded and me with alarming gold gleaming eyes.

"You heard him," Mag spoke. The tense energy lingered. It was starting to feel like a preheated oven. Defensively, tattoos instantly sparked red on my forearm. "Where are you taking him?"

No one wanted to volunteer the answer right away.

"Temcaltiaf's Secret Service. They're Awcers," Laurenx nodded to the men. "I'm headed for prison."

"For what?"

Laurenx looked away. "I've been a wanted man for years."

I shook my head, disbelieving. "This isn't right. You helped me."

On Mag's signal, the men nudged him abruptly forward. "It's fine. Worry about yourself," Laurenx said. Before I could say another word, Laurenx walked away with the two men. They flashed out of the room. He was gone.

"I am pleased to see you awake," Mag told me. She spoke as if nothing happened.

"Why is he arrested?" A wind picked up in the room. Mag didn't move a muscle. Unlike Laurenx, her lack of reaction over the Po'luxnann made me nervous. I practiced deep breathing. When I was calm again, the wind stopped.

"He is an escaped convict," Mag said. "He will await trial like any criminal would."

I couldn't believe it. "He helped save my Passage. Your world, too."

She took Laurenx's empty seat. "That is correct. For now, he has been granted a trial on the account of assisting in preserving the Gates and Passages. He has been arrested for his thievery against the kingdom, and recently treason, kidnapping, murder, and conspiracy against the late Temcaltiaf king. More counts of conviction are going for his head."

"Laurenx didn't steal from the king; he was set up by Parpagg. He never sided with Parpagg," I said. "None of us did."

"I know," she answered simply. I was able to feel Laurenx's emotions and the Awcer's energy. With Mag, there was nothing beneath the waters. It's as if she was an empty vessel.

"Sixa and several members of the Council are claiming his involvement in the disappearance of the Po'luxnann. Vaora will vouch for him." She paused briefly. "And so will you as king."

When I didn't respond Mag changed the subject. "The Awcers outside are insurance in case you plan to run away with the Po'luxnann. To everyone, you might as well have conspired for the Po'luxnann. You must first set foot in D'uthne and await an official meeting.

"I'm under house arrest?"

"Yes."

"When will they know I'm innocent? When can I plead my case?"

"I have told you. We will wait for an official summons meeting in D'uthne by the Council."

I frowned. I finally took a seat on my bed. "Anything else?"

"Before he died, King Razhatlab ordered me to take part in the Council of Temcaltiaf. This decree is not made public, and only one other Council member knows the true reason I was allowed to sit through the meeting that declared your sentence under house arrest." She whispered the last part. "This visit is presumed I will take note to who was involved in the Po'luxnann conspiracy. I am a Council member representing my people: the R'uttri, Frih Kio, and all the creatures of Imudmid."

"But you know I Princess Vaora, Laurenx aren't responsible. You knew all along what would happen. King Razhatlab told you."

"More or less."

"So why,"

"There is a certain order that must be completed. If I were to present the truth without evidence, I could possibly put you and the royal family in jeopardy. I suspect there are many other foes at work. We need to take the proper steps to detain them as well." That triggered my temper. "Why couldn't you just stop Parpagg from attacking me? None of this would have happened. King Razhatlab wouldn't have died."

"Perhaps," she shrugged. "But Parpagg's, Sixa's, and now Frih Kio's plans wouldn't have been revealed. Frih Kio is a ruthless being that controls R'uttri. He was behind the planned attack to infiltrate the Bror and Temcaltiaf Passage. Many events were key in the discovery of this fact."

She regarded me calmly. She grabbed one of my hands and peered into my eyes. I wasn't comfortable staring at anyone at the risk of a Death Lock, but Mag encouraged me to.

"King Razhatlab knew you'd be king. He believed in you. He perceived you had to grow strong on your own so you could stand for what lies ahead of you," she said. "If you had not gone through what you endured you would still be that same lost boy who was in love, infatuated by his own problems and his own worries. You have grown to care for others who do not look like you." She motioned to her gray, pale skin. "You did not give in to your desires, your weaknesses, and withstood against the Po'luxnann. You are worthy to be Bearer of Po'luxnann. You are worthy to be king of Temcaltiaf."

She abruptly stood. "I must depart now. I have exceeded my time."

I looked at her, suddenly feeling lost. "What do I do now?"

"Be still. Remain steady and unmovable. Live on."

***

My friends visited on the third day I awoke under house arrest. Eli and Karin both gave me an earful when I finally contacted them the day before. I let them know I needed the time to think, and that was the reason why I disappeared on them for over a week. They knew that was a load of bull and Karin promptly told me to go screw myself.

Karin and Eli sat on my bed. They were very confused to the ten men in the living room. Mom and Logan moved around them as if they didn't notice they existed. I finally confessed what had been going on since Gavin's party.

And of course, as my friends, they thought I was making things up. Then I showed them my left arm. It was permanently bigger than my right. Also, my scars and tattoos on arms and my chest- those would never fade. At first they thought I self-harmed myself and illegally inked my skin. When I accidentally started a little wind in my room because I couldn't hide my irritation, they started to believe.

Karin and Eli left fearful, excited, and confused. I had Eli calling me at random times asking random questions. "Can you see the future?"

"I told you, it doesn't work like that, Eli."

"Oh c'mon. Can you tell me what college I should apply to? Or what about horse races? We can bet big like my cousin Ernie did- except he lost it all again in another horse race- we need to invest, you know? In our future." He would hang up until another bright idea came to him.

Karin didn't call me two days after I told her everything, and it wasn't for answers. She sounded like she was crying before I picked up the phone. "I need to talk to you," was all she said.

She and Eli both came over to my house. "I'm not going to give you the gory details but the football team threw another party for the New Year. Yeah, I know," Karin rolled her eyes at my expression.

"The first party was a hit so I guess they wanted a part two," she said. "The New Year's Eve party was unsupervised so of course everybody was either getting drunk or having one night stands. Chessie was doing both."

"Hey, don't exaggerate," Eli said. It didn't go over my head they were sitting at the far end of the bed. They were being very cautious around me.

"Whatever," Karin replied. "You know because of our deal Chessie was invited to my Mom's New Year's Eve gala, right?" I nodded along.

"You're lucky you didn't make it. Saved you from dying of boredom," Eli said.

"So Chessie didn't come," Karin said loudly over Eli, "and I have to admit, the gala was dull as hell, but she would have landed herself in far less trouble if she did," she explained. "Chessie went out and chilled at another party then got arrested for illegal drinking. The football player who was hosting the party got himself arrested for being underage and promoting underage drinking. Guess who it was." She didn't wait for a response. "Gavin."

During the time I've been under house arrest, I didn't call Chessie. My gala ticket sat on the nightstand, reminding me of what could have been. Chessie was all I could think about, though. She was the missing link to a puzzle I hadn't solved, so I tried to distract myself. I'd eat, play my old games on my phone, or watch mindless television and movies. My Awcers weren't interested in speaking to me; Mom and Logan didn't know I existed. After all the near death experiences I've had last week, nothing else occupied my time. I didn't know how to react to this new information about Chessie.

"My dad was one of the officers who was called to the party," Eli said. "Dad told me Chessie's parents came and they were 'shocked' their daughter was acting this way. They never thought she'd do something like that."

No one really did. Chessie has been hurting since the day she was raped and she hadn't been the same since. She was always looking for attention in all the wrong places. I believed it was her way of numbing the pain she was holding on to after the incident.

"I don't know what to do," Karin said. She sounded close to tears. "I can't stand her guts, but Chessie used to be my best friend. I don't want her to end up doing something so stupid she'll wind up dead."

Seeing Karin this way was opening up a flood of emotions. In that moment I finally admitted to myself how I really felt.

I hated Chessie. It was an automatic gut feeling I couldn't shake out of my heart and soul until my mind caught up to the idea.

I hated her. I hated how she made Karin worry and the stupid decisions she made. I hated how much she cared more about looking pretty and popular than the way she treated me. I hated how she never wanted to change. I wanted to rip up the gala ticket and burn it to pieces.

I had to forgive her. I needed to, so I could let go of the past. I couldn't hold onto this hate that was leaving me bitter. I still loved Chessie and it hurt, but I had to move on. It was easier said than done.

There was a knock on the door. Without waiting for a reply, an Awcer stepped into the already tight space.

All Awcers looked similar. They wore dusk colored coats with an embroidered design of two overlapping suns, black boots, had similar golden skin, wooly auburn hair, and liquid clear eyes. The Awcer had to bend his knees to enter my room.

"The Council has summoned Sir Seth Castillo for a meeting." I've been waiting for something to happen. Now the moment had come, I wasn't feeling ready.

Karin looked at me worriedly. "What did he say?" She and Eli didn't speak Everyman.

"I have to go to D'uthne."

Eli's face paled. "Do you know when you're coming back?" I shook my head. This was it. There was no turning back.

I turned to the Awcer. "I need to do a few things before I leave. I need to run a couple of errands."

He disregarded my request. "No. We have our orders."

"Look, I need to do this."

He didn't move a muscle.

I set my jaw and drew the line in the sand. "I am Bearer of the

Po'luxnann. You don't want me using it on you."

His bicep flexed. He didn't respond to threats very well. "I need two-no, just one hour, and we'll go on our way."

He didn't answer. I took it as a good sign.

I grabbed my backpack and duffel bag, already packed for the road, and started out my bedroom. I went to the kitchen and found Logan and my Mom there. Mom was at the stove fixing him a meal. Because I didn't exist to her, she didn't leave any for me. I hadn't tasted her food in what felt like a year. I missed her cooking. "I love you Mom," I whispered in her ear. "I'm sorry Aunt Evangeline died. I'm really sorry." I touched her shoulder as she fried the hotdogs.

"I'm not leaving you because I hate you. I stopped blaming you for Dad leaving us." I hugged her close. "I'm sorry I ever did." Her arm stopped moving. A tear escaped her eye and I looked at her expectantly.

"How many eggs do you want with your hotdogs?"

For a brief moment I thought she was speaking to me but then she turned, gazing at Logan. He was busy reading on his cellphone when he looked up. "Three eggs sound good." Mom smiled as she wiped her tear away. "Okay."

I let my hand drop from her shoulder. I looked at Mom for the longest time as she went right on cracking those eggs.

I kissed her on the cheek and said a final goodbye. The main Awcer, Karin, and Eli waited in the living room. Eli gave me a pat on the back.

"You alright?"

I couldn't look at him. "Yeah." I motioned to the Awcer. "I'm good to go."

After a stop at the Quik Mart for a pack of Slim Jims, we flashed on the corner of Chessie's house. The Awcers flashed somewhere nearby, except for the main Awcer who stood close. He had a tense grip on my shoulder.

"Forty minutes remain," he announced.

We rounded to the front of the house. Chessie's father's car was parked in the driveway. "Who's going to talk first?" Karin said nervously as we walked up the front steps. Mrs. Jensen swung it open before Karin's knuckles rapped against the door.

"Chessie is not accepting any visitors," she told us. Mrs. Jensen was usually a made-up woman but today she wore sweatpants and her brown hair was in a ponytail; she hadn't bothered to put on any makeup. Mrs. Jensen glanced up at the Awcer's great height and blanched. Karin cleared her throat.

"We're not here to see Chessie, Mrs. Jensen," Karin said. "We needed to speak to you and Mr. Jensen."

That made Mrs. Jensen pause. "What is this about?"

"If we can have a minute of your time," Eli said graciously. "We'd like to tell you inside what we know concerns you."

"He's an uncle," I said as her eyes traveled back to the Awcer. Before we left my house, I convinced the annoyed Awcer to chuck his coat aside and wear a pair of Logan's jeans, my jacket, and a shirt to blend in. It didn't disguise the otherworldliness of his presence and his height. The jacket and borrowed sunglasses covered most of his golden skin and hid his liquid colored eyes. He could pass for the Terminator's cousin.

"He's only here to see if Chessie is okay."

Mrs. Jensen's shoulders deflated. "Come inside." She held the door open and allowed us inside. She then led us to the study room.

I've been to their house a million times but everything now seemed foreign. The piano in the living room was still there, the couches were still beige, and the house carried the scent of vanilla, Mrs. Jensen's favorite.

The house was quiet. Chessie's brothers were probably at music or karate practice, or at a school club. Mr. Jensen himself was rarely home before six but we found him in his study. He narrowed his eyes when he saw me. The last time I was in his presence his restaurant almost burned to the ground. He didn't have many fond memories whenever I showed up.

I handed Mrs. Jensen the cookies I baked earlier and Karin helped prepare them. Mrs. Jensen accepted them and placed them on the center table in the study and we sat on the cushioned seats. I was glad we weren't in the living room because it reminded me of that day. It was already hard enough being inside this house. Karin cleared her throat again.

"I don't know how else to say what is on my mind, but I'm just going to say it." Karin took a deep breath. "Chessie needs help but she doesn't want it."

Mr. Jensen frowned. "If you're talking about recent events, those boys pressured her to do inhumane things."

Karin and I exchanged glances. Eli hid a surprised snort. "With all due respect, Chessie hasn't been the same since she was raped," Karin said. She struggled to keep her tone even. "I lost my best friend the day it happened and I admit, I haven't been a friend to her for a while, but I always had her best interests."

"Do you mean when you took her to parties and had her home late at night?" Mr. Jensen accused.

"It's not like I held her against her will," Karin rebutted but Mr. Jensen spoke over her.

"You were a bad influence on Chessandra the minute she met you."

"Edgar." Mrs. Jensen said.

"Sir, we didn't come here to bash Chessie," I interjected. "We came because we care about her."

Karin went on. "Yeah, I know I'm no princess but you don't know what Chessie does behind your back, sir. She's still hurting and you guys sit here blaming everyone for her problems."

"Karin!" Mrs. Jensen exclaimed. Mr. Evan's face was red as a bullfrog.

Karin held her ground. "I'm sorry Ma'am, but I have to say it." Her eyes welled with tears. "It's like we're all afraid of talking about the issue because it hurts," she said. "Chessie is doing things you pretend not to see. She's not only a smart girl who got straight A's. She's damaged inside."

"Enough!" Mr. Jensen leapt from his chair. Just then there was a knock on the door. No one moved for a second. Mrs. Jensen gave me a stern look. "It is time for you to go."

"Gladly," Eli muttered. Karin chewed on her lip as she held back her tears. Eli took her hand. "Let's go." Karin hesitated but Eli helped her off the couch and led her out. I quickly fell in step behind them. Eli opened the front door to his father in uniform.

We figured Mr. Goodchild had to wait outside fifteen minutes just so we could chat with Chessie's parents.

Eli's Dad nodded to us as we said our goodbyes to the Mr. and Mrs. Jensen. Before we rounded out the door, at the topmost stair in the grand hall was a shadow of a girl with long brunette hair. I took one long look at her before I walked out the door. Eli's father greeted Chessie's parents.

"Hello Mrs. Jensen, how are you? Mr. Jensen sorry for intruding, but I'm here regarding your daughter Chessandra Jensen? She was one of the children I arrested at Martin's household for illegal drinking," he said diplomatically.

We didn't get to hear the rest.

I didn't realize how bad I was shaking until Eli gave me a nod. I put my hands in my pockets, playing off I was cool.

"You did good," Eli told Karin. "Thanks."

Karin squeezed my hand and I locked up. Karin nodded to me. "You did good too," she said and softly squeezed my hand again. That simple gesture allowed me to let go the weight of guilt I held on for so long.

It was right there I decided I could move forward. Someone else could look out for Chessie better than we ever could.

Once we were out in the driveway, Karin looked worried.

"Do you think they'll go for Chessie getting more counseling this time?"

Eli rested a hand on her shoulder. "Dad came with a bunch of pamphlets just in case. They might take a cop more seriously than us."

Karin wiped away a tear. "Good."

By doing this little step for her, maybe Chessie would try and help herself get better. Maybe not. Eli stretched his arms high and squinted at the sky.

"Man, I haven't seen the sky so blue. It feels like forever." Karin nodded meekly and grimaced. "It's been rainy, windy, and cold for two straight weeks."

For us living in Miami, Florida, it was unusual for us to go without seeing the sun for that long. The city itself had flooded, and many residents were forced to stay indoors. Schools and businesses were closed except for places that housed food and shelter, and a few mini stores were left running.

Fortunately, Miami was recovering quickly from the storms than any other part of the state. Some signs of the massive downpour and tornadoes were the toppled trees and hanging power lines, debris, and two feet of water that covered most neighborhood yards.

"No one knows you saved Florida from drowning," Karin said, motioning at the flooded, dirty street. "No one will even think you saved this world. All worlds." We stood in our rain boots in murky water, looking up at the clear sky.

I shrugged, but what she said was true. I was too busy enjoying the warmth of the sun. It felt so nice on my skin.

"So Seth, I was wondering," Eli started, "about your powers. Do you think you can send us to Tokyo? I wanted to grab a couple mangas."

"Who are you kidding?" Karin said. "You want to see girls dressed in cosplay."

"If not Japan, how about hopping us to heaven?" Eli said. "I'm not too picky." Karin rolled her eyes at him.

The main Awcer emerged behind a tree, wearing his cloak.

My shoulders dropped. "I have to go."

Eli and Karin froze. "You can't," said Karin.

"I have to," I told them.

"We'll go with you," said Eli. Karin and I looked at him. The Awcer began his march toward us. I was running out of time.

"You can't just go through the Gates and their Passages when you want to," I said for the hundredth time. "Only Passagekeepers, Awcers, or whoever is authorized is allowed. There's a reason why the Passages are sealed behind the Gates."

The Po'luxnann took it upon itself to speak. I had given up the pendants to Laurenx so it was free to interrupt my thoughts whenever it wanted.

You have me, the Po'luxnann Gejruvhet. I created the Gates to each Passage. Your friends are free to cross.

You didn't think to tell me this before?

The Awcer abruptly halted before us. "It is time."

My pulse quickened.

You did not bid them to join. This information was not necessary at the time. Unless you wanted them to come all along?

I didn't answer directly. Who is going to bring them back if something happens to me?

Mag will bring them back home safely.

I didn't trust Mag, but King Razhatlab did. Eli and Karin were waiting anxiously.

"They're coming with me," I told the Awcer.

Eli and Karin automatically grinned. The Awcer looked surprised.

I shook my head at them. "It's not safe. I'm a prisoner, for God's sake."

"And we don't care," said Eli. "What's life without a little risk?"

"Why do you want to come along so badly?"

"We want to protect you," said Karin.

I almost laughed. "With what powers?"

"You need someone on your side if you're going to stand trial, idiot," Karin said.

Eli clasped a hand on my back. "Yeah, Mack, don't be an idiot. You know you can't stop us," he chided. We all knew very well I could, but it was the thought that counted.

I stared at them. "Are you sure?"

Karin stood between us. "Positive." She linked her arms with mine and

Eli's. The Awcers circled us.

I couldn't see Karin and Eli's expressions; the sunlight was now directly behind them. We were all going to enter another world blind, not knowing what we were getting ourselves into. I faced the main Awcer.

"We're ready."

He nodded sharply.

I looked forward and instead of my friends, I saw the sun. There in the middle of the flooded road, we all flashed out of sight.

ABOUT THE AUTHOR

Sam Suffrat grew up in sunny Miami, Florida where she always dreamed of producing movies, manning her own space shuttle, and traveling across the world. One and a half of her dreams came true. She's continuing to pursue her dreams abroad, from South Korea, France, and beyond.